The Lady Takes It All

Unexpected Heirs of Scotland
Book 1

Terri Brisbin

ARE YOU SIGNED UP FOR DRAGONBLADE'S BLOG?

You'll get the latest news and information on exclusive giveaways, exclusive excerpts, coming releases, sales, free books, cover reveals and more.

Check out our complete list of authors, too!

No spam, no junk. That's a promise!

Sign Up Here

www.dragonbladepublishing.com

Dearest Reader;

Thank you for your support of a small press. At Dragonblade Publishing, we strive to bring you the highest quality Historical Romance from some of the best authors in the business. Without your support, there is no 'us', so we sincerely hope you adore these stories and find some new favorite authors along the way.

Happy Reading!

CEO, Dragonblade Publishing

Dedication

I'd like to dedicate this story to my local romance readers' group that I've been a part of for 20 years. They started monthly meetings at a nearby Borders store, moved to a Barnes & Noble and then continued meeting at diners when that wasn't available. They've been enthusiastic historical romance fans, have supported me through all my books and some of us have even travelled together. Though some of the group has moved away, we're still in touch.

To Bonnie, Deborah, Deb, Maria, Karen, Nicole, Lena, Denise, Amanda, MaryJane and Kathy – thanks so much for all your support!

Acknowledgements

When I began putting this series together, I decided that in addition to the stories centering on people who unexpectedly inherit money or titles in Regency Scotland, I would use my "crushes" as the heroes. And I did! The hero of this book is a thinly disguised, fictionalized version of explorer, adventurer, archeologist and Discovery TV celebrity Josh Gates.

I love watching Josh's exuberance in traveling and searching for obscure places and events and details, and his self-deprecating humor when faced with challenges that don't always work out his way. I had the chance to see him in person and he is a wonderful storyteller, too. So, if you see a little of the real person in my fictional character, I hope you enjoy it!

And, my thanks to everyone at Dragonblade Publishing for their support and help with my first project with them.

Prologue

Batna Province
Algeria
December 1799

F INALLY.

They'd travelled from the last small town, across rolling lands that skirted the verdant grasslands and entered the beginning of the great desert. The winds dried now as they journeyed farther and farther from the humid coast and the heat intensified with each mile crossed. The group had passed into a valley, following the river, and they climbed as the landscape filled with hills.

As leader of this motley group of travelers—some visitors to this country, some natives, some representing the Bey and some he knew not at all, Joshua Robertson led the way to the crest of the nearest hill and caught sight of the first artifact. To the untrained eye, a piece of stone exposed by the shifting desert sands was just that. But to an explorer familiar with both what the area should look like and what the potential explanations were, the possibilities were. . . exciting.

He stumbled down the other side of the uneven mound, rushing forward even as he knew he should walk calmly. Fighting the urge to run and filling with a sense of calm detachment that surprised him, he proceeded in a slow, orderly fashion towards what was the discovery of a lifetime—a long-buried Roman city.

The rapid and hard beating of his heart echoed in his ears until he could hear nothing else. He could not draw a deep breath into his lungs. The hat claimed by the winds in his haste to reach the bottom of the rise, rolled past him and he grabbed for it. And missed.

When he reached the level ground, he strode to the nearest pale stone, part of a deteriorating column, and touched it to prove to himself it was indeed real. He ran to the next one and the next and the next until he could neither speak nor think with any certainty of reason.

But how could he when faced with the accomplishment of a lifetime, one he'd dreamt of for. . . too long. One for which he'd borne more than two years of humiliation by the Bey of Algiers. One for which he'd bided his time like a loyal subject of His Majesty would, allowing other opportunities to pass him by while he waited. Joshua stood and simply stared from one piece of carved stone to the next, as he now realized that hundreds, nay, possibly thousands of pieces lay spread over the acres before him.

Each one needing to be identified and exposed to view and appreciated by visitors. Each one revealing the history of the mighty Roman Empire's presence here.

"Is it everything you'd hoped?"

Startled by the voice of his companion, Joshua turned to face the Italian man he'd first met when assigned to serve the British government in Rome. Recommended by his cousin, the Viscount of Dunalastair, Luigi Balugani was, among other things, an artist, and his sketches would immortalize the sight before them. Tempted by this discovery to wipe the slate clean of the problems the man had created in Edinburgh, on their travels and in Rome, Joshua would withhold that decision until they could sort out the parameters and name of this long-buried town.

"The rumors were not exaggerated," he said as he tugged the scarf wrapped around his lower face and neck loose. Reaching over to reclaim his hat before the winds took it once more, Joshua glanced once more over the expanse before him. "I cannot believe we are the first to see it."

"The reports of it reappearing from under the desert sands have only just begun recently," Luigi said. "And the Bey controls all foreigners on his land. While he kept you where he wanted you, he did the same with the others who'd sought his permission."

He studied Luigi's olive-skinned face. Where Joshua's pale Scottish complexion tended to burn, hence his attempts at covering up, Luigi's darkened over their many days of travel beneath an unrelenting sun. Being mistaken as an inhabitant of this region had both opened many previously-closed doors and allowed the man liberties otherwise prohibited. It was those liberties that would be the cause of many problems.

"Just so."

"We are permitted to stay here only four days before we must move on."

"And so much to see."

Plans of an orderly tour of the whole area then a closer examination of important parts formed in his thoughts, even as Luigi called out orders to the men who'd traveled with them. A camp must be set up. Supplies organized. Water brought from the river they'd crossed just before reaching the valley here. Luigi handled those matters on their travels.

"I will meet you near that—" He stopped and stared, not believing his eyes. "Near that Roman archway."

The overwhelming feeling of awe and wonder did not leave him that day or any of the days spent there at the place where the Emperor Trajan had established a town and fort. On the morning of their second day, Joshua identified the arch as one in honor of the emperor himself. By the third day, carvings confirmed that this was indeed the lost Roman city called Thamugadi or Timgad in ancient sources.

On the morning before they would be forced to leave by the Bey's orders, Joshua came upon a site that could only be an amphitheater. His attempts at a professional, methodical approach to the ruins crumbled as did he—his legs gave out and he landed hard on the sand next to the keystone of the huge building. Still buried under the sands, it would take years to uncover the rest of it, but when faced with the proof of it, his sensibilities failed him and he could neither stand nor speak for some time.

So many artifacts and buildings. So many acres of history untouched for centuries. So many treasures to be found, both personal ones giving names to the thousands who would have lived here and those that were evidence of the wealth and power in such a place as this. Spread out before him, and he knew he would never see the completion of such an extensive project.

As the sun rose on that fourth and final day, Joshua Robertson prepared to return to Algiers before leaving for home. There might be other journeys, other searches for lost history, but his discovery here must be revealed first and confirmed.

It would be an auspicious beginning to a reputation as not only a minor Scottish diplomat, but also as a scholar, an adventurer and discoverer, and as a man of travel and history. It would gain him entry into the highest levels of academia and even society. He would speak at the respected organizations and academies, and even the Society for the Preservation of Historical Antiquities in Edinburgh would be open to him now.

His future lay open before him—wide and sprawling and appealing.

Sadly, his future did not turn out as he'd expected, but instead as he'd feared any endeavor connected to Balugani might.

Chapter One

Edinburgh, Scotland
Spring, 1815

THE MEETING WAS starting at half-past eleven sharp and Joshua knew he'd be late. Even picking up his pace would not help this morning, for the streets between his home near the University and the building where the Society met were filled with carts, carriages, riders on horses, cows and other creatures and those persons who lived and worked in the area.

There was only one word that could clearly describe the situation—chaos. Whether the recent storms that turned some intersections into small ponds and others into muddy puddles were to blame, he knew not. All he did know was that he would never reach the headquarters on Cowgate off Parliament Square in time.

His stomach burned at the thought of making a late entrance into the meeting. Although he was a member in good standing of the Society, the whispered insults and sly glances spoke the truth—he was not welcome there. Even the title that had surprisingly come his way had not changed the disdain with which he was treated. With his thoughts elsewhere, he tripped on a crack and bumped into someone on the sidewalk.

"Pardon," he said as he touched the edge of his hat and shifted one pace over to move around the person. Only then, as they passed by, did the realization that he'd felt soft curves and a feminine shape against him strike.

Joshua stopped and turned to apologize but the woman, with brown hair covered by a hat with a very distinctive feather at the back of it, continued on down along the street away from him without a backward glance. For a few long moments, he watched the sway of that feather as it rocked from side to side with her every step. Only when another passerby jostled him again did he realize he'd been standing and staring down the street after the woman.

And he'd be later to the Society meeting than even he'd expected. More stares. More surreptitious whispers. Damn it! Turning back, Joshua rushed through the crowded streets and slowed only as he climbed the stairs to the door of the Society's building on Cowgate. Slipping in through that back door rather than the main entrance, he wanted to melt into the members in attendance unnoticed. When a familiar voice called his name, he lost all hope of that.

"Dunalastair," the man called again. Joshua watched as those in the corridor connected that name with him and then looked away just as quickly and directly. "Dunalastair, I did not expect to see you here today." Sometimes Jamie Hepburn could be an arse. But it was the times when he was the best of friends that kept Joshua from doing something drastic to him. Times like just now.

"Hepburn," he said, lifting his hat and handing it to one of the footmen standing nearby. He kept his walking stick in hand. "Has the lecture begun?"

"Nay, the meeting continued longer than planned and the speaker is delayed."

"Why are you not in there?" Joshua walked along the wainscot paneled corridor towards the large and currently boisterous chamber at the end of it. From the sound of the raised voices, the usual business considered at a meeting had given way to some other issue. He paused as Hepburn opened the door and the raucous yelling and laughter spilled out into the hallway.

"Now you see?" Jamie said. Shaking his head only served to

send his unkempt long hair swirling over his eyes and back again. In all the years Joshua had known his friend, his appearance tended to be on the messy side of things. "I cannot abide it when they lose control in these. . . these trivial matters and pay no heed to the important ones!"

Which meant the hunt for and discovery of old books for Jamie. The man could never pass an antiquary bookstore or museum or library collection without losing hours within them. Watching the grimace pull his friend's face taut as more yelling emanated from within the main chamber, Joshua shrugged.

"Tempers run high and loose when everyone has their own interests and wants them to be of the highest priority to the Society," he said. "Are you going in?"

"Aye," Jamie said on a sigh. "I was but waiting for your arrival."

"Come then," he said.

With a nod of his head to the doorway, Joshua stepped closer and then pushed into the large, historic room. With its dark wooden paneling, heavy carved, pulpit-like lectern and individual seats that resembled desks, the main meeting room of the Society for the Preservation of Historical Antiquities was in equal measures a church for believers, a school for education on ancient artifacts and places, and a gathering place of unruly men. But for a bar to serve ale and spirits, it could have been a pub, too.

As was his practice, he headed towards the back of the room and sought out two seats together. Unless. . . .

"Is MacDonald coming today?" he asked over his shoulder.

"Nay. He has some other appointment or matter demanding his attention."

The sarcasm was so strong in his friend's tone that Joshua winced against it. The only matter demanding Alexander MacDonald's time or attention was the young woman, formerly an opera singer and lately his wealthy friend's "companion." Of the three of them, Alex was most comfortably situated here in Edinburgh—with a title, another coming upon his father's passing and so much wealth it bordered on obscene.

Joshua saw two empty places in the far side of the rows and led Jamie towards them. That the men before him stepped away, both making a clear space and avoiding any close contact with him, still stung. They were all self-righteous, pretentious twits, but it never ceased to hurt his conscience and his self-regard. How long would it take before their pettiness stopped or would no longer bother him if it continued?

"Come now, I see others eyeing up our seats," Jamie said before Joshua even realized he'd slowed down nigh to a stop, staring at nothing as he did. "I would rather not stand for this."

Joshua wanted to thank his perceptive friend, but did not wish to continue considering the matter or it would lead to anger he could not control. And that, he did not wish to allow them all to see. He would rather be thought of as a man who was not smart enough to understand the cuts given him than the one he was—a man with much to hide about his past. A man unwilling to expose the truth he knew. Moving along, he allowed Jamie to pass him to the more inside seat and he took his place in the one on the aisle.

With no one behind him, he could view the proceedings and not worry about someone getting too close without him noticing. It had been just over four years since the last attack, but he would never stop watching. Another legacy of the Timgad discovery. Those who should have believed him had not, and those who did believe him wanted something. Something he did not have because it did not exist.

With calls from the presiding member to pay heed, the audience quieted and the speaker, a historian and amateur archeologist from the southwest of the country, began explaining the methods he'd used in his discovery on the Duke of Argyll's lands. Joshua would speak to the man later, but for now, he let the man's enthusiasm break through his own growing disenchantment.

At some turn of phrase, Joshua thought he saw himself in the speaker's description of the moment of discovery. Had anything been more glorious than that moment of vindication and success for the speaker, or, indeed, for himself? If only that moment could have been preserved much as the exposed relics had been. Collected, protected, displayed under glass to keep them from decay and tarnish.

"I can almost hear your melancholy thoughts, Joshua," Jamie whispered as the speaker finished his remarks. "I do not ken why you even attend these gatherings when all they do is—"

"Inform. Educate. Enlighten. That is what they do, my friend." Joshua stood and faced his friend. "There is always a need to report discoveries and study them."

Jamie studied *him* with a narrowed gaze for a few long moments. "But at what cost, Josh?" The shortened version of his name made him smile. It reminded him of exactly how long ago he and Jamie became friends. And what epic adventures of their own they'd had, as lads then young men and even more recently. Lifting his walking stick, Josh tapped his friend's lapel with the handle of it.

"The costs have been paid, Jamie. Worry not." A soft huffing sound was Jamie's only reply, but it was filled with disbelief and frustration. Sentiments that he'd often experienced. Turning his topic as he stepped from the row into the aisle, Joshua tapped his stick on the floor. "What are your plans this day?"

As he asked his friend, Joshua remembered his own schedule. Glancing at his pocket watch, he realized that, for the second time this day, he would be late. By the time they escaped the crowded chamber, reclaimed their hats, and made their way out to the street, Jamie had declined any invitations to accompany him on Joshua's next task.

Apparently, interviewing a prospective housekeeper was more than his friend could do, even on being reminded of their friendship. The two parted ways and, eschewing a hack, Joshua made his way home on foot. The traffic had eased, strengthening his suspicion that an accident or some such occurrence nearby had caused the earlier congestion. He reached his house, a townhouse on a respectable block near to the university, and approached slowly.

He had experience in interviewing or choosing some servants and staff, though he relied on the opinion of the butler who oversaw the household. In the four years since inheriting his title, that butler had handled most matters of this kind as he had for Joshua's late cousin. But a passing comment, overheard as he searched for a book in an out-of-the-way shelf in the dark corner of the library, gave him pause.

The former housekeeper, another servant inherited from the last Viscount of Dunalastair, whispered a warning about Pottles to another one of the housemaids. Since he'd heard that and even without more information about the reason for the warning, he'd found himself less confident in his butler's actions. Hence, his decision to be part of the process of hiring a new housekeeper.

Joshua fought *not* to reach for the doorknob—another leftover vestige of his previous life—and, as he expected, the door opened as he approached. Graham, the older of the two footmen who served him, stepped back to allow him entrance.

"My lord," the young man said, with a referential nod of his head. "Pottles and the next candidate for the housekeeper's position are in your study as you directed."

After handing off his hat and stick, Joshua walked down the hallway to the room he'd claimed as his. Formerly the viscount's library, he found it made his tasks easier to have all his research books and maps and such at hand when he needed them. Pottles had objected to that in his humorless manner, but as "lord of the manor," Joshua's wishes were followed. He paused before the closed door, listening for conversation on the other side. A murmured exchange of voices without anything he could identify as either man or woman.

"Here, my lord. Allow me." Graham appeared soundlessly at his side and turned the knob, making his arrival known quite clearly. "The Viscount of Dunalastair," he announced.

Pottles could see him from the place he sat—in Joshua's chair, positioned against the far wall, but the woman could not. As Pottles rose, so did she. For a moment, all he could see was the back of her. Brown hair, swept up under a brown hat with a feather that seemed too gay for the rest of her somber, staid brown pelisse and dress. Before she turned to face him, he spoke.

"Ah. At least now I get the chance to apologize to you, Mrs. . . . ?"

Luckily, he'd spoken, for he lost the ability when she lifted her face after a respectful curtsy. Most house servants tried to appear unassuming, dull, unremarkable. This woman clearly had not.

Her heart-shaped face was surrounded by a fringe of dark brown curls that spilled down from under her hat. Lashes of the same color outlined her eyes and formed delicate brows above them. Her mouth. Her lips were lush and full and a deep pink and meant for. . . .

"My lord, a pleasure to meet you, though I ken not the reason for any apology," she said. Pottles cleared his throat, making it clear he thought her comment impertinent. "Forgive me, my lord. I am Mrs. Lewis, Mrs. Clara Lewis, my lord."

Judging from her name she was following the convention of polite society that required every housekeeper to be called as a married woman would be—even if they were not. Was she truly?

Joshua walked to the chair near hers, motioning to a scandalized Pottles to remain at the desk, as Joshua took a seat where he could observe her as she spoke to Pottles. "And Mr. Lewis?"

"Sadly, my lord, my Edgar fought in the war on the continent and was lost. Three years past."

"I am sorry for your loss, Mrs. Lewis." So many had perished in the war against Napoleon Bonaparte, a Corsican who'd claimed France and then tried to claim the rest of Europe. Joshua had barely escaped the man's forces in Egypt after his time in Algeria and even now, battles yet raged. He paused and met her gaze, nodding his sympathies. "And you are lately of?"

This time she did not hesitate or speak other than to his question. "Arbuthnott, my lord. I was in the countess's employ there."

She'd worked for the old lioness and survived? That spoke of true strength of character, courage and fortitude. The countess was known to eat several servants before noon. Mrs. Lewis rose in his esteem at once. Pottles held out a paper to him, but Joshua shook his head. It must be her letters of reference. He was more interested in her.

"I've not visited my godmother in years. How is she?"

The surprise on her face disappeared mere moments after he spoke. The rosy blush in her cheeks had drained away in an instant. Her full lips thinned and her eyes—the same hue as her hair—blinked quickly until she pulled herself under control.

"When I last saw her, she was hale and hearty as usual, my lord." A nice recovery that gave him no information. His godmother was always hale and hearty. And obnoxious and infuriating. And opinionated. And sometimes, just mean.

"How long did you last there?"

"My lord?"

"How long were you employed there? And please, sit." He motioned at the chair behind her. Her movements did not hide Pottles' sound of shock that he'd been displaced from the conversation. She sat and crossed her hands in her lap. A small reticule dangled from one gloved wrist. Brown. She was awash in only that one color.

"My lord, her letters from Lady Arbuthnott's housekeeper and others are here for your inspection." Pottles once more held out said papers. Joshua held up a hand to ward them off.

"I have been there for nigh on three years, my lord." As she sat, she angled herself to face him more fully, making that ridiculous feather sweep to and fro with every move she made. "After Edgar, I lived with a relative there and I sought work. I was hired by the housekeeper to help with several special events at the house and then kept on."

"The housekeeper is still the same one?"

"Mrs. Brander? Is she the one you remember from your visits, my lord?"

"Aye. Mrs. Brander! You've worked with her then?" Pottles moved the blasted papers again at his question. "Pottles, I will read those later. For now, let us ask Mrs. Lewis the questions those pages do not answer." Pottles was, for a moment, without words and so Joshua turned back to the possible housekeeper.

Something was bothering him, whether her words or something else. Mayhap it was something else. Nay, not bothering him but intriguing him. He could not help but notice the way she sat on the edge of the chair, while still moving enough to make that feather sway. He watched as the light streaming into the library— another reason he'd claimed it—reflected in her dark brown eyes.

"Aye, my lord. Mrs. Brander made me her assistant and trained me as a housekeeper. When I saw the advertisement in the newspaper, Mrs. Brander suggested I apply."

"She believes you qualified for the responsibilities of running this house?" His household may not be the size or breadth of the countess or other great and grand estates, but it was a respectable one, of a good size and more when the country house was added into consideration.

"As her letter indicates," she glanced at the damned pages sitting at the edge of the desk. "Aye, my lord, she does."

Letting out a loud sigh of resignation, Joshua picked up the papers and stood. As did Pottles and Mrs. Lewis. He waved them to sit and walked over to the window to read the polite words of his godmother and her housekeeper.

"I interrupted your interview, Pottles. Please go on while I read these."

He turned away, giving them his back while never missing a word they said. Pottles asked some questions meant to elicit the woman's methods in dealing with staff, managing the household's duties and other specific tasks that Mrs. Lewis would oversee. Her answers seemed adequate to him, but from Pottles' various noises Joshua understood that his butler would not be hiring this woman. His reaction was not logical. It was purely made by reflex, but those instincts had saved his skin and his life on his journeys. He'd learned to listen to and follow them years ago.

"Pottles, have you discussed salary and rooming arrangements yet?" Joshua had not read a word on the papers and he placed them back by Pottles on the desk.

"No, my lord. I have not." Though his demeanor was one of complete self-control, Pottles had several tells that all was not well with him. His hands curled into fists. His breathing became more rushed. And his left brow lifted and twitched. "That only comes when—"

"I understand, Pottles." He glanced over at the prospective employee to find her examining the top of the window as though not the one under consideration. It was the polite way to react in a situation like this. "Would you excuse us, Mrs. Lewis?" Joshua walked to the door and waited for Pottles to follow.

"Of course, my lord." She stood and nodded, watching them leave.

Pottles followed directly behind him and Graham, still on duty at the door, closed it quickly and stepped away.

"I wish to hire Mrs. Lewis for the position, Pottles."

"But, my lord, she is not the most qualified applicant." This was new, for Pottles had objected so rarely to any of his wishes, whims or orders, that Joshua could not remember when it had happened in the past. "I think that Mrs. Mathieson is a more satisfactory candidate."

He'd seen several of the others coming or going but had not spoken to any of them until Mrs. Lewis. So far, Pottles had interviewed women who were. . . staid. Older. Experienced in all manner of housekeeping duties. And any one of them would probably be a safer choice. Yet, that tightness in his gut pushed him to do this.

"I wish to hire Mrs. Lewis, Pottles. Make certain the offer you make is enticing enough to gain her agreement."

"But, my lord, this would be her first position as a house-keeper and, your godmother's, I mean, Lady Arbuthnott's recommendation aside—"

"I learned early in life to never, never, disregard any opinion offered by my godmother, Pottles." He cut his butler off with a look. "Hire this woman. Now."

"Very well, my lord," Pottles said as he offered a curt nod of his head in acceptance.

"I will let you see to the details." He turned to walk away, needing time alone to sort through the reasons he'd reacted this way, when another thought struck. "And Pottles. Let not this disagreement between us spill over to your regard for or treatment of Mrs. Lewis while she is in our employ." Joshua waited as his servant took a few more seconds than he should have to accept that directive.

"Of course not, my lord," Pottles said. After a bow, the man turned back and opened the door.

As Joshua passed by, he glanced in to find Mrs. Lewis standing just as she had when they'd left her. She met his gaze and he noticed it narrowed as she realized he was not entering with his butler. That gaze, the color of the dark chocolate he favored, exposed something to him—this woman would never be subservient to anyone. She could pretend and bank the determination in her eyes when needed, but in this moment, Joshua knew the truth of her.

Mrs. Clara Lewis was much more than the woman she presented herself to be.

More? Aye. Different? Aye that, as well. Dangerous? Mayhap that, too. And seeing a momentary flash of something that resembled vulnerability in that warm and lush brown gaze made the decision for him. No matter the lack of logic or critical assessment of it all.

The door closed and Joshua walked along the corridor and up the stairs to his chamber. Entering his dressing room, he sought the small closet to which no one else had access where the strongbox lay hidden away in its own secret place. Only his most valuable belongings and books and papers were stored there. Every so often, the need to confirm that the box was indeed locked and the artifact safe grew strong and brought him here.

Why now, he knew not, but he checked the lock and the only key that was also hidden away, in a specially made nook in the paneling of the wall next to the fireplace. Once he knew both were safe, Joshua tried to make himself comfortable in a large, overstuffed chair by the window and opened a book he was destined to not read.

The front door below him opened and closed and his new housekeeper stepped onto the pavement. Lifting her hand, she adjusted the pins holding her hat in place before taking off at a brisk pace back in the direction from whence she'd come. As he watched her walk away, the damned feather swaying in time with her steps, Joshua tried to figure out why he'd gone against his butler in this matter.

A knock on his chamber door pulled him from his reverie, but only after more than an hour had passed and only after the woman in his thoughts had long since disappeared from his view.

Chapter Two

I T TOOK ALL her self-control to keep from running. Something within her wanted to break free, jumped down the three steps leading to his house and run the rest of the way back to the boarding house where she was staying.

Laughter bubbled up from inside, pushing to be released. But hurrying down the street, laughing like a madwoman would gain her nothing but attention. Attention she did not want and certainly did not need. Reaching a wynd along the Royal Mile, she turned into it and sought out the alcove she knew was located a half-block down the steeply inclined cobblestone path. At last, she slipped into the shadowed corner and pressed herself against the wall before allowing it free.

The tension inside her, a force that had grown stronger yet more brittle with each passing day since her arrival in Edinburgh, did not let go completely, but the peals of laughter took the sharp edge off it. When a man walked by the opening and glanced her way, she covered her mouth to muffle most of it. When it became difficult to breathe, she leaned down and forced her lungs to empty out several times.

A riot of emotions shot through her as she stood there. Frustration at the length of time these arrangements had taken. Relief to finally be starting her true efforts. Fear of failure to find the truth and fear of exposure as she moved into this false identity and life. But the strongest remained the grief at her loss. She allowed a moment for that to weaken and pass before the anger settled in her belly once more.

Anger had been her friend for a long time. It supported and enervated her in a way that wanting or needing never had. It gave her the strength to seek out a method and to plan her subterfuge. Now, it would need to sustain her efforts during the next dangerous weeks or months—however long it took to find out what Lord Joshua Robertson, Viscount of Dunalastair hid and where he'd hidden it.

She'd worked too hard and searched too long to allow herself to weaken now. Taking one last fortifying breath, she straightened up on her feet, brushed some dust from her pelisse and gown, and stepped out into the walkway ready to take her plan to its next step.

Her hand moved without thought to the small brooch she wore under her clothing. Its value lay not in the cost of it, for it was a mere replica. Nay, it was priceless to her because her father had it made for her. A reminder of the betrayal that destroyed him and of the vengeance she'd sworn to seek on his behalf.

Now that her plan was underway, she had much to accomplish. She must move into the Dunalastair townhouse and take control of his household. Mr. Pottles would be a challenge, for his dislike of her had increased tenfold when his lordship interfered with the interview and clearly demanded his butler hire her. But, she would not allow anyone to block her way now that she was so close to discovering the truth and forcing a confession from the man who had singlehandedly destroyed her family.

Joshua Robertson, now Viscount of Dunalastair.

He had broken trust with her father, causing his early death. He had lied and accused her father of scandalous behavior, without proof and without remorse. Then, faced with the repercussions of her husband's death, her mother had deteriorated rapidly, and she'd died soon after he did.

Because of Lord Joshua Robertson's cavalier words and threats, she'd lost her entire family and was thrown on the mercy of others. An old friend of her mother who lived in Arbuthnott had taken her in more than eight years ago and had seen her trained in service where she worked. It was not the life she'd wanted, but what could a young woman with no family do except allow the well-meant kindness with gratefulness and use it as a means to the end she sought. When she'd accepted it, she'd no idea it would become the vehicle of her revenge after all.

Now, Arabella MacGibbon, daughter of Luigi Balugani and Sarah MacGibbon, would have her chance. Even if it was *Mrs. Clara Lewis* who attained it for her.

Gathering her wits, she walked back to the boarding house and climbed to her room three floors above. It took but minutes to pack her clothing and belongings into two satchels, for she did not have many of either. Mr. Pottles had said the position was available immediately and Arabella was more than ready to begin.

Though one of her references was a bit grander than the truth of her experience, it would stand up to scrutiny if anyone sought out its verification. As she suspected Mr. Pottles would, if for nothing more than his own need to do so. And to gather ammunition against her for future battles. It had been her experience that men who felt threatened usually responded in that way. Well, she had gathered her own ammunition, so she was prepared.

Glancing around the small room, she understood she would never return to this chamber or to the freedom she had in this moment. If she failed, against a peer of the realm, there would be consequences for certain. If she was lucky, she might be able to flee to Italy and find her father's family there. If she was not, prison might be her next home.

As it did when uncertainty attacked her resolve, the memories of her father's humiliation spurred the anger and she allowed it to fill her. Diplomat or not, explorer or not—indeed, viscount or not—Joshua Robertson would pay for his misdeeds and face the repudiation of those he respected. It was his turn to suffer as her father had.

She carried her bags out into the hallway and pulled the door shut. Mrs. Taylor's nephew would take them to the viscount's house for a coin or two and Arabella, or rather Clara, would make her way there later. On the morrow she would begin her duties and, once established in his household, start her search.

Then and only then would Luigi Balugani rest in peace.

MR. POTTLES' ICY reception did not surprise her, nor did it signify for she had his lordship's approval. A frisson of something crept along her spine at that realization, for she knew not why he'd done it—countermanded his butler and hired her. The interview was unlike any she'd ever had before. As she'd sought various positions in households, she'd only ever spoken to the butler and, or, the housekeeper involved. She understood this would be different for the very reason of hiring a housekeeper. But still, speaking as though equals with a viscount was unexpected. Speaking with this particular one and in the manner of a conversation was shocking.

No matter the butler's attitude, the understaff all seemed welcoming of her in their household. Comprised of two upstairs maids, a kitchen maid, two footmen, one man who oversaw the stables and grounds, another who was coachman, the cook, his lordship's valet along with herself and Mr. Pottles, it was, well, manageable for her. By the time they'd finished their evening meal, a call to the library surprised her. Though she'd hoped for time to explore the housekeeper's office before her first full day of duties, it would have to wait until after she'd seen to his lordship's matter.

Checking to see that her notepad and pencil were in her apron's pocket and that her cap was in place, she climbed the stairs and made her way to the library. Arabella took a deep breath, trying to ease the tension before knocking. At his acknowledgement, she twisted the knob and pushed the door open. He sat behind the desk now, wearing spectacles that lay on the bridge of his nose. His glance, over the edge of the eyeglasses, narrowed for a slight moment before he invited her to sit.

She stood, hands clasped in front of her, and wondered about that strange glance. Though this was not her best dress, it was black, clean, well-fitted and most appropriate for a housekeeper's garb. And her apron was almost new, and she'd only put it on before their meal. Had she somehow torn it? Tempted to look down to check it, she resisted that urge.

"You called, my lord?"

"I did, Mrs. Lewis." He removed the spectacles and rubbed his eyes, leaning back against the chair as he did. Once again, his gaze lowered momentarily before meeting hers. "Have you moved into your room? Is it acceptable?"

It was all Arabella could do not to sputter at his question. Household servants were given room and board and accepted whatever they were given. Though a housekeeper should be assigned a larger, more comfortable room, most servants' quarters were barely more than austere. Her room below was both comfortable and spacious. With its small dining table, desk and separate sleeping area, it was larger than the space she'd rented at the boarding house.

"More than acceptable, my lord." She finally remembered to respond to his question. "Certainly, more than I expected." The viscount stood and circled his desk until he stood before her, forcing her to tilt her head to look at him.

"Pottles explained about the clothing allowance?" Her surprise must have been clear, for he shook his head and leaned back, sitting on the edge now. "You are provided with whatever garments are necessary for your work."

"My lord, that is simply not necessary!" She pushed the chair back as she stood to give herself room to rise. "I am quite able to supply my own clothing." Allowing him to buy her clothing felt. . . too personal and certainly uncomfortable.

"I did not intend any insult, Mrs. Lewis. I provide the livery for my footmen and suitable clothing for my other servants, from cook to stablemaster." His words were slow and measured. Instead of the challenging sparkle that had filled his green eyes during their first meeting, now all she saw was exhaustion.

Why she'd taken his words as she had, she knew not. And, damn him, Pottles had not mentioned this funding. Arabella did not doubt it was done apurpose and for his own reasons, but it had opened her up to an uncomfortable situation between her and her new employer. Gathering her control, she nodded.

"I beg your pardon, my lord. I did not comprehend your generous offer." She lowered her head as she apologized, not wanting him to witness the confusion in her own eyes, for a part of her was truly sorry she'd questioned him so readily. Even while another part of her believed he could be capable of such a dishonorable offer. She must behave as the servant she portrayed until she could prove her suspicions. "I will see to the purchase of clothing appropriate for your household."

"It has been a long day, Mrs. Lewis. I fear exhaustion is claiming me even now," he said, giving a reasonable explanation for her reaction to his words.

Stepping around her, he opened the door, dismissing her. Arabella nodded to him as she walked out. Just before she turned towards the back of the house and the servants' stairs, he spoke.

"I hope you find your time in my household satisfactory, Mrs. Lewis."

"I am certain I will, my lord," she answered. "And I hope you find my work to your expectations."

The corner of his mouth lifted as a smile lit up his face at her words. He nodded to her, as one of his brows lifted, too, and she could not identify the feeling that flooded her. Arabella turned and walked away, fighting that urge to run from him for the second time in just this one day.

His heavier footfalls climbed the front stairs up to his chamber above and she gave into the urge to rush away. When she reached her rooms downstairs, she closed the door and collapsed against it, unable to draw an even breath for some time.

Arabella had prepared herself before they met to hate this man. He was the destroyer of her family. He needed to be brought down from his high and mighty place. His pompous attitude would be humbled after she was done.

Pushing away from the door, she prepared quickly for bed. Her first full day in this position would begin early and she must be well-rested and clear-minded to face the challenges coming her way. From staff unfamiliar with her. From a butler intent on redress for the slight paid him in her hiring. From the practical demands of running such a household.

But, after she blew out the candle and as she slipped under the bedcovers, so many thoughts and doubts and questions plagued her that sleep would not come. As the minutes turned to hours, the matter that disturbed her sleep the most was. . . him.

Joshua Robertson, Viscount of Dunalastair, was nothing like the man she expected him to be.

Having had only a few glimpses of the man prior to the interview this afternoon, and no chance to actually converse with him, she'd built a preconceived idea of him and his personality. Meeting him, speaking to him—more as person to person than lord to servant—tore those notions apart.

Worse than that, he intrigued her.

Why would he speak so freely to her, a prospective employee, a woman? Why had he overstepped Pottles' expected right to choose employees under his oversight and chosen her?

Did he know who she truly was?

A shudder coursed through her body, not caused by the chill in her chamber but the fear that she'd given herself away already.

By the time she'd examined each encounter several times to make certain she'd played her character well and thoroughly, the weak light of another dreary Edinburgh morning fought its way into the chamber through the small window high on her wall.

And, it was time to begin putting her plan into action.

Chapter Three

"**M**RS. LEWIS?"

Arabella startled, both at the sound of his voice and its nearness to her. Gathering her wits, she turned to face him. Nodding first, she tucked her notepad into the pocket of her apron.

"My lord. You startled me."

"I had spoken your name twice before you heard me." Before she could offer an apology, he continued, "But you were so intent in your observations of the housemaids, I suspect you did not hear me." She stood at the doorway, tucked to one side and out of view from the two maids presently cleaning the lord's library.

Why did he always seem too rational? That was not how her father had described him. He'd used words like *unbalanced, moody, unpredictable, daft* and worse—*mad*.

"Aye, my lord. I was that." She nodded once more to him. "But that is no excuse for not hearing your call." She gathered her hands in front of her. "Have you need of something?"

"Are you spying on them, Mrs. Lewis?" Arabella felt her eyes blinking rapidly and closed them for a moment to gain control. Spying? Aye. On the maids? Nay.

"Of course I am, my lord," she said. Stepping away from the door so the maids did not hear their conversation, she nodded.

"Any housekeeper worth her reputation must ken everything that goes on in the household. And a new one must gather that knowledge quickly. So, I am spending my day spying on all the servants, my lord." It was the truth, though she might not have used those words to describe her current observations.

Lord Dunalastair watched her closely for a few moments with those intense green eyes before bursting into laughter. The sounds within his library stopped, for the maids had heard it. She stepped to where she could be seen.

"Continue your work," she said. When the sounds of their activities began once more, Arabella looked back at her employer. Laughter changed his countenance into something more dangerous than the stern visage she'd seen directed at Mr. Pottles. Something more. . . appealing. Which was more of a threat to her.

"Most housekeepers, and butlers for that matter, would never admit to that behavior, Mrs. Lewis." Another hearty laugh followed and she turned her gaze to the floor between them to avoid staring at him. "I, for one, am glad to ken that you are about your duties so quickly." He stepped back as if to leave and she stopped him.

"My lord, if I might?" When he canted his head, listening to her, she went on. "When the maids have finished their work, or now if it is more convenient for you, could I ask you a few questions about how you wish your library and desk and records handled? I do not wish to intrude or examine things you wish not touched."

"Mrs. Lewis, you have overstepped yourself." The gasp escaped her before Arabella could control it, surprised by the silent approach and condemnation in Pottles' tone.

"Mr. Pottles?" she asked as she turned to face the butler. Oh, she had an idea of how she had, but 'twas better to meet this challenge straight on.

"Pottles?" Lord Dunalastair asked.

"My lord, 'tis the butler's responsibility, my duty, to express your wishes and needs and requirements to the staff." The butler faced the viscount and never looked in her direction. "I can assure you that I ken the way you wish things to be taken care of in your home, my lord." Pottles bowed to his lord and continued. "And I will guide Mrs. Lewis in her duties."

She opened her mouth to speak but stopped when the viscount raised his hand between his two servants.

"Pottles is one of the finest and most experienced butlers in Edinburgh, Mrs. Lewis. And one from whom you have much to learn." A side glance at the man revealed a slight rise to the corner of his mouth, a sign of his vindication by his master's declaration. "But he has always lamented over my inexperience in and lack of regard for and adherence to the correct ways of society."

For a moment, a single one, shock shone brightly in Pottles' gaze. Then he blinked and it was gone, and his steely control was back in place.

"Mrs. Lewis, if you have any questions after Pottles explains the details of my personal and work habits, I would be available to speak to you."

His green eyes positively shone with merriment, as though tweaking his butler's behavior was a thing done. He confused her more with each encounter. Glancing between the two men who held the most power in her life in this moment, she understood which one would be the most immediate trouble to her.

"Mr. Pottles, of course I would seek your counsel and direction before proceeding. I await your convenience to discuss this matter more completely."

Now Lord Dunalastair glanced at her, then his butler, as though assessing her truthfulness and whether she was sincere or simply complying. A small huff of air was the sign of his acceptance, before he nodded and turned to walk away, entering the library as the maids left.

Pottles spared her not a word as his disgruntled harumph made clear his attitude and opinion of her. She could not afford to make an enemy of him before she'd even had a chance to learn the household and *his* ways. To find the proof she needed. So, for now, she would play the part of obedient, grateful servant to both the lord and his man. The good thing was that she was indeed a talented housekeeper and could hide behind those skills.

Arabella had little time to do much more than carry out her responsibilities for the next two days and learn about the people under her control in the household and the roles they held, and how they carried out their duties. Only then did she request that discussion with Mr. Pottles.

And, at half-nine the next morning, she presented herself at the butler's door and waited for him to summon her within.

AFTER HE'D SPOKEN to both of his most senior servants, Josh wondered if he'd accidentally set up a feud worthy of ancient Scottish clans within his own household. Pottles was furious, that was clear in spite of the ever-polite demeanor of his butler. Well, the polite behavior he saw or heard. What happened belowstairs could be another matter.

Having lived in a number of households here in Scotland while growing up and then in dozens more during his travels, he should have understood the uncrossable lines that existed when it came to the duties, responsibilities and perquisites among servants. Candidly, he found he'd enjoyed the less stringent ambiance in Rome and on the road on his journeys across northern Africa and up the Nile River. The tribal communities who spoke in languages and had customs of which he had little knowledge somehow felt safer than the current situation between the estimable Pottles and the newly-arrived yet seemingly-skilled Mrs. Lewis.

So, understanding that a strategic retreat could lower the hostilities, he'd accepted several invitations to visit and sup with friends over those next days and nights. In an attempt to give the household servants a chance to adapt to this change, he worked on his newest travelogue late into the night in his bedchamber instead of using his library.

Uncertain of the reason he wanted Mrs. Lewis hired over Pottles' clear disinclination, he worried that he'd made an irreparable mistake... again. Though, in the history of his inheriting and stepping into his title, and all the things expected and unexpected that came with that, this was not the largest one he'd made.

A knock on his door interrupted his inevitable review of his lack of preparation for his position.

"My lord." Pottles spoke as he opened the door.

"Aye?" He waited for his butler's explanation.

"I wish to inquire if you will return to your previous schedule and host the weekly dinner this Thursday evening?"

He had told his friends he would not be doing so in the next few weeks, but the situation seemed to have settled somewhat in his household. *Begin as ye mean t' go*, his cousin would have said. He'd failed at that so far. . . .

"I do, Pottles."

"I will let Mrs. Mathieson ken." The edge of the door slid almost soundlessly across the thick carpet of his bedchamber and was about to close when Josh spoke.

"And Mrs. Lewis."

"My lord?" Pottles turned and stepped back into the room. "As housekeeper, Mrs. Lewis has no oversight of dinners you hold."

"Are we going to argue over this again, Pottles?"

"I would never presume to argue with you, my lord." The butler drew up to his full height, filled with insult.

Joshua stood then, placing the copy of the latest *Scotsman* on his table. He, too, straightened as he stood.

"You and I and Mrs. Lewis are partners in this household, Pottles. The success and standing and position depend on us. We play our parts and set the tone in which we wish to live and as an example to the understaff. There is no excuse for, nor will I accept, keeping you or Mrs. Lewis in the dark about anything that happens or is planned to happen in this household. I expect the same from you," he said.

Pottles met his gaze for a moment or two longer than usual as though judging Josh's resolve. So, he added the last warning he would give.

"If you cannot carry out the duties I expect of you, I'm certain I can find someone who will." A flash of surprise in the older man's gaze followed by acquiescence. "Good night then."

Dismissed, Pottles pulled the door closed.

Hepburn and even MacDonald had been chaffing to get a look at his new housekeeper, no doubt because they knew he'd defied old Pottles to hire her. He admitted to himself that he was interested in seeing her reaction to his weekly dinners and those who attended.

His was a bachelor's residence and he frequently entertained his friends and their particular *friends*. Mrs. Lewis was more familiar with service in the stodgy and formal household of an elderly though cantankerous lady. And a household in which guests and family behaved with the decorum of the matriarch.

This week's gathering was a motley group of friends and acquaintances of his from the University. Though only Alex would bring along a female companion, others would sometimes arrive with an unexpected guest. The spontaneity and openness appealed to him, but Pottles was uncomfortable with it. *A proper nobleman's table was set and not a thing that ebbed and flowed with every knock at the door*, Pottles had complained to one of the footmen under his breath. His butler had not realized that Josh stood directly behind him, and he'd never commented again.

His gatherings were informal, mostly small, always friendly, sometimes boisterous and filled with discussions and arguments on all manner of topics. Someone had suggested he'd created his own salon, but Josh thought that too grand of a description, preferring to keep it as a gathering of friends. And, he would admit, it was one of few times and places when he was completely at ease.

That small detail was the entire reason he continued, in spite of his butler's disdain. In spite of the snubs of some influential people he'd invited. In spite of knowing he should cultivate acquaintances who could help ease or even resolve his difficult position. Because being with friends who accepted him—poor minor diplomat and vindicated adventurer no matter what others said or did—was comfortable for him.

And so, his mood improved as Thursday approached. And it continued as each of the three invitations extended was accepted without delay.

"HOW WAS YOUR Spring term, Professor?" Jamie directed his question to Gill MacIvor, who taught humanities at the university. "Successful for you then?"

"Successful enough I suppose," Gill replied. "Not living in poverty yet, though 'tis a close thing." Though his tone was jovial, Josh knew him to be speaking the truth. Since the university was controlled by the Edinburgh Council and paid their professors differently than Cambridge or Oxford, many of them lived in poverty or sought additional employment to supplement their incomes. Only a small number of the best-known or most experienced had full classes with the income that those generated. "I am hoping for a private commission or two to see me through until next term."

Since they were without female company, they remained at table to enjoy their port after dinner and Pottles did not argue over it, so it must be not heinous on his list of infractions. Soon, the servants cleared away everything but clean glasses and a fresh decanter of port and the comfortable conversation continued for some time. He'd just suggested that they move to the comforts of the drawing room next to his library when loud voices erupted from the hallway, drawing their attention. Pottles, he recognized, but the other, the other was a woman's voice. Not his housekeeper or cook, or any of the maids it seemed. Before he could react, MacDonald jumped to his feet, even as his countenance took on a green hue.

"Alex?"

"I will handle this myself," his friend said as he reached for the door. Just as he touched the knob, the door was forcefully pushed open, knocking him off his balance. Alex stumbled back as what could only be described as a force of nature entered.

Reaching barely to Josh's own shoulders, the well-dressed young woman rushed at his friend, fists raised and flailing, and beat against him. Though she said no words Josh could understand, her sorrow-filled wailing made clear her pain as she continued her attack. When he would have intervened, Alex motioned him away, wrapping his arms carefully around the woman, whispering words only she could hear. Even knowing that Pottles and his footmen were more than a match for this lass if needed, Josh whispered an order to Graham to summon another and the footman ran off.

Whatever MacDonald said helped not one whit and the woman's sobs turned into accusations. Alex tried to guide her from the room, planning, Josh thought, to get her out of the house. Any thoughts of that ended when the woman collapsed, sliding out of Alex's arms and landing on the floor. Before either of them could react, Mrs. Lewis arrived. Josh began to explain, but her words forestalled him.

"If I might, my lord?" He thought she'd spoken to him, but one glance and he realized she was asking Alex for permission. And one look at Alex told him his friend had no idea of what to do when faced with an overwrought woman, so Josh nodded permission anyway.

With a few softly spoken orders, Mrs. Lewis took control and, within a very short time and with the help of the footmen, had the young woman removed from the chamber and ensconced somewhere else. When silence reigned once more, Josh retrieved the carafe of port and added some to each man's glass before taking his seat once more.

Meeting Alex's gaze, he waited for some explanation. At the least learning the identity of the unexpected guest would satisfy.

Gentlemen or noblemen would not expect Alex to reveal details or personal bits.

"I did not think she would follow me here," Alex said before swallowing the contents of his glass in one large mouthful.

"This is your opera singer?" The woman was much younger than most entertainers Josh had seen, so he could not help but doubt this was her.

Alex looked away, clearly chagrined by Josh's questions. Alexander MacDonald, as an earl, answered to few other than his duke of a father. He cavorted around town and out in the country, spending a fortune on entertainment and folly of all sorts. He'd not had a serious thought in his head in years, and Josh suspected he was bored rather than empty-headed. Actually, of the three of them—Alex, Jamie and himself—Alex was probably the most accomplished in academic studies.

But, in the ways of the world, and of women, he was sometimes the most inexperienced. Before another word could be spoken or Alex's amorous companion's identity was revealed, Gill rose and placed his glass there on the table.

"If you dinna mind, I will see myself out, Dunalastair. My thanks for the good evening," MacIvor said. "MacDonald. Hepburn." The professor was not a close friend, so this development added tension to what had been a comfortable evening. With a nod, he left. Josh passed the etched-crystal decanter once more before asking, since Alex was not forthcoming.

"Well, the opera singer or another you have not mentioned yet?"

Alex leaned his head down and rubbed his hands over his face. The shake of his head admitted the complexity of the young woman's presence.

"She is from Miss Adam's establishment."

"You brought a wh—"

"I did not bring her here." Alex stood, hands fisted, as he tried to defend himself.

"Why would she come here? How did she ken to find you

here?" Josh studied his friend's face.

"I may have mentioned our Thursday gatherings to her."

"Alex."

"Josh."

He let out a long exhalation, feeling frustrated with his friend's dissembling non-answers. "Truly, Alex, I want an answer in this. Why did this particular woman come to my home and why was she so hysterical?"

"Miss Anderson came here because she was led to expect a marriage proposal, my lord. And her condition was brought on by the denial of such an offer."

The voice, the voice threaded with true anger, came from behind him. Turning, he found Mrs. Lewis standing in the doorway. For a moment, she gave not the appearance of a housekeeper but that of an angel of righteous anger. When her gaze turned to his friend, Josh nearly let out a sigh of relief that it was not directed at him.

Chapter Four

HER CONTROL SLIPPING, Arabella clenched her hands under the apron she wore. Though Lord Dunalastair was not to blame, his kind were—privileged, wealthy men who thought they could play with people's lives and discard them when finished with them.

And his friend, Lord Finlaggan, was responsible for what had just happened here.

"Pardon?" Lord Dunalastair said. The culprit himself did not speak, as guilty men so often held their tongues. But there was enough of some tone, a warning mayhap, in the viscount's question that she tempered her reply.

"The young woman is abed, my lord. I gave her a small dose of laudanum to calm her nerves. She could be moved with assistance."

"Finlaggan, Hepburn, this is Mrs. Lewis, my new housekeeper," the viscount introduced her to his guests. She'd not met them before, but she'd seen them as they arrived this evening. Glancing around, she only then noticed that the tall, red-haired man was missing. She'd been engaged abovestairs and had not seen him leave.

"My lord. Mr. Hepburn." She nodded to both.

Arabella paused and waited to be asked a question rather than speaking freely. She must remember the role she played, no matter what she'd like to say at this moment. Just when she thought she'd regained control, Mr. Pottles entered the room.

"Mrs. Lewis, may I speak with you?"

He would draw her out of the room, away from the horrible man responsible for the woman now sleeping and give her orders. To keep her place, she would have to follow them, and she knew deep within it would mean tossing the young woman out. She'd turned away, forcing herself to move when Lord Finlaggan spoke.

"I ken it is a complete and utter overstepping here, but could I impose on your hospitality and ask if—" He paused and she waited to hear his request. "May Miss Anderson be permitted to continue rest here until she is feeling stronger? I will come in the morning to see her. . . home."

"Home?" The word slipped out before she could keep it behind her teeth.

"Mrs. Lewis!" Pottles hissed under his breath.

She expected that no matter what Lord Dunalastair decided about Miss Anderson, Arabella would be given leave for speaking so boldly to his friends. Pottles would make certain. And her plans to avenge her family would fail.

All because this unfair and cruel situation had enraged her.

She had no illusions about the profession of the young woman who now lay in drugged oblivion in the guestroom upstairs. And, as a god-fearing woman, she should be scandalized by her presence. But, growing up as she had, relying on the charity of her mother's friends, Arabella had seen the other side of the line between poverty and comfortable living and understood the realities of life and how classes mattered.

"I beg your pardon, my lord," she said, bowing her head to her employer and then to his guest. And she stopped then, not adding another word or trying to explain.

If she lost her position because she chose to defend or at least support this unfortunate, then the two of them might be availing themselves of the services of the Edinburgh Asylum for Women.

"Pottles. Mrs. Lewis. I will join you in a moment," Lord Dunalastair said. His voice, now flat, gave her no indication of what to expect. Arabella nodded and followed the butler.

Graham closed the door, but even that stout barrier was not enough to contain the raised voices within. Though the content of the yelling was garbled, the loudness could be heard even when she reached the landing on the first floor. The guestroom was near the back of the house on this story, so they walked the long corridor to it in silence.

Then, the sounds of doors opening downstairs followed by slamming and footsteps up the staircase foretold of the viscount's arrival. Pottles had not spoken, but his glare did not cease.

Part of his reaction was surely meant to intimidate her. But somewhere within he must be battling the perfect butler's need to serve perfectly, and the indignation of a man bred and raised to recognize those acceptable people in society and those not unacceptable.

Like the young prostitute only a few yards away.

"I understand how irregular this is, but I have given permission for the young woman to remain here overnight. In your care, Mrs. Lewis, if you would?"

"Of course, my lord," she said. He'd surprised her once again. She'd expected that he would side with his friend and hide the unfortunate indiscretion.

"I do not wish the other servants, especially the younger maids and such, to be involved. Pottles, speak to Graham as well."

"My lord," Pottles nodded as he spoke. "I have already."

The viscount glanced at her as though he would speak but did not. Instead, he told Pottles to settle the house for the night before taking his leave and walking to his own chamber. Pottles glared at her once more but left without another word as well.

Arabella opened the door of the guestroom and checked to see that Peigi Anderson was still sleeping. The worst thing to

Arabella was how young this lady of pleasure looked now that the draught had calmed her. Young. Much too young for such a life.

Making her way down to the kitchen, Arabella checked on the progress of the servants in cleaning up after dinner and carrying out the other chores needed to put the house aright before seeking their rest. Her plan was to return upstairs and stay with their guest in case she awakened. And after arranging with Mrs. Mathieson for a breakfast tray to be prepared in the morning and some other light nourishment readied in case needed overnight, Arabella then gathered a few items from her own room to take with her.

The house settled as it did each night, with fewer and fewer footsteps moving about, the creaking of old joints in the wood of the walls and floor and finally the spreading silence. Claiming the comfortable chair in the corner of the guest room, she turned up the oil lamp on the small table and began reviewing her notebook and lists. If she needed to be here to monitor their guest, she would not waste time since many tasks were yet left in her own day. So, once the meals were reviewed, she moved on. Checking the current and upcoming orders from the butcher, chandler, grocer, miller, fishmonger and other merchants was next.

When later she stood up to place the notebook and papers on the table, her back reminded her how long she'd been sitting. As she leaned over the bed, a shiver from the chill in the air gave her another task. With other guests, the housemaids would tend the hearths, but not this one and not tonight. It took only a few minutes to get it burning. Deciding that a fresh cup of tea for herself and some broth for Miss Anderson would be a good thing, Arabella walked quietly across the chamber and turned the knob.

Not expecting anyone to be there, she walked into him.

Directly into him.

Arabella grabbed for something to stop her fall and found her fingers clutching the smooth silk of his banyan. Stumbling back, she lost her balance and would have fallen if he'd not taken hold of her shoulders and held her there. His strong and warm hands kept her from tumbling.

And held her close enough that she could smell the scent of the shaving soap his valet used hours before. Close enough to see his valet could have shaved him again now.

"I did not mean to startle you, Mrs. Lewis," he said as he released her and stepped back. That small shift in their positions revealed that she yet held onto his robe. He glanced down and then back at her face. She let go of the smooth fabric and cleared her throat. "I wanted to check with you about our guest."

"I was just going to the kitchen to bring back some tea and broth," she managed to say in a quiet tone. "While Miss Anderson remains asleep."

"I will walk with you then. We can speak there without disturbing her rest."

And he did, following her along the corridor to the stairs and down. If she thought he would not continue to the lower floor, the territory of the servants, she was wrong. He did so without hesitation. When they reached the bottom, she led him into Mrs. Mathieson's domain.

The kitchen took up almost half of the lower floor, not including the storage closets, or cellar for foodstuffs and spirits. Always warm because of a constant fire in either the hearth or the stove or oven, the overwhelming heat tempted Arabella to open a window. But this level was accessible from outside and the threat of thievery was ever-present here in Edinburgh. Unless the kitchen was well occupied, the windows remained closed.

Other than a low fire burning in the main hearth with a large pot of water on one hook over it and another pot of broth left warming on the stovetop, everything else was stored away until morning. The huge chamber was deserted and quiet. The viscount stopped at the doorway, not yet entering the chamber. He'd walked down here at such ease, so she'd not expected him to stop before entering. Most lords would never have come belowstairs, but he'd not shown himself to be the usual kind of lord.

"Would you care for some tea, or would you prefer something stronger, my lord?"

"Stronger, but only if it is to hand."

Her brow rose on its own for, as housekeeper and servant, she would be expected to retrieve what he needed when he asked for it regardless of its location. And she would have, also regardless of its location, because that's what she should do. But, there was an adequate supply of various spirits close by the kitchen in the locked closet nearest to the butler's room.

"I have something here, my lord," she said.

Though not frequently imbibed here belowstairs, there was whisky, brandy and even some wine kept here in case of need. Selecting the necessary key from the chatelaine hanging from her belt, she opened the locked cabinet near Mr. Pottles' office and selected the bottle of whisky. Back in the kitchen, she found a glass in another closet and poured a goodly amount into it. He moved closer now, pulling a stool closer to the main table in the center of the room as he did. Once he sat, staring into the cup, she ladled some of the water in the pot into a kettle and placed it on the stovetop to make a small pot of tea.

Arabella used the time it took her to get a small, ovenware jug from Mrs. Mathieson's collection and fill it with the broth waiting on the stove to try to calm her breathing. The tension around them increased with every moment of silence. The memory of the cool and silky feeling of his banyan sliding over her fingers made her skin tingle even now. The small shake of her head did little to clear her thoughts, for she knew that it was not only wrong, but also dangerous to look at him as a living, breathing man. Instead of remembering that he was simply her enemy. Her cup clattered on its saucer as she poured the tea into it too quickly. Steadying it was difficult, knowing that he was watching her.

"Was there something in particular you wished to ken about Miss Anderson's condition?" she asked. Walking to the table, she waited for him to speak.

"Do you think she needs more attention than we, you, can provide? Should I summon a—"

"Nay, my lord." Arabella scooped a small spoonful of sugar and a splash of cream into her tea as she stopped him. "The young woman is simply overwrought."

"I expect she is." He drank most of the whisky in his glass in one mouthful before meeting her gaze. "It was not well done of him. Lord Finlaggan has assured me he will sort it out with the woman."

He'd surprised her once again. Taking the side of an unfortunate instead of his rich friend was not what she'd expected from her father's descriptions. Not what she'd prepared herself to face in her quest. Lord Dunalastair finished his whisky and stood, as did she.

"How old do you think she is?" he asked.

"She did not say, but I would estimate her to be around ten-and-nine or possibly a score." A few years separated her from the unfortunate woman.

"So young then to be at such a thing." He glanced over at the hearth for several moments before turning back to her. His gaze intense, his words were almost whispered. "Summon me if you need help with Miss Anderson." He put the glass in the sink, something she'd never seen a nobleman do before and he must have seen the disbelief on her face, for she could not hide it.

"Should you not summon me?" he asked. "I think Pottles would suffer apoplexy if you asked him to tend to this guest."

"I will do what you wish, my lord," she said. His eyes darkened at her words and the air rushed from her lungs at the sight. She recognized arousal in a man's gaze—any woman in service could. "I mean, I will seek you out as you've requested if Miss Anderson needs anything with which I cannot assist."

She offered a bow of her head and waited on his further orders, holding the edge of the table to stop their trembling.

"What do you need to take upstairs?"

"A tea tray, the jug of soup, my lord."

"For both of you?"

"Tea for both but soup and bread for our guest. Mrs. Mathieson suggested a strong broth for the young woman upon awakening to strengthen her. The tea is for her, as well."

"And the whisky?" The bottle she'd forgotten sat there on the table.

"As much as I am tempted to put a good dollop of your fine whisky into my own cup, I will resist the urge and need to do so, my lord." She was met with a smile when she chanced to look at him. Arabella secured the bottle in the locked cabinet.

"As long as you do not overindulge, I have no objections to a wee dram when needed or wanted, Mrs. Lewis," he said as she walked back into the kitchen.

Had he jested with her? It felt like one, in the softening of his voice and the hint of a smile in the corners of his mouth. He stood then and she stepped over to shelves to get a tray to carry all the necessary items up to the guestroom. After refilling the tea pot with more hot water, she placed it in the center of the tray.

"Can I help you with that?"

"Nay, my lord. I can manage it." Arabella heard her scolding tone, almost as bad as Pottles' when he corrected someone, and would blame it on her shock once more. A lord carrying a tray for a servant? Unthinkable! But she began again, not wanting to give the wrong impression. "'Twill not be so heavy that I cannot carry it, my lord."

"Will you be insulted if I order you to allow me to carry it?" This time, she controlled her surprise. Just barely though.

"Insulted? Nay, my lord, if that is your order." She put another cup, the sugar, cream, spoons along with the jug of broth and an empty bowl onto the tray and held it out to him. Adding a napkin to it once he took hold, she held onto her own cup, prepared to make those her chore. "I welcome your help."

The journey to the guestroom was made in silence even while she was aware of each movement he made as he climbed the stairs ahead of her. As the light from the candlelit sconces along the corridor and steps made it possible to see their path, all she could see was him.

Her too-close inspection of his form even as the silky banyan swirled around him made it difficult to slow the rapid beating of her heart. The way his legs, outlined by the tightness of his pantaloons, easily climbed the steps. The strong arms that did not waver as he maneuvered the tray without anything spilling or tilting. He reached the top of the stairway and walked to the guestroom without pause and it was her hands that shook. Her teacup clattered on its saucer.

If she had not looked up at that moment, Arabella would have walked into the man again. Luck was on her side for once, for she had seen him stop. And she waited while he moved out of the way so she could open the door.

With quieter steps than she would have thought possible, he carried the tray in and placed it on the top of the chest of drawers she'd cleared earlier. Shifting it a bit, he released it. As he turned, the robe shifted in the front and she noticed for the first time that he did not wear a cravat to keep his shirt closed. Because of his height to hers, it was difficult to miss as he stepped away. Her mistake was in meeting his gaze after seeing his chest exposed to her.

A moment spun out between them as neither moved nor looked away. Another strange thought occurred to her—she noticed the reflection of the flames in his eyes—his *green* eyes. Only a spark snapping in the fire next to them brought her back to her senses. The last thing she should be doing was looking at him as anything but her foe, her enemy. The weight of the cup in her hand gave her a reason to move away.

Arabella silently crossed the bedchamber and put her tea on that small table again. Miss Anderson did not move, seeming deeply asleep.

"My thanks for your help, my lord." She nodded her head.

"Glad to be of service." Her eyes widened at his words, and she could not help it. Lord Dunalastair had his hand on the knob when he turned back to her. "You are not like any housekeeper I've ever met, Mrs. Lewis."

"And you are like no viscount I have ever met, my lord."

He blinked at her and let out the beginning of a laugh, before stopping himself and leaving the chamber quickly. A moment after what was mayhap her worst indiscretion, her worst misstep, since beginning her plan, she stood watching their guest sleep and wondered if Miss Anderson, or she herself, was the bigger fool.

Chapter Five

W HEN NEXT HE encountered Alex, days after their meeting when he came to retrieve Miss Anderson, his friend looked serious. As Josh entered the Society's library wing intent on beginning the next chapter of his work, they passed in the corridor.

"Dunalastair." Alex nodded in greeting. "Are you coming or going?"

"Just arrived." His friend looked past him and then met his gaze.

"Not a good time for a drink then?" Something in Alex's tone made Josh believe this was not simply his friend passing the time.

"Let me claim my spot in the library and I will meet you upstairs."

Continuing on, Josh walked into the chamber where he preferred to work. After placing his leather satchel on a small table in the back corner, also his customary location, he went off to meet Alex in the drawing room for members of the Society. His friend, seated in the back of the chamber against the wall, had two glasses ready on the table between the two chairs. Sliding down into the plush cushions, he took one of the glasses—of whisky apparently—and held it up in a mock salute before tasting it.

"There was no session today and you have not taken up a

new project that you have shared—" Josh waited for Alex to give a sign that something was underway. "So, what brings you here on this lovely Edinburgh afternoon."

Alex did glance out one nearby window and smile at Josh's jest. The rain was pouring down in torrents, the large drops splashing off the glass panes only to be replaced with more.

"I came to speak to you."

"You could have called at my house," Josh said. "I have been there most days."

"I ken." Alex shifted in his seat and drank some of his whisky. "I'd rather not."

Josh studied his friend. The serious mien was new. Though he sipped at this drink, Alex seemed more alert, less drunk, than was his habit.

"Why is that?"

Even as he asked the question, the image of Mrs. Lewis entered his thoughts. Not the one he witnessed every day as she went about her housekeeping duties in her neat black gown, clean white apron and her dark brown hair tucked into a cap. Well, all of her hair except that one unruly, untamed lock that seemed to escape and curl down the back of her neck, drawing his attention every single time she passed him.

Nay, what he remembered was the way pure, unadulterated fury in her brown eyes as she entered the dining room and spied Alex there. After she'd spoken to Miss Anderson. When he would swear she'd wanted to throw a punch at his friend. But, in an instant, she'd tamped down her ire and, other than one word uttered with disrespect, he could not find fault with her behavior.

"You do not wish to encounter Mrs. Lewis."

Alex swallowed the last of his whisky without looking at him. A nod answered his question.

"She is a servant."

"My own illustrious and imperious father is unable to cause the guilt that your housekeeper did with a word and a glance. He could learn a thing or two about putting someone in their place from your Mrs. Lewis."

"She is not *my* Mrs. Lewis." He surprised himself with the strength of his denial. He took a breath. "So, it would seem that you do have a conscience after all?"

"Bloody hell! How can you ask that?" Alex's voice rose and the slam of the heavy crystal glass drew attention.

A footman rushed over with fresh glasses, thinking as most around them had, that the Earl of Finlaggan was in need of more spirits. Though Alex grabbed up the new serving, he held it, not drinking, until the footman returned to his place near the door where he oversaw the needs of the members in the chamber. Even then, he did not drink.

"For a long time, I have watched my oldest friend fall headlong into a life of overindulgence, aimless meandering and even destructive folly. I guess our society sees nothing wrong with that, expects it really, considering your title and wealth. But nothing has seemed to matter to you, nor no bad behavior or excess has given you pause." Josh leaned closer and lowered his voice. "I worry."

After looking at his glass, Alex put it, the whisky untouched, back on the table and pushed it away. Josh leaned away too, sensing his friend needed a bit of space.

"Miss Anderson has been given a settlement and a position away from her. . . former place of employment. She is, as it turns out, a proficient seamstress and there is an opening for her at a successful shop, in Leith."

Of all the things Alex could have said, that was completely unexpected. Alex stared at him now and Josh did not know what his friend was waiting for him to say.

"And she is content with these arrangements?"

"Aye, very." Alex reached inside his jacket pocket and withdrew an envelope. "I ken Mrs. Lewis was kind to Peigi and I appreciate that. If you would give this to her, I would be in your debt." Accepting it, Josh saw it was addressed to his housekeeper.

"I can do that." Josh took the envelope and the glass on the table in his hands and stood. "Will this ease your way back into my house?"

"It may." Alex stood and nodded to him. "Send me an invitation to your next gathering."

Josh watched as his friend left and, for the first time in many, many months, he worried a bit less about him. Making his way back to the library where his latest chapter awaited him, he decided to return home to give this envelope to Mrs. Lewis and see her reaction. He might even ask her about the contents, rude as that might be. A laugh escaped at the memory of Alex calling her *Josh's* Mrs. Lewis.

Reaching the table where he'd left his satchel, Josh stopped before it, stunned by what lay there. And what no longer did.

A few books remained on the table, but now scattered rather than the neat pile he'd left.

His satchel now lay on the chair, unlatched and open.

Pages he'd written, along with his notebook were strewn over the surface, some ripped into pieces and other pages clearly torn from the notebook.

Only one page seemed put into a specific position so that he could see it there.

A drawing from years, decades ago, drawn by Luigi, on the morning of their first excavation.

In Timgad.

He did not need to lift it closer to recognize the item.

Drawn as they'd found it, the ancient Roman brooch contained several large jewels in a variety of colors arranged around the perimeter of the metal disk. Until Luigi had dropped it, they'd never seen that it was two different pieces that slid together in one ornate piece.

Shivers of dread raced along his spine at the sight of it, causing an unease to race through his blood. Sweat broke out on his brow and more ran down his back.

As beautiful and well-crafted as it was, Josh swore that it was the beginning of everything bad that had happened to him. To his reputation. To the rest of the visit to the old Roman fort and his travels to other places in Africa and home to Scotland.

Glancing around, he saw no one close to this back table. An attendant sat at the door but could not see around the tall shelves into this alcove. So, whoever did this, whoever rummaged his belongings, destroyed some of his pages and, from his cursory examination, took others, had not been seen. Only as he quickly gathered everything together and sought out his greatcoat and hat did he see the disturbing clue on the floor.

A line of wet footprints led from the slightly open window a few feet away, to the table he'd used and back again.

Someone had managed to know where he was. Someone watched and took advantage of his short excursion upstairs to sneak in through the window. Someone knew what he carried with him and searched his belongings looking for something they thought he possessed.

Not just any item.

The piece of the brooch in the sketch.

And in spite of his denials, hundreds or thousands of denials over the years, it was the only thing he had from that dig. No one else knew that it was locked away in his safe lockbox at home, hidden behind a fake panel that only he knew about...

But, if Luigi's local guide had been correct, an old legend said that the purpose of the brooch—to reveal the location of a richer, larger treasure left behind in the ruins—could only be accomplished if both pieces were entwined together, lining up the stones with the lines carved into the gold.

In other words, a map. A map to untold wealth.

An artifact he'd tried to keep hidden, especially since the other half was lost forever. A relic of long dead Romans, buried with them and uncovered by accident by his team. A guide to rumored riches. But, people had died because of it already and Josh had sworn to never let it see the light of day again.

He almost dropped the satchel to his side as the reality struck him.

Someone else knew of the legend and had other plans to pursue it.

Again.

SINCE HIS PRACTICE was to spend most of the day at the Society's library while working on a new project, he knew he'd surprised his servants with his early and hasty return.

"My lord?" Pottles approached him before he got past Graham or removed his greatcoat. "Is there something you need? Did you leave something behind?"

Josh waved him off, needing to get to his chamber. Needing to see the lockbox there. That it was. . . there. And locked. And its contents still locked and safe. As he moved past his butler, Pottles spoke again.

"If you have need of something, simply send a message and I will have it delivered to you, my lord."

Since attaining his title, he had made it a practice to take the pretentious man's instruction in how to be a proper nobleman in his stride and to explain himself or his actions. But, in this moment, he needed no such lessons and would give no such explanations.

"Silence!"

He had not raised his voice in speaking the word. Indeed, he'd pushed the word through clenched teeth in a low voice. But the effect was as if he had shouted. Pottles backed up and straightened to that perfect-butler pose and closed his mouth, all in an instant.

Graham had caught up with them, so he shrugged his dripping coat off before climbing the stairs. Leaving Pottles and Graham behind, he sought his chamber and slammed its door closed so no one would disturb him. His chest tightened with each step towards the key's hiding place next to the fireplace.

So many years trying to keep it safe. Rather, trying to keep others who believed in the folly of such a relic safe from the inevitable greed its legend caused. Safe from those who would pursue it without regard for others. Away from those who would murder to find it, regardless of the truth.

Had he truly failed?

Now in front of the false compartment, he reached out to the place on the wooden frame of the mantel that would free the latch. The trembling of his hand made it difficult to touch exactly the correct place, so he shook it free of the tremors and tried once more. The small panel popped open and Josh could see the pouch tucked in the back of the enclosure. A bit of relief surged when he touched the sack and felt the key within it.

He wanted to hope that all was well. But the previous attacks of years ago yet lived in the back of his consciousness every moment. Every time someone heard about his journey to Timgad, Luigi's stories surfaced and led to dreamers and criminals seeking out the Treasure of Trajan.

Treasure of Trajan? More like a curse!

It was one of the reasons he remained quiet when faced with too many questions about that journey. One of the reasons. A rough laugh escaped into the quiet around him. It had been Luigi's questions that had caused the attention in the first place.

Pulling the key from its hiding place, he walked over and locked the door, then walked into his dressing room, seeking out the closet within and the strongbox in it. His breath held, he put the key into the lock and turned, opening the lid.

Nothing looked disturbed or moved. The small wooden box that held the brooch lay just where it should, under layers of papers and documents and a few other personal items. Releasing the mechanism that kept it closed, Josh offered up a brief prayer that all was well.

And it was.

The brooch, or the part of it that he possessed, lay exactly as he'd left it. The gold disk was smaller than his palm and crisscross lines were carved into its surface, looking very much like a rudimentary map. The decorations along the edge were done by someone with experience in working gold, for they were masterfully done, delicate marks and designs. A small projection in the center appeared to be the place where the second disk would attach.

The part of the disk that contained the jewels shown on the drawing left for him. The one that would supposedly lead to the treasure. Closing his eyes for a moment, he allowed relief to fill him.

The brooch was here. Safe. At least it was at this moment. As he placed it back in the box and then back into the larger, metal strongbox, he knew he would need to take further actions to protect it now.

Someone was searching for it, following him at the least, and he would not allow it to be found. Or endanger others in someone's quest to take it.

After the strongbox was secured back in its place and the key hidden away, he considered his choices.

Over the next few days, he would vary his schedule, never doing the same thing at the same time. And, he would warn Pottles not to allow unknown workers or delivery boys for merchants to enter the house. Also, a word to Pottles about locking the doors and windows.

Then, after retrieving his small notebook of names and addresses in the drawer of the table next to his bed, he examined those listed who were known to him as sellers and brokers in antique jewelry and historical artifacts. He would seek out a few of the more unsavory ones, traders in items that authorities would be interested in finding.

Sadly, there were many who would—even some of his well-titled, educated acquaintances would be willing to look away from the legalities if they could buy the brooch or the treasure it would lead them to. The worlds of academia and historians were filled with as many cut-throats as any other business where fortunes could be made.

And, if he was the one stirring this pot of unseemly characters, he would have to think about making arrangements for more vigilance around his house. Possibly even guards hired to patrol the immediate area.

Tucking his notebook into his waistcoat pocket, he returned downstairs to speak to Pottles. He would speak to the footmen separately so that his butler was not insulted. The next hours were spent trying to sort through the necessary things needed to secure his house and to investigate this newest threat.

Only when he changed clothing for dinner out did his valet find the envelope still in his waistcoat pocket. When he asked for her to be called, Ewan—the footman on duty outside his chamber—reminded him that it was Mrs. Lewis' afternoon off and she was expected back later.

That envelope, along with Alex's attempt at redemption, were the only good things about this day and he wanted to see his housekeeper's expression and reaction to the news within it. For some reason, as Alex had, it was important to him for her to know about the change in Miss Anderson's circumstances.

Sitting on the edge of his bed, he realized that his reactions to her—when they'd spoken that night, or when he watched that dangerous lock of her hair dangle loosely down her delicate neck, or when he shared a conspiratorial glance after Pottles made one or another command—were not appropriate.

She was in his employ, and he was not one of those men. Men who dawdled with servants or who pushed their own will on others. Part of his attitude was his past—growing up less than noble and witnessing of that behavior. Part of it came from the fact he did not feel noble or entitled. Indeed he felt like an impostor most days and especially when called by the title that had unexpectedly come to him.

But, even knowing and understanding the problems inherent with attraction to women in one's employ, Josh could not help that he liked her. He did admit that much to himself. He liked the way she dealt with others. He liked the way she defended those unable, or unwilling, to defend themselves. He liked the gentle way she cared about others. And the way she moved with a confidence unusual in someone as young as she.

But worse, he worried over the truly dangerous appeal of that curl that always escaped her cap and led his eyes down to watch the sway of her hips as she walked. The fullness of her lips, whether while speaking or especially while smiling. The directness of her mahogany brown eyes when they met and even when they held his gaze. The moment when they were together in the guestroom and everything around them, even time, seemed to pause repeated over and over in his memory.

Staring at the envelope in his hand, turning it end over end, Josh understood that in spite of the danger, in spite of the fact that he should not, he liked Clara Lewis.

Chapter Six

H ER KEY TURNED in the lock on the servants' entrance door but the door itself did not budge. Gazing through the frosted glass panes, she could see no movement within the entranceway or rooms beyond. She checked her pocket watch and saw that she was later in arriving back at Lord Dunalastair's house than she'd planned, but it was not so late that she should be locked out for the night.

Arabella tucked the watch back into the small reticule on her wrist and peered in once more before knocking a few times. Unsuccessful at drawing the notice of anyone inside, she decided her way into the house must be through. . . the front door. The only other alternative was to return in the morning and that was not something she was willing to do. Better to scandalize Mr. Pottles than spend the night. . . wherever. With the cool haar swirling in and filling the streets, wynds and closes, she did not wish to stay outside for much longer.

She walked up the steps from the entryway below street level and stared up at the front door, wondering if she should indeed be bold and knock on the front door. Lord Dunalastair was out for the evening, or for dinner at least, so he would never know. Fortune smiled on her in that moment as the front door opened and Ewan stepped out.

"Mrs. Lewis," he said with a nod. "I thought I heard knocking below."

"Aye, Ewan, you did," she said. Standing at the bottom of the steps, she waited a moment before climbing up to the door. "My key seemed to work below, yet the door would not open."

"His lordship ordered new locks on the doors, Mrs. Lewis," he said, as he moved aside to allow her entrance. "He said to watch for you."

"New locks?" She turned to face the tall young man as he closed the door. She could see the additional lock, a sliding bolt, above the current knob and keyhole. "Was there a—"

She stopped the rest of her words, knowing that somehow Mr. Pottles would hear her questioning Lord Dunalastair's decision. Luckily she had, for Mr. Pottles stood just a few yards away watching her enter.

"If you had returned at the correct time, you would have learned of this when I spoke to the staff after dinner, Mrs. Lewis."

Arabella took in a breath and began counting to herself as she released it slowly. One of these times when Mr. Pottles harassed her, she would indeed lose control, but she could not until she found what she was looking for. Before she could address the butler, she nodded to the footman and dismissed him.

Ewan threw the new bolt that now secured the door closed and walked back to the back stairs. In seeing that, Arabella learned that the viscount was already home. And he'd been considerate enough to have Ewan wait on her return after his own.

"Well, Mr. Pottles, if there's nothing else needed, I will retire."

"Actually, there is something, Mrs. Lewis." She'd almost made it past him when her words stopped her. Facing him, she waited for the rest. The smug expression he wore most of the time when dealing with anyone but Lord Dunalastair was firmly in place now. "His lordship wants to speak with you about some matter."

She'd avoided being alone with his lordship after that encounter in the guestroom, seeing him only as they each went their own way each day. He consulted her on matters of the household a few times, but he was a busy man, overseeing his affairs and his properties and working on his new project.

He'd gone on to travel elsewhere on the African continent after his, their, initial discovery, she knew that. And now he was writing an account of that second, longer journey, probably stealing once more from records and sketches her father had made all those years ago. The thought of that continued misuse of her father's years of efforts *had* stoked her hatred, even though it was his behavior the rest of the time that was making it more and more difficult to keep that in mind.

Like having a footman wait for her when he knew she would not be able to enter on her own.

"Now?" She glanced at the staircase that led to his bedchamber.

"In the morning. His lordship will be taking his breakfast in his. . . library and wants you to join him there."

His lordship never liked to be disturbed in his library in the morning. Even Mr. Pottles remained outside the door, clearly resisting the urge to knock or enter until the viscount opened it and signaled the end of his self-imposed work session.

"His library? Truly?" Not really a question, more an expression of disbelief, for she'd not gotten a good chance to explore that chamber since her arrival.

Mr. Pottles simply stared at her, as though waiting for her to explain how she was permitted, nay invited, into his lordship's privacy at the time when no one else dared. Arabella blinked several times before speaking.

"Very well, Mr. Pottles. I will attend his lordship in the morning."

Though his lordship rose and began his day much earlier than many nobles, she would still have several hours in the morning to finish her own tasks before answering this summons. She'd found him to be more scholarly, like an academic or professor, than similar to his noble and gentlemen friends in his approach to servants or his lifestyle.

With a nod, she took her leave of the butler, as he stood—still staring at her as though trying to sort out in his mind the reasons behind this extraordinary breach in daily schedule and practice. Walking to the ground floor, she first made her way to the door and did indeed find the same thing as the front entry—a sturdy, new bolt above the existing know and keyhole.

Something had happened. While she was taking her afternoon off, something had happened. Something that resulted in new locks on the doors. She would need to find out before she spoke with him in the morning. Forewarned and all.

THE CHORES OF the household, from cleaning rooms and preparing meals to accepting deliveries of supplies, began early each morning. In any household, repairs and mending needed to be done as well as care of the stable, carriage and horses. This one was no different. Though her training and experience was not quite as broad as the letters of reference made it sound, Arabella had actually witnessed and assisted Lady Arbuthnott's very efficient housekeeper. And so far, she'd not run into a situation or problem she could not handle.

And this morning, after a night of restless sleep—when it did come—she needed things to run smoothly. Mrs. Mathieson had shared some of the details from yesterday's sudden visit from a locksmith, who worked quickly under Lord Dunalastair's constant oversight. In spite of what the cook did know, she could not explain what had brought these changes on.

Finally, just before dread and anticipation could grow too strong, the time came for her to attend the viscount in his library. After taking a few minutes to change her apron and cap and wash her hands, she walked up to the servants' staircase and made her way to his lordship's library. Pottles stood in the corridor, glaring at her when she reached the doorway and as she knocked. And as she waited for permission to enter. She did not hesitate when the word came.

"Good morning, my lord," she said as she closed the door. Walking over to his desk, she curtsied. "I was told you wished to speak to me."

Whatever she'd expected in his reception of her, the smile that greeted her was not it. It was strange how such a simple thing could change his countenance so much. Though he was fifteen years older than her, when he smiled it was hard to tell. His green eyes shone as though filled with mirth and she found she was less intimidated than when she'd opened the door. He ran his hands through his hair, pushing the longer strands back in an affectation that was almost intimate.

His valet must despair of his lord. Now, as she waited for him to speak, she realized that he was never a stickler over his appearance. Sometimes he would rush in from some appointment or another without his hat on and his wind-blown hair all askew and she imagined that's what he looked like on his journeys. Across the desert. Along the Nile River.

Shaking herself from these shocking thoughts, thoughts that should be repellant to her considering her past. Their past. His responsibility in her father's humiliation and death.

"Mrs. Lewis, please sit."

"I beg your pardon, my lord?" She glanced down at the chair that remained in the exact same spot as it had during her interview. "Sit?"

"Sit," he repeated in that quiet voice that sent commanded without volume. So, she did. "Would you care for some coffee?"

This time her mouth dropped open before she could control it. Arabella stood at the unexpected offer. "My lord?"

"Please, Mrs. Lewis. Pour yourself a cup of coffee and sit while I explain the reason I've called you here."

"My thanks," she said, lifting the coffee pot and filling the empty cup near his full one on the tray. A touch of milk and a sprinkle of sugar was all she needed before she did as he'd ordered. "Did something happen, my lord? The new locks?" She was watching his face over the edge of her cup as she took a sip and saw his expression shift to wary and then back to the relaxed one that had greeted her on her arrival.

"Reports of attempts to rob several houses in the area," he said. His tone was even, but somehow, *somehow*, Arabella could hear the lie in his words. "I thought it best to be safe."

"Ah, I did wonder over the haste to have them placed. And, my thanks for having Ewan look out for my return. I will not be so late again, my lord."

"Mrs. Lewis, no one is more aware than I am that you have not taken the days off that were agreed to when you were hired. I understand you left word before you went on your way, so I have no objections that you were out of the house last evening."

No one is more aware than I am. . . .

Luckily, she'd placed her cup on its saucer right then or she might have dropped it at his words. A chill raced through her at his words even as heat crept into her cheeks at the thought that the viscount was *aware* of her. She reported to Pottles every day. Twice a day at the least. He was the man who was in charge of her activities each day. And, under the utter surprise caused by his words, a frisson of fear settled deep in her belly that his awareness might include having seen her searching some of the shelves and storage cabinets.

"Now to the reason I asked you here this morn." He stood and circled the desk until he stood before her. "This is for you." He held out a small envelope to her.

"What is this, my lord?" He turned it so she could see her name written on the front. Still, she did not take it and he leaned against the desk, holding it out.

"Open it and see." Mischief shone in his eyes as she took it from him. "I promise there is nothing dangerous within it."

Since she knew very few people here in Edinburgh outside those in this household, she could not imagine who would have written to her. Arabella glanced up to see he was watching her. . .

and smiling. Confused, off-balance and wary, she accepted his letter opener and lifted the seal. There was an insignia on the wax, but she had no way of knowing to whom it belonged.

"You are very slow at this."

"I am not in the practice of receiving letters such as these, my lord. Pardon my lack of haste." She'd offered the words dripping in sarcasm, forgetting her place completely, and he surprised her by laughing. It felt like warm treacle pouring through her— deep and warm and soothing somehow.

"I am chastened, Mrs. Lewis," he said, bowing his head in a mock salute.

When he stood and moved away, something within her did not like it. And then her sensible side realized she must not allow this familiarity between them. The viscount walked slowly around the perimeter of the library, acting quite clearly as if he was not watching even while waiting for her to read her letter.

Unfolding the expensive sheets of paper, she found the beginning and read it. After only the first sentence, she turned it over to see the writer's name.

"Lord Finlaggan? What business has he with me?"

"Read on, Mrs. Lewis," he said over his shoulder. "Read on."

The pages slid through her grasp as the memory of her rude words and behavior that night. Was he angry over her insulting question of him about Miss Anderson? Or her not-well-veiled comments on the morning when he arrived to escort the woman out?

"You might discover it if you would simply read his words."

He'd noticed her continued delay. He stood by the window now. Still watching her. And she suspected he already knew the contents of this letter. So, she read on.

And gasped at what she found there.

A nobleman explaining his actions to a servant and a stranger at that? She was shocked at everything she read, shocked by his tone and his words and even more so by the actions he'd taken. Arabella did not even realize she was crying until she noticed the handkerchief in Lord Dunalastair's outstretched hand.

"Thank you, my lord," she said. Placing the papers on his desk, she accepted the linen square and wiped away the tears. He remained close and continued to watch her. The need on her part to move away grew stronger.

"Are you well, Mrs. Lewis? Unless there is more in that than he told me, I did not think that Lord Finlaggan's words would distress you." She met his gaze.

"So, you knew then?"

A nod. He slid over a bit when she began to stand, giving her room enough to move past him. Which she did not hesitate to do, taking a few paces to the window where he'd been.

"I saw him at the Society's rooms yesterday and he asked me to give it to you. He also explained the arrangements for Miss Anderson."

The unexpected kindness on his own part to her as well as that of his friend towards a young prostitute shook her deeply. Whether the stark solitude of her own life or her less-than-charitable treatment by nobles and gentlemen, she knew not, but her control and calm evaporated in that moment. Worse than just reacting with a few tears, she burst out crying.

Leaning her face into the borrowed handkerchief, she tried to muffle the sobs she could not contain. She might have been able to stop herself, but the feel of his arm sliding around her shoulders and holding her made it worse... and better in the same moment. He leaned in and whispered something against her head, and all she could tell was that he was trying to comfort her.

No one had done that since her mother had passed away.

On her own for years. Alone. Left with only her anger to sustain her, Arabella struggled against her need to sink into his embrace and accept the comfort he offered—as one person to another. It took only another moment to realize what she had succumbed to and to pull free from him.

"I did not expect such softheartedness from you, Mrs. Lewis. I

knew you were a kind woman, but this is more than I suspected."
He lifted his hand and gently smoothed the loosened strands of
hair from her face. Then he wiped the last tears away with the
back of his fingers. She stepped back one more pace before he
could move nearer, and he dropped his hand.

Looking at him now, she cursed that softheartedness and the
overwhelming need to move back into his embrace. It had been
years and years. . . . And worse, she was lying to him with every
word she spoke and every action she took. She cleared her throat
only with great effort.

"I am glad for Miss Anderson. A chance at a new life, a new
future, is a wonderful thing."

She scooped up the papers and folded them back into a neat
square, placing that into the envelope. She would consider all the
details later, including the joy she felt for this young woman
leaving behind her precarious life for one with a possibility of
success and even happiness. Right now, in this moment, Arabella
needed to pull herself back under control before everything she'd
worked towards was irretrievably lost forever. Tucking the
envelope into her apron pocket, she pushed her shoulders back
and stood taller.

"Was there anything else, my lord?"

The puzzlement at her behavior—the quick change from
weeping woman to efficient housekeeper—was clear on his face.
He shook his head and returned to his chair. She'd always
presented herself in a calm manner, been unflappable in most
situations here, even pretending or bluffing when she had no idea
of what to do. So this complete breakdown was an unspeakable
breach of behavior.

"Only to ask if you have any issues with Lord Finlaggan's
return?"

"My lord?" His question confused her. But following on the
heels of her emotional outburst, she wondered if she'd taken
leave of her senses. "I do not understand your meaning."

She wanted to run. Someplace away from here to hide away

until things made sense. Until she could sort out the morass of conflicting emotions that filled and unbalanced her.

A lord asking her opinion about his friend.

A man she should hate giving her more and more reasons not to.

A need deep within her to throw her plans aside gnawed at the other need to set things aright.

"Lord Finlaggan was very concerned with your reaction to his arrangements. He said that you scared him more than his father, the duke," the viscount said. "And since I ken the duke very well, that is quite a compliment."

"I ken not what to say, my lord," she answered, with a bow of her head. Of all the things she would have guessed his friend would say, this was not one. "He, pardon me, Lord Finlaggan is your friend. 'Tis not my place to have anything to say."

"I kenned you would say that, Mrs. Lewis." He stood then and walked to the door. Instead of opening it, he remained in front of it until she met his eyes. "I think you do not understand the effect you have on others. Somehow you managed to reach my friend who was on the brink of something dangerous and pull him back."

He turned the knob and tugged the door ajar an inch or so. Arabella wait, for his hand did not move. She thought he had something else to say. And his next words took her breath and nearly her resolve for her goal away.

"In championing young Miss Anderson, you made a difference in someone I have always counted as a good friend. So, that night, you saved two lives. And I will always be in your debt on his behalf."

With that, he smiled once more and opened the door, stepping back to allow her to pass. Only the sight of Pottles in the corridor stopped her from a foolish reaction. Hastily, she tucked the handkerchief into her pocket, not wanting Pottles to see it, and nodded to the viscount as she left.

Arabella would see it returned to him later, but for now she clutched it as she made her way down to her little office. With most of her chores for the day finished, she would only need to check on the housemaids' progress in cleaning and be available if Mrs. Mathieson called on her for something. She could accomplish either of those without much thought or concentration.

Thank the good Lord for that because her thoughts, her memories, her feelings and her plans were beginning to melt into one big heaping pile of confusion. When she'd begun this endeavor, she was certain she knew the man, knew the way he would be, what he would say and do. But every day here demonstrated her folly, her complete lack of true preparation in this attempt of hers.

Oh, she'd thought herself prepared and ready to face the man who'd stolen her father's accomplishments and claimed them as his own. The man who erased her father from any link to the discoveries and successes that Luigi Balugani had actually achieved.

But the man she'd hated for years was not the man she knew. Nay, this man who cared about his friends and who was happy over the fate of an unfortunate woman could not be the same man. Had he changed that much? Had he felt the guilt that a deceiver and absconder should feel?

By the afternoon, she took to her bed with a megrim, seeking the dark and silent place so she could sort this out. And to decide if her path still made sense. And what she could do if it, as she suspected, it did not.

Chapter Seven

H E'D LEFT THE house right after speaking to Mrs. Lewis, a different time than his usual to depart for his day's business. Two meetings already scheduled could not be moved so he would have to work around those and shift a few other plans.

Two things distracted him through the next several hours. First, the memory of those footprints leading from the window to his papers. And second, the way that Mrs. Lewis' shoulders shook when she sobbed into her hands after reading Alex's letter.

And of those two, Mrs. Lewis, for better or worse, was his biggest concern.

The feel of her so close was torture. When he leaned down to whisper to her, he could smell the scent of whatever soap she used. As he slipped his arm around her shoulders to give her support, Josh realized he was breaking a barrier with his actions. Good intentions meant naught when it came to violating society's, and decency's, restrictions. If he continued, he'd be no better in his actions than Alex had been.

He needed to do what both his friends and the estate solicitor were telling him to do—marry and produce an heir to secure the estate and title. That would place his focus on a critical thing that needed doing and mayhap reduce this recent lust for his house-keeper.

Thinking on it now, Josh realized it had been weeks, months really, since he'd carried out anything of an amorous nature. A few friendships with a few very willing widows over the last years since inheriting had sufficed in that regard. Any attempts to find a suitable bride and arrange an engagement had been impossible as Josh's purported questionable past and rumors about his expeditions rose each time.

He let out a scorn-filled chuckle as Hepburn's carriage turned onto his street.

"Are you well, Josh?" his friend asked. They had been at their club for several hours, but nothing seemed to settle him down this night. "You are quiet now after hours of the fidgets."

He had not shared this latest disturbing news with Jamie, or Alex, or anyone but the head of the agency he was hiring for additional protection. This could be a completely coincidental robbery—someone saw his unintended satchel and made a hard search, tearing pages and tossing things around.

"I asked you a question." Jamie's serious tone caught his attention.

"Just. . ."

"Has it happened again?" Damn. Just when he'd underestimated Hepburn's attention and memory, his friend surprised him.

"I wish to keep this quiet, Jamie."

"So, it has then? And, 'tis connected to. . . before?"

Josh closed his eyes for a moment and pinched the bridge of his nose. He'd almost put aside the memories of the attacks that ended years ago. Oh, the habits developed during the months and months of mysterious robberies, muggings and even more dangerous threats had served him well. But as quickly as they'd begun, they stopped.

"I suspect it may be." At Jamie's indrawn breath, Josh shook his head. "I just do not ken yet. So, please do not share your suspicions with anyone, especially Alex."

Jamie sank back into the plush cushions and for a few moments, only the sound of the wheels and horse on the cobble-stones filled the carriage. Josh could almost hear the workings of his mind.

"Whatever you need."

Jamie was the amiable sort of friend, but with little drive or ambition other than surviving on the allowance given him by his mother's brother. His offer was. . . extraordinary.

"We will speak on it when I ken more," he said.

The carriage drew to a stop before his house. After climbing out, he waited as the coachman shook the reins and called out to the horses. Jamie nodded at him. Josh stood a bit longer, lost in his thoughts as a few others passed by in carriages, on horseback and on foot as well.

He only heard the approach at the last second, just before the blow to his head.

"MY LORD?" THE voice cut through the thick fog and pain, but he could not sort out who it was. "My lord, can you hear me?"

Josh struggled to open his eyes. The soft touch on his cheek caught his attention. Then the scent he recognized now as *hers* swirled about him. Forcing his eyes open a slit, he found Mrs. Lewis staring at him with concern in her dark brown gaze.

From only inches away. The searing pain in his head now could not be ignored. Lifting his hand, he reached up to find out the source of it. Until she stopped him and guided his arm back down to rest on his stomach.

"Remain still and have a care, my lord," Mrs. Lewis said. "'Tis bleeding heavily and will need stitching."

Only when he tried to rise did he realize that he'd been resting his head on her lap. Flashes of light and colors filled his vision at his attempt to sit up and he fell back. With a soft gasp, she guided his head down, easing him back.

"That was a stupid thing to do," he whispered through teeth clenched against the pain that made it feel as though his head would explode.

"Aye, it was."

He would have replied but the way she stroked across his forehead and wiped his face with her own handkerchief distracted him completely. But when she pressed against the wound, he could not ignore the pain.

"What happened?"

"Someone struck you from behind," she explained. "And, whoever did this tried to rob you."

"What?"

"Some of your pockets are all torn away. The thief or thieves were too hurried to do a slow search for your treasurers."

"Treasures? What do you mean by that?" Did she know? How could she?

"I think you will find your pocket watch and your purse along with that fine pen you carry are gone."

A flurry of activity began—he thought it was her calling out orders, the approach of footsteps and Mrs. Lewis' shifting beneath him—told him help had arrived.

"Please remain still until Ewan and Graham move you. I worry that you will fall unconscious again and do more injury to yourself if you attempt to rise on your own efforts again."

A wave of nausea washed over him suddenly and his belly roiled as it did when he was ill. He clutched his stomach as she spoke.

"Ewan, step back. Graham, take his arm. Now, do it now!" She could be every bit as imperious as Pottles was and she did not even know it.

He wanted to smile but too many things happened at once. That was his last coherent thought for what must have been a long time, for the next time he opened his eyes—carefully, slowly—he was in his own bed. Lying fully clothed in the garments he'd worn out for the evening.

Then he also realized that people were speaking outside his door in the corridor. Pottles and Mrs. Lewis actually were not speaking—they were arguing. More surprising to him was the fact that his housekeeper was not giving his butler an easy time of it. In spite of the slamming pain in his head, he smiled.

The heated exchange gave no sign of ceasing so Josh took advantage of being alone to examine his head and the wound. A bandage wound around his head, covering the injury but even the pressure of his fingers on it caused more pain. He would know if they'd done anything substantial, wouldn't he? About to try sitting up, he was stopped when the discussion ceased, and the door opened.

"You are awake, my lord." They spoke the words in one voice before rushing into the room. His valet followed and waited by the door.

"What happened?"

The two senior servants glanced at each other before speaking, with Mrs. Lewis giving way with a slight nod of her head. Only then did he take in the whole of her and see the blood on her apron.

His blood? It must be. Seeing his reaction, she quickly untied, removed and rolled up the apron and held it out of sight.

"Duncan, help me up," he said, holding his arm out as his valet approached. He was not foolish enough to rush it and he allowed Duncan's strength to aid his movements. His ascent to upright was in degrees. It took several minutes before he was sitting on the edge of his bed and not falling back down—though the bedchamber spun a bit in a blur before his eyes.

"Mrs. Lewis, I remember. . . ." But when tasked with explaining himself, he could not actually remember anything after watching Jamie's carriage drive away. A slight feeling of being close to her, inhaling her scent, then nothing else. He started to rub his head from the ache, however even the pressure of his hand caused the pain to increase. "I do not remember."

"My lord, you were struck down after Mr. Hepburn left," Pottles explained. "The surgeon was called to see to your injuries."

"Thank you, Pottles. Efficient as ever."

Pottles' face puffed up and turned bright red. He shifted his stance looking very uncomfortable, very unlike the smooth, unperturbed butler he knew. Something was amiss. If he doubted that, the glances exchanged between the two people who ran his household confirmed it.

"Did anyone see it happen? Surely there were people on the street?" They'd left their club near the university early enough that the streets were busy with coaches and horses and people. Had they stopped elsewhere? He rubbed his forehead as he tried to force the information out. It did no good.

"I did not see anyone around, my lord." Mrs. Lewis replied instead of Pottles. Josh turned to face her.

"You were there?"

"Aye, my lord. I found you there."

"Pottles? Did you see anyone nearby?"

"I, ahem, I was, ahem," his butler stammered in an uncertain manner until Mrs. Lewis spoke.

"'Twas Mr. Pottles' evening off, my lord. We sent word to him as soon as we moved you inside."

The reaction from Pottles, a sort of mixture of snorting and choking was the first time in the five years since accepting the title and moving into this house that Josh had ever seen the older man come this close to losing control.

"Pottles, as I told Mrs. Lewis, you are both entitled to take the time off from your duties that you are due, so do not let your absence weigh on you." Josh stretched his shoulders as pain began to creep down his neck and into his shoulders and back. "May I speak to Mrs. Lewis in private?"

He should feel guilty for tweaking at his butler's temper with such a request, and yet, he did not. If Mrs. Lewis had seen it happen, he wanted to question her away from others. And he wanted to do it before time passed and she forgot small details.

"Very well, my lord." Pottles bowed and left without hesitation. Duncan followed with a nod but before he could follow, Mrs. Lewis reminded his valet of something in a low voice. In a few minutes, he was alone with her.

"Here now, my lord," she said. Rushing to his side, she helped him stand and walk to the chair nearest the hearth. "Sit here until Duncan can help you prepare for bed."

The movements made everything worse. Crossing the small distance to a chair felt like a monumental accomplishment but it took most of his strength to do it. He'd not been knocked unconscious before, and the head pain was worse than anything he'd experienced. He leaned his head back slowly, allowing it to rest on the cushioned chairback.

"The surgeon placed stitches and said to keep the injury covered until his return." She went to the table next to the bed and took a packet from a small box of them sitting there. After filling a glass with water from the pitcher, she stirred the contents of the packet into it. "This should help the pain in your head."

Josh took it and held it up, examining the color of the concoction before drinking it. Her laugh surprised him.

"Begging your pardon, my lord. You looked like a young lad given his tonic by his governess and refusing to drink it." She cleared her throat and grew serious. "You have a severe concussive injury to your head and must have a care these next few days. That needs to be taken before retiring and in the morning." He stared at her, not really wanting to consume the bitter liquid even while knowing he must. She lifted the glass from his hand after he'd forced the contents down. "You must follow his instructions or. . . ." Mrs. Lewis turned her gaze away for a moment though he noticed the concern there. Then, he took advantage of that pause.

"What did you see, Mrs. Lewis? What happened that I do not remember?"

"If you promise that you will return to your bed once I have, I will." He waited to see a smile and, when he did not, he understood that she was not jesting.

"Rather bold of you, Mrs. Lewis. Blackmailing your employer."

"As I said, I have discovered that injured men sometimes act like lads and not the adults they are. So, I do not feel the least bit wrong in using some. . . encouragement to do what's necessary."

"Well, I ken not what kind of men you've met, but I like to think that I am open to following the sound advice."

If he'd not been watching her when he said those words, he would have missed the veil of pain that passed over her gaze and was gone in a moment. When he expected a swift retort, she remained silent for a long pause before she took several paces around his chamber, pretending to fix this and adjust that. Unfortunately, watching her walk in circles made his stomach roil.

"Would you please be seated? Your circles are. . . making me dizzy."

She took one look at him and, he must have appeared as badly as he felt, for she dropped into the chair nearest his without an argument. Once he nodded, she did speak and on the subject of the attack.

"I had sent Ewan to the kitchen to fetch something for me, so I waited at the door in case you returned sooner rather than later." She clutched her hands on her lap and he noticed the bloodied apron was no longer in her grasp. She must have passed it to Duncan to remove. "I heard the carriage approaching and as I opened the door, I saw someone, someone tall, a man, walk up behind you and strike you."

"Nothing other than that? A tall man? Well-dressed or not?"

"He looked. . . *appropriate* to this area, my lord. Not shabby." She stared off for a moment and then shook her head. "That's all I remember. When I saw you topple from the blow, I confess, I did not pay much heed to anyone else around." Her hands now shook on her lap as she looked at him. "I called out for Ewan and Graham and ran to help you."

His thoughts were muddled as he tried to think about his attacker. Muddled by the admission that she was the one who came to his rescue, too. Watery visions of her face about his came to him. Trying to apply her description to probable assailants was impossible for it was too vague and could describe half of all the middle-class men in Edinburgh.

Many women would have remained in safety and just waited for the footmen to come. Many would have run in the other direction when danger was afoot. But not his housekeeper. Not Mrs. Lewis who ran to his side when she could have been attacked. She didn't wait.

Clara took action. Clara ran to him.

Shaken by the possessive feeling rushing through him, shaken by the line it crossed, Josh closed his eyes and tried to regain his control. Before he did something foolish.

Changing the topic seemed the thing to do in this weak moment.

"Would you tell Duncan I will be ready to retire in five minutes, Mrs. Lewis?" If his emphasis on the honorific was too strong, she gave no sign.

"Of course, my lord," she said, rising. "I brought fresh linens for the bed and a clean nightshirt for you as well. The blood—" She stopped quickly and he heard the soft epithet she whispered at herself. "If there's nothing else, I will send for him."

"What were you arguing with Pottles about?" She did not speak and did not look as if she would. "I heard your raised voices when I woke."

"I'm sorry that we disturbed you, my lord." She did that little curtsy bob and reached for the doorknob. She was not going to answer.

"Mrs. Lewis." She stopped and faced him.

"He was angry at me, my lord." He narrowed his gaze at her until she continued. "Once Ewan and Graham were able to move you inside, I summoned the surgeon. You must understand, the amount of bleeding, the severity of the injury and the way you kept losing consciousness worried me."

"And how was that the wrong thing?" Josh could not sort out why this would anger the butler.

"Mr. Pottles said I should have waited for his return after we sent word to him and let him decide the course of action."

"I see." She had taken control of the situation and Pottles had missed out.

"He will report my impertinence to you directly, I am certain, but we did not dare wait."

"*You* did not wait." She straightened up to a pose worthy of Pottles and he understood she thought him blaming her or her impertinence in acting. "You have my thanks for not delaying."

"Let me summon Duncan, my lord."

His strength waning, he watched her leave. She may have saved his life tonight. If she'd not responded quickly, if she'd not called the surgeon, things could have turned out worse.

After a lackluster attempt to stand, or even sit up straight, on his own, he waited on Duncan's assistance. His efficient valet entered and had the bed linens and his bloodied clothing removed and replaced within minutes. The few paces to the bed took whatever strength he had, but he fought to escape sleep's grasp.

He hurriedly gave Duncan instructions about who to summon for morning meetings, what Pottles should be told, and orders for the entire staff. He knew in his bones that this attack was linked to the incident at the Society's libraries. And that was so clearly related to. . . .

The ache in his head, dulled by whatever was in that concoction, left him feeling confused. He knew there were other things he must see to, important things, but sleep was stronger than his resolve.

"Duncan, my satchel. Make sure it's. . . in. . . my. . . ."

And he fell asleep.

Chapter Eight

I T WAS ONE of those rare times when she both needed a stiff drink and had one. Three actually if she was counting. And after the events this night, she would be better served by half a dozen, but Arabella stopped herself after the three.

She sat at the small table in the housekeeper's chambers, sipping the good whisky and staring at the bag there on the table. Since he carried it with him nearly every time he left the house and had it next to him on the floor when he sat at his desk, Arabella was familiar with Lord Dunalastair's leather satchel. Standing outside his door after she'd left and summoned Duncan, she listened to their exchange while the valet aided him to bed.

Oh, her intention was an admirable one—to be at hand in case Duncan needed help. But when his lordship mentioned the satchel, all of that changed. After watching from the stairs as Duncan entered the library and then left in just a brief time, empty-handed, she went in and found the leather bag. Covering it with a folded sheet, she carried it down to her chambers and locked the door behind her. Now, after some fortifying spirits, she felt ready to search it.

That he'd wanted it secured told her he thought it was linked to the attack on him. That he was safely abed gave her the chance to look at its contents. But neither of those bits lessened the guilt or the conflict about feeling guilty that raged within her. Her gaze fell on it once more and this time she reached for the decanter instead.

The fourth *wee dram* went down smoothly. As with the others, this one did not ease any of the swirling emotions inside of her, so she cursed under her breath and reached for the damn bag.

Opening the leather strap and buckle that held it closed, she examined the contents without touching any of them. She would need to place them back in the correct order or position and studying it first made sense. Then she slid the whole pile out and onto the table before her.

Loose papers along with several notebooks and other books—nothing unusual or surprising—filled the bag. Trying to proceed in a logical manner, she began to quickly skim over each page as she turned it over onto the surface. Looking for anything that seemed familiar or somehow connected to her father's dealings with the viscount, she flipped page after page until she reached the first notebook. Although these first papers were his writing, they involved his more recent travels and not those with her father years ago.

The notebook appeared untouched, almost never until she opened it and read a bit. This was his record of the books and sources he used in his research. Titles, authors, dates, and a brief description of each book's contents followed along in order of the alphabet. Not finding anything of interest, she continued on.

And on. And on. Uncertain of how much time had passed and growing exhausted from. . . everything this day had demanded of her and four large portions of excellent whisky, Arabella was about to give up when she noticed a piece of paper folded and tucked into the second notebook. This notebook was missing a number of sheets from its binding, and she opened it with some care fearing that more pages might loosen.

Tension spiraled within her as she began to unfold the page. As the drawing was revealed, everything—her breathing, the sounds within the room, the sounds outside her chamber, even time—seemed to stop. Once she saw the whole of it, her hand moved on its own to her neck to feel the chain on which her pendant hung. Sheer panic struck when she could not feel it and it took several moments to remember that she'd hidden it away in the trunk under her bed to keep it safe and not allow its accidental exposure.

There on the page was the complete pendant as drawn by her father. The jewels almost glittered in the candlelight, so realistically was it portrayed. But this showed another piece—a flat disklike backing that was scored with lines across its surface and all around the curved edges. She'd never seen this before—only having the replica her father made for her.

Exquisite and more colorful than she'd expected, this artifact was the only one her father had drawn in its entirety. His other sketches were of parts of the ruins he'd visited with the then Mister Joshua Robertson. Broken stone pillars, temple and house walls, scattered pieces of a long ago forgotten city that the desert had claimed for hundreds of years. Until her father had guided *his friend* to it.

Glancing back at the drawing while angry memories tried to flood her thoughts, she realized that, though she'd never seen this version of it, it must be significant. A significance that added veracity to her father's claims. Did she dare another serving of whisky to calm the anger? Was it getting in the way of examining the contents of his bag or was the strong liquor giving her the courage to continue?

Nay. More whisky would lead to a bigger headache in the morning than she'd had earlier today. And it would make it more difficult to acquiesce to the imperious butler. Worse, it would make it nigh to impossible to keep her true aims hidden, which she must.

With care, she closed the drawing after taking one more close look at it. Part of her wanted, nay needed, this piece of paper that she knew her father had handled as he created the image on it.

But taking it now would be noticed, especially after this attack and. . . .

Tucking the paper back into the notebook as it had been, something bothered her. Some sort of piece to this puzzle niggled in the back of her thoughts as she finished the rest of the contents and placed them back within the bag. His lordship had brought this back from the place where he researched his next work—the libraries at the Society for the Preservation of Historical Antiquities. Just after his return, he'd ordered more locks and a firmer control on the flow of workmen and merchants to the house.

Had something happened at the library? Or on his way home? The papers were all mixed up and the one notebook was seriously damaged, with chunks of pages torn out and missing as far as she could tell.

Someone had searched through his satchel and taken some pages from his notebook. She removed it once more and took a closer look at its contents. As she opened the book, the first thing she noticed was that the front half of it was gone. Reading the first few of the remaining pages, Arabella realized that this part, the part left behind untouched, was about his current work. From the dates on the cover and opening page, she could tell that someone had ripped out the entire section about his earlier excavations.

About Timgad.

About her father.

Her gasp echoed through her chamber. Someone else was looking for information about that journey, that city, the lost artifacts. Someone desperate enough to attack and rob the viscount. Which meant that someone else was watching him.

"Oh God!"

Arabella stood, a little too quickly for the amount of whisky she'd imbibed, and had to grab the edge of the table to regain her balance. This was not the night she should have succumbed to the need for spirits. Fear, though, was an efficient catalyst to clear away the comfortable feeling the whisky had provided.

This bag may yet contain important information and she suspected it did, or else it would not weigh so heavily on him that he ordered his valet to confirm its location. So important that he fought off the effects of the medication administered in that mixture she'd given him.

Torn over taking it back or keeping it, she decided to return it, but to the viscount's bedchamber rather than his library. Being on the first floor, it would take little to no effort for someone to smash the window and grab it before anyone knew. Then it would be lost to Lord Dunalastair and to her. Better that she place it in his bedchamber and try to get a more thorough look at it later.

So, she once again put everything back inside of it and quietly made her way upstairs to his rooms. There was no sign of anyone as she walked along the corridor and stopped before his door. Her hand shook as she touched the knob and turned it slowly, pushing it open with a care so as not to wake his lordship with her entrance. It would be better, certainly easier for her, if he slept through her arrival and did not ask questions.

Candidly, she did not trust herself to be able to answer without babbling some nonsense. Worse, she would be held to it later. Not speaking of it now gave her more time to craft a good explanation for later.

The room was warm, but not overly so. A snuffled breath followed by a soft snore told her he slept. The bedlinens looked as smooth as when the housemaids finished their efforts on any given morning, which gave credit to Duncan's skills. And it spoke of how deeply his lordship was under sleep's control. She stared at him and noticed how much younger he appeared when at rest.

His light brown hair was tussled now, much like his friend Mr. Hepburn wore his as his style. The viscount always seemed comfortable in less than formal attire, and now, looking at him she could almost imagine him riding a camel in the desert, a scarf around his face and neck, as her father had told her was the custom, to protect him from the sand and the heat. He could not have even been a score of years old back then. Young and thrilled at the discovery of a lifetime.

The crack of a spark in the fire brought her back to her senses and her location. First, the bag.

Where she stood, close to the head of the bed, she could see a space next to the legs at the head of the bed that was just big enough for the satchel. She could place it and it would be safe. Arabella had misjudged the weight of it and barely managed to place it before losing her balance. Resting her hand on the pillow next to her to keep from falling, the touch on her face startled her even more.

"Mrs. Lewis." He stroked down her cheek with the back of his hand. "You are back."

"My lord—"

"I did not thank you before." His hand dropped, as though he could not keep it raised. Then, he opened his eyes and met her gaze. "Clara."

"My lord, I'm sure you did—" She could hear her own uncertainty at his personal address to her.

He stared at her and the moment stretched out forever. The touch of his hand was gentle as he reached up and slid it around her neck to draw her near. His thumb stroked along the edge of her jaw sending bursts of fire into her. But that sensation was nothing compared to the flames that raced through her veins at the touch of his mouth on hers.

Once. Twice. And again, he pressed his mouth to hers, each time claiming a bit more. She should pull away. She should stop him. She should. . . .

"Whisky," he whispered against her. He took advantage of her gasp to move his tongue inside her mouth as though tasting her. "Sweet," he said against her lips. Then he dipped back within her as though searching for more of it. "Smokey. Lovely Clara." Could he truly taste it? A shiver coursed through her whole body at his words and his kisses.

She wanted to taste him back. In that moment, she lied to

herself that she simply wanted to know. Know how it felt. Know him. Then she would stop this madness.

Then she would walk away from him and this.

Then she dared to kiss him again, her tongue imitating his and searching for the flavor that she would always remember as. . . *him*.

The only thing that finally stirred her common sense was the sound of her name as Duncan spoke from the hallway.

By the time she righted herself, the viscount was soundly asleep and she wondered if he even knew what he'd, what they'd, done.

"I heard his lordship's voice," Duncan said as he entered. "Has he awakened?"

She smoothed her gown and apron down with her trembling hands and prayed her lips were not so swollen from his attentions to give away her. She let out her breath and nodded in reply.

"Briefly. He is sleeping once more." Arabella searched the valet's gaze for some sign that he'd witnessed her indiscretion when he entered the bedchamber. Duncan met hers and there was no indication of it. "The surgeon said to check him often through the night."

"Aye, Mrs. Lewis. He told me the same thing—which is why I came." The tall man walked to the bed and straightened a non-existent wrinkle in the bedcovers. "I will come back in a few hours."

Arabella's eyes went to the satchel, barely out of sight, by the bed. Duncan would surely see it as he tended to his lordship.

"Duncan," she said, turning to face him. "I heard him speak to you about his bag and it sounded serious. So, I brought it here where it is closer to him. Where it will be safer than downstairs."

"A good idea, Mrs. Lewis."

"Ring if you need anything later."

She clasped her hands together as she walked towards the door. One hand was on the knob when his lordship spoke.

One word.

Her name.

"Clara."

The whisper could have been shouted for the shock of it. The intimate tone made it worse. So much worse.

She waited for Duncan to acknowledge it or for some reply to come to mind, but between the sizzling kisses and then this, nothing happened.

"Good night, Mrs. Lewis," Duncan said, moving around her to open the door. If he'd emphasized her supposed married state or if she'd imagined it, she knew not.

"Good night, Duncan." And after a quick glance at the viscount in his bed, she left.

Well, she ran back down the stairs, into her chamber and slammed the door behind her.

Chapter Nine

T WO DAYS.
He slipped in and out of a light and disturbed sleep as the hours passed. Oh, he heard the voices and the movements of those in his bedchamber, but he could not rouse enough strength or interest to reply to questions or add to conversations.

Two days had passed, they revealed that when he finally refused the next dose of the concoction from the surgeon. But it had taken another day to be clear of the effects of the ingredients in the bitter brew. Well, he was not exactly clear, for he felt as though his mind was filled with cobwebs even while the pain from the stitches throbbed in the background. Less certainly than the hours after the attack, but strong enough to have him clenching against it when it came in waves.

The clamor outside his door might be a good thing or a sign of something bad but he welcomed the change from the monotony enforced on him and apparently his servants. From Pottles who arrived after Duncan had seen to his ablutions, to the housemaids who cleaned the chamber when he was allowed to sit in a chair, and even the almost-absent Mrs. Lewis whose visits were momentary, everyone observed a strict dictate to silence that they'd been given by. . . someone. So, the noise in the hallway sounded like a great interruption to too much quiet.

"My lord, the Earl of Finlaggan and Mr. Hepburn," Pottles announced as he opened the door and stepped aside. His voice was quieter than normal, so he was still obeying the edict someone gave.

Josh had just gotten settled in the large armchair next to the fire so at least he was not greeting his friends in his bed. As his friends entered, their demeanor changed. Each one walked across the chamber as if the carpet on the floor was something fragile and breakable. Instead of their usual boisterous greetings, they nodded and sat down without a word. And they both glanced towards the door, almost looking for approval. The flash of a black dress moving away from the doorway explained much.

He watched as Ewan carried in a tray and Pottles saw to his friends. After setting a cup of coffee next to him, Pottles bowed and left. Jamie and Alex waited a few moments before their barrage began.

"What happened?" Jamie said.

"Why did you tell him not to tell me?" Alex added.

"I swear I did not realize you'd been attacked, Josh. My coachman said he saw nothing as we left you off."

"I cannot believe you did not tell me about—" When he reached up to massage his forehead, they stopped talking. Then he realized that they were. . . .

"Why are you both whispering?" When he heard his own voice, he spoke again, this time in a regular tone. "I asked Duncan to send word to you. Candidly, I could barely put words together and explain what had happened."

"What have the constables said? Did any watchmen report anything nearby?" Alex asked. "There's a box just across the way. If you'd like, I can ask my father to—"

"No need, Alex." The duke was a General Commissioner, one of the highest-ranking peers who served in an honorary position and oversaw the police in Edinburgh. "And since I've been held prisoner in my chamber for the last three days, I have not spoken to any official or constable yet." He took a mouthful of the coffee and savored it, allowing its flavor to remove the dryness and bad taste left from the tonic.

"Prisoner?" Jamie asked. His friends exchanged a glance before facing him.

"Well, not precisely a prisoner," he admitted.

"I presume your Mrs. Lewis is the chief gaoler?" Alex asked. Once his friends had the bit in their teeth. . . .

"Again, she is not *my* Mrs. Lewis, Alex." His words sounded hollow even to himself. Worse, a memory of her mouth on his and the flavor of whisky on her tongue filled his thoughts as he denied that she was anything other than what she was—his housekeeper. A housekeeper.

The housekeeper.

"I'd thought Pottles was in control here," Alex said. "But then this happened, and I suspect the balance has shifted."

Josh could not help it, for something in his friend's words showed Alex's begrudging respect for Clara and he laughed aloud. Another chuckle escaped and managed to reverberate through his head reminding him of the injury. When he reached up to touch the still-swollen area on the back of his head, Alex shushed them.

"Not too loud!" he warned again.

"Fine," Josh said. He gave in not only because Alex looked genuinely worried but also because he hurt less when they lowered their voices.

"So now what?" Jamie asked. "Tell us what we can do while you are still housebound?"

"If you could check with the Society about any out-of-the-ordinary happenings? Anything missing? Damage to the building, too."

"What else can we help with?" Alex asked in a whisper.

Josh paused and thought about the other inquiries he needed to make. Items he must check. The security company he'd interviewed and now needed to speak to. The boxes and boxes of documents stored at his house in the country. And he could not forget about. . . .

Someone should. . . .

Someone. . . .

Suddenly, the room grew very hot. The walls began to shrink and then expand back to their larger size. Sweat trickled down his forehead and burned when it splashed in his eyes. Pain struck and his vision filled with flashes. Mayhap he should not have refused that bloody concoction.

"Josh?" He heard his name being called, but he could not reply.

"Lord Dunalastair?" Now a woman spoke to him. "Your head is bleeding again. I will need to fix the stitches." He forced his eyes open and there was his rescuer again.

"Clara."

"Could you ring for his valet, my lord?"

At first, Josh thought she meant him, but Alex spoke. "Of course, Mrs. Lewis."

She began giving orders when Duncan entered in a quiet but firm voice. His valet and even his friends did as she said, and he wanted to laugh again. But, all that happened was fatigue dragged him down again.

"Forgive me, my lord. This is going to hurt. Duncan?"

Damn but it did hurt! His valet supported his head as she went about the nasty task. He thought Jamie moaned and he heard Alex warn him off. Everything went blank after that until Clara spoke his name.

"Lord Dunalastair, we're going to move you now." Would she ever speak his name and not his title?

He could almost walk, but the room racing around him made it impossible to balance on his own. Lying down definitely made a difference in the dizziness, and he'd been foolish to push too hard and fast. He just could not accept the forced inactivity when so many questions needed answers and certainly not when danger had come to his doorstep once more.

The dark specters of his past were rising.

"Drink this now." Clara held out a glass to him as Duncan lifted his shoulders to steady him. "My lord."

"Must I?" He hesitated, not wanting to fall under the control of that sleeping draught.

"If you wish to avoid fainting every time you get out of your bed, then, aye, you must. But just for two more days." She whispered something else under her breath he could not understand, yet he knew their meaning. He drank the contents of the glass quickly to get it down.

"Thank you, Clara."

Alex and Jamie looked shocked when he met their eyes, but they remained there watching as his valet and housekeeper settled him back on the bed. Knowing Jamie's weak stomach when it came to blood and gore, he was surprised that his friend had remained this close for this long.

"My lord?" Pottles' voice echoed across the quiet chamber. "What is going on here?"

"He—" Jamie started to say something but was interrupted.

"His lordship's stitches tore, Mr. Pottles," Clara answered.

"I will summon the surgeon." Pottles nodded to him and stepped back to leave.

"No need to call him, Mr. Pottles. I replaced the ones that pulled apart." She stepped away from his side and he almost reached out for her hand. Damn, but the medicine was strong for making him want what he could not have. "He—" She cleared her throat. "His lordship has taken the next dose as the surgeon ordered. All his lordship needs is to rest and not be disturbed." Josh almost laughed because her gaze fell on his friends now, with an especially prolonged glare at Alex. "Lord Finlaggan and Mr. Hepburn were just leaving, Mr. Pottles."

The two stood there, caught between butler and housekeeper, and not certain what to do. Knowing how uncomfortable Alex was, he took pity on him.

"If you and Hepburn can do as I asked?"

"We will," Jamie said.

"Come back and let me ken what you learn." Alex threw a glance at his perceived nemesis.

"No matter the hour, Alex. Call on me when you learn something." Josh hoped that would make clear that Alex would be welcome any time, day, night or even in the gloaming.

Pottles opened the door wider to allow the two to leave. Clara gave no indication of doing the same, so he dismissed Duncan with a nod. Soon, the chamber was empty but for him and her. And the tonic and the exhaustion weighed him down. But first. . . .

"I owe you an apology."

"For being foolish and refusing your medicaments?" she said. A smile tugged the left corner of her mouth up just a tantalizing bit. He liked her sense of humor, inappropriate as it sometimes was.

She made her way around the chamber, straightening this and repositioning that while never looking at him. He'd overstepped—both with the kisses and his late habit of calling her by her given name. Now that he'd crossed those lines, he discovered that he did not wish to step back.

"I think you ken as well as I do the reason," he said. Sliding up to lean against the headboard, Josh wished she would look at him. "Or would you prefer I simply blame it on the potion's effects?"

"There is that," she whispered.

"And the whisky?" If there was even the smallest excuse, he would offer her the refuge of it.

"Aye, that as well." For the first time since he'd met her, uncertainty filled her lovely brown eyes when she finally looked in his direction.

"And you have been avoiding me these last three days because of it. I do not like knowing I made you uncomfortable, Clara." He didn't think he could go back to calling her Mrs. Lewis. In spite of the niggling of guilt coursing through him, he decided she was Clara to him now. "Please tell me you accept my apology."

Surely he should not be craving the very act even as he was asking for forgiveness for it? But he was.

"I accept, my lord." She picked up the basket from the table and gathered up some linens. "Now, you must rest, and I must go."

He was able to watch her leave though he could not stay awake much longer than that. Two more days and this inactivity would be done.

Two more days and he could no longer blame a medicine for his behavior.

Two more days and he could only blame himself.

ARABELLA WASN'T SURE which encounter was worse—the one that ended in whisky-filled kisses or the one just now when he apologized for those kisses. Pressing the back of her hand to her cheek, the heat of a blush revealed her body's reaction to even speaking about it with him.

She stopped outside his door to try to catch her breath before the inevitable confrontation with Pottles belowstairs. As she leaned against the wall, she dropped the basket next to her on the floor and the linens on top of it. But, no matter how much she wanted to, she could not fool herself into believing that her breathlessness and feeling of danger had nothing to do with the growing attraction to the man within. The man she wanted to destroy. Arabella pressed her palms on her apron, wiping the nervous moisture from her trembling hands.

This had gone so wrong.

In the weeks since her arrival here in his household, her hunt had been fruitless—she'd found nothing. Oh, her searches had not been as thorough as she'd have liked, but, until finding the drawing in his satchel, she'd failed in her quest. The viscount had clearly made certain that anything tied to Timgad was hidden away well, if it was even here in his home. A hiding place at the Society's building was a possibility, though he only ever mentioned that place's libraries.

Well, she hadn't been a complete failure in finding something surprising—she had found a viscount who was a decent man completely different from the one she expected she would find. Now, she doubted that this man could have defrauded and ruined her father. With the passing of each day in his household, she worried more and more that her resolve was crumbling and her oath would be broken.

Then she'd opened that paper and saw the broach drawn on it and hope and fear had blossomed within her. The tendrils of hope that she indeed had found something that could help her prove his perfidy while the fear grew that the knowledge would be in her grasp, and she would be forced to use it against him.

Arabella gathered up her strength and the basket and linens and made her way down to the lower floor, placing the used linens in the bin and her basket on the table in the laundry room. There was no sign of Pottles so he must be in his own office, working on household inventories so she began to refill the used items in her basket. Sorting through her needles and threads, she searched in the drawer of the cabinet for the correct thickness and color. This task, or one like it, usually calmed her and allowed her to organize her thoughts as her hands arranged her supplies. It was only later when she glanced at the clock that she realized it was mid-afternoon. And she may have continued on if Pottles' voice had not carried into the room.

The reckoning was here.

Even expecting it, the knock startled her. She bade him enter and stood waiting for his entrance. The butler saw her and nodded before closing the door.

"What can I do for you, Mr. Pottles?" She closed the open drawer and clasped her hands in front of her.

"Has his lordship spoken about my lapse to you, Mrs. Lewis?" Of the endless possibilities of conversation opening lines, that was not anywhere in consideration. Though his tone was calm and even, unexpectedly so, the question revealed a vulnerability.

"To which lapse do you refer, Mr. Pottles?"

"My absence the night he was attacked."

"Only what he said to the both of us that first night—that he does not begrudge us the time we are owed."

Pottles glanced away, turning his gaze to the wall past her shoulder for a long pause. "And he does not think. . . ?"

"Think, Mr. Pottles? I'm not certain I understand your meaning?" She was not being difficult. She just could not comprehend what he was worried over. As butler, he was entitled to more time away than even she was as housekeeper, and considering the number of years he'd worked here, more than anyone else on staff.

"That I was somehow remiss in locking up or in my oversight of the security of the house and grounds?" Pottles unsettled was nothing she could have anticipated.

"His lordship has only spoken highly of your abilities, Mr. Pottles. And I would think that unless anything has changed, you are in good stead with him." The sound he made, something between a huff and a harrumph, told her that Pottles was worried.

"No matter what he said then, he has ordered that you are in charge of his recuperation and care. Ordered that his visitors must now be approved by *you*." He mumbled something then which was very out of character. Stunned by this admission, she searched for the right thing to say.

"I am certain that this is due to the medicines ordered by the surgeon. They can cause a man to act out of character when taken. . ." The heat of a blush crept up her cheeks as she remembered what else the viscount had done while on the medication. The butler glanced up and Arabella knew he'd seen the flushing of her face.

"I think there is more than you either ken or more that you do not see for his lordship's orders."

Arabella fought off the pleasure that filled her at the thought that he trusted her—it was for all the wrong reasons. And the guilt. Oh God, the guilt! This acceptance by the viscount, placing her in a position of authority, was something she should not feel badly about. It meant that she was succeeding in fooling him and everyone here. Her disguise was working.

"I am not so sure of that, Mrs. Lewis." He met her eyes and she realized he'd raised his tone as he'd said her name. "I am not the only one who has noticed his attentions to you."

Clara.

Her name had echoed across his bedchamber and right in front of Duncan. And he'd used it not only that time when half-asleep, but several times when his friends were present. Her stomach tightened in anticipation of what else he would say.

"This man, this Viscount Dunalastair, does not abide by the expectations of his position, Mrs. Lewis. He does not understand them, nor does he wish to, and he has rejected them since ascending to his title." Pottles' voice was unlike she'd ever heard him speak. "Worse, he had made his attraction to you obvious."

"Mr. Pottles, I am certain—"

"This may not end well for you, Mrs. Lewis. Not well at all. Have a care." He nodded at her, ending his part of this strange conversation.

Stunned speechless by the encounter, she could only stand and watch him leave the room. From the voices outside, Mrs. Mathieson had supper for the staff underway. With the viscount abed and taking only broth and bread in his chamber, there was no need to plan more. Right now, with Mr. Pottles' warning echoing in her ears, she knew she would be unable to eat anything. Pottles was correct but he had no true idea of the full scope of the situation. And if the butler's suspicions were true about Joshua Robertson's attraction to her, it was worse than she ever thought it could get.

This would not end well for her. Not well at all.

Chapter Ten

FINALLY, THE BEDCHAMBER was empty and she had the perfect excuse to be in it.

After his recovery and the removal of the stitches by the surgeon, the viscount had left the room as if the very devil himself was on his heels. He'd even demanded that Duncan prepare the hottest bath ever and to use the washroom off the kitchen to make it possible to keep the supply of water coming.

When Duncan was allowed his way, his preparations of his lordship to go out could take more than two hours. His lordship could barely tolerate it on days when he had more formal engagements to attend, and it became something of a challenge between the two men—one trying to rush through and the other dragging it out. This morning was different, for after so many days abed, without a proper shaving or haircut, the valet informed his lordship that it could take the better part of the morning and the viscount did not argue.

Arabella gathered up the housemaids and borrowed the kitchen maid from Mrs. Mathieson and let them loose on the long-untended chamber. Soon, with the windows opened wide and the draperies thrown back, the sickroom smell was gone. The bed was stripped of its layers of sheets and blankets, and everything sent down to be washed. Eilidh and Edmee were very efficient girls and with Mary helping them, the chamber was swept, washed, cleaned, polished and returned to the condition expected for his lordship's comfort.

Promising Duncan she would send down clean clothes to the washroom gave her the perfect excuse to remain behind and to be in the dressing room and closet unattended. First, she gathered the garments and put them near the door so she could have them at hand if interrupted. Then, Arabella began her search.

Her father had often told her about the way that archeologists searched a field or town or a new find, moving in a methodical way across the length and breadth of the area so as to not miss a spot. Oh, he had freely admitted he did not have the patience for such a process, but those he toured with certainly did and he described it to her often. So, she organized her thoughts and started.

Drawer by drawer, trunk by trunk and section by section, Arabella opened, searched for anything that should not be there in his dressing room and then moved on. She dared not take too much time in each. Then she went into the large closet and looked among all the garments, hung neatly and organized by type. Nothing seemed out of place here, Duncan would not permit such a thing from the appearance of it.

Nothing.

Unless he had some secret compartment or a safe box in another place, she could not see a place for it here. Realizing that too much time had passed, she smoothed out the clothing she'd searched and turned to leave.

"Clara."

Instead of the invalid of the last days, the viscount stood before her shaved and groomed and wearing some sort of foreign garment in a shade of beige cotton with embroidery around the neckline and front edges in a deep green that matched his eyes. Unlike his usual banyan over trousers and a shirt and waistcoat, it appeared that he wore little to nothing under this loose, flowing robe. Her mouth went dry at the sight of the dark brown curls that covered his chest—exposed when the front of the garment gapped as he moved. She clenched her hands into fists to control the urge to touch him there and run her fingers through it.

Idiot! Arabella looked away from the view of the strong muscular chest only to notice he was barefoot. And that he did indeed wear something under this robe, for his feet peeked out from a loose pair of. . .trousers in the same fabric. How could a man's feet be attractive? She was not daft, she was simply mad. She had never seen him in this state of undress so she could be excused for being overwhelmed by it. And though he thought her a widow, with some experience or knowledge of a man, she'd had little of that kind.

"Are you looking for something?" he asked, stepping inside the small, enclosed area and closer to her.

"I thought you might want the blue banyan you favor so much." Surely that made sense. "I did not ken that you had. . . that."

"It is a kaftan, from my travels to Algiers and Marrakesh."

She did not wish to study the garment for it meant staring at his body. And the more she noticed that, the more her own body heated, and a throb began deep inside her.

He stepped closer and she breathed in the scent of the soap from his bath. His hair curled more when damp. Somehow he seemed taller though without shoes or boots on, he should not be. Her gaze went back to his bare feet which were now only inches from the toes of her shoes. When she dared raise her head, he was staring at her mouth.

Her lips tingled as she remembered the touch of his lips, the taste of him and the heat he created with each kiss. Still she kept her hands tightly closed at her sides, fearing that she would lose all control and sense if she reached for him.

"I will not be able or willing to blame a potion this time," he whispered.

Josh waited then, wanting her, wanting to kiss her, but not willing to take what she would not offer. Days of watching her and feeling her touch as she tended his injury and cared for him left him in need of her. She was a widow who would understand the physical needs of a man and a woman, and she could make her own decision. But it must be hers.

"I will not trespass where I am not wanted," he said.

Her breaths were shallow and quick, and he could see the flush of arousal fill her face, coloring her cheeks with an appealing shade of pink. He leaned down slowly, while waiting on her word, aching to kiss her. Aching for more than that even if it was out of bounds for them. He would settle for a kiss, given freely and with no medicament or spirit to blame.

Josh slid his hands around her shoulders and drew her gently towards him. If she glanced down again now, his own arousal would be clear, for the soft, flowing kaftan hid nothing. She did not resist at all, allowing him to bring her closer still. Releasing his hold, he caressed down the backs of her arms until he reached her hands. As he encircled her wrists with his fingers, he closed the final inches separating their lips, leaving a space large enough for only a breath to pass between them. Her heated breath against his face and the nearness of her body made him burn with desire.

He could read the indecision in her eyes even as her body seemed intent on moving closer.

"Clara?" he whispered, his lips so close now he could feel hers trembling against his as he spoke.

All she did was close that minuscule gap between their mouths with the lightest touch of her lips to hers, but that was all it took to give her assent. Her mouth was on his and she leaned her body against his. Josh released her wrists and slid his hands around onto her back, caressing across it as she kissed him.

The touch of her tongue, teasing across his lips until he opened was a glorious thing. His body arched against hers and his cock, readied and hard, pressed against her only separated by the layers of cloth between them. The friction as he rubbed against her made him swell and harden even more. When she lifted up on her toes and wrapped her hands around his shoulders, fire surged through his blood, and he felt alive for the first time in such a long time.

Clara kissed him again, tasting him and tilting her mouth until she could thrust her tongue deeply in his. Sadly, no whisky flavor in this kiss, but the taste of her intoxicated him. He shifted his hands to her waist and stroked the underside of her breasts. She inhaled but did not stop him or pull away. He tilted away a scant inch, wanting to watch her face, her eyes, as he touched her.

He smiled with each little gasp that escaped from her open mouth now as he moved his thumbs across the tight buds of both breasts. She stumbled and fell back, their bodies ending up against the back wall of his closet. From hips to shoulders, there was not an inch or several not touching. Clara's breathing grew shallow but when he tried to move off her, she held him close.

Josh kissed her and stepped back. If they continued, if he did, there would be no going back. She might be a widow, she might be in service, but he should know better. He should be in control. And if he couldn't or wouldn't have something honorable to offer her, he shouldn't take advantage. No matter how much he wanted to.

"Mayhap we—"

"If we take this further, Clara," he said, choosing to call her that, "more apologies will definitely be needed on my part."

He gave her more room and held her hand as she regained her balance. The passionate partner disappeared as he watched, each tug or shifting of her garments or repositioning of her cap and tucking her hair back into its confines, Mrs. Lewis did indeed reappear there before his eyes. She'd neatened everything back into place just as Duncan called out.

"My lord? Are you here?" He touched his finger to his mouth to silence her. Walking out into his chamber, he nodded at his valet.

"I am." He walked over to the chair and sat down.

"You look flushed, my lord. Are you well?"

"I fear I may have overdone my first hours of freedom, Duncan."

"Should you rest? Even a short while might help."

"Very well." He capitulated and leaned his head back. "Wake me in an hour, Duncan. I should dress since the Earl of Finlaggan and Mr. Hepburn will be calling later."

Duncan closed the door as he left, and Josh let out the breath he was holding as the valet's footsteps moved down the hallway and the stairs. The closet door opened slowly, exposing her inch by inch.

"It should be safe now," he said. He stood as she left her hiding place and walked to the door. "I do thank you for all of your hours of care over this last week, Clara. I think you should take a few days off."

"Pardon?"

"A few days, to rest and see to your own cares." A short break would be best for both of them, he thought. "The household will hold together."

"If that is what you wish, my lord." He could see his suggestion hurt her somehow. She curtsied to him which felt very strange to him considering what they'd just been about. She'd reached the door and had her hand on the knob when she faced him.

"I forgot to tell you, my lord. Your satchel is just there." She pointed to the leather bag tucked almost out of sight between his bed and the wall. "You seemed concerned when you were first awake, so I brought it here to keep it safe until you could deal with it."

He glanced at the bag and then back at her. Had she opened it? Did she know what was inside? Did she even know about his past before the title passed to him or only since he'd become viscount?

"Clara, did you look within it?"

For a moment she looked afraid, as though she would not

answer him but instead would flee like prey spotted by the hunter. A curt nod gave him her reply.

"Did anyone else?"

"Nay, my lord. I'm the only one who opened it here."

He stood and walked towards her. He could not risk dragging her into this latest round of danger.

"And you read the contents?" He stood only a few feet from her, close enough that she had to lift her chin to meet his eyes. Her shoulders drew back and she stood straighter.

"Aye, my lord. I did." Her lower lip curled just a bit, almost as though she was challenging him in some way. She had no idea of the danger.

"Tell no one, Clara. Tell no one what you saw." He covered her hand on the doorknob and leaned closer. "If anyone knows you've seen it, I fear you could be in grave danger." He turned the knob but did not open it yet. "Give me some time, take your time off, and we will speak of it afterwards."

She only tilted her head enough to acknowledge his order and then she pulled the door open. Checking that the hallway was empty, she stepped out of the chamber.

As he pushed the door closed, he offered up a prayer that no one knew of her actions. Anyone who saw his notes about Timgad could be in danger.

Anyone.

When his head began throbbing, Josh thought it was more than just the injury flaring up again.

Chapter Eleven

"Y OU SEE, JOSHUA. It is not painful at all."

Josh raised one brow as he stared over his glass of watered down ratafia at his godmother who also managed to be a distant connection on his mother's side. The woman who had arrived in town unexpectedly and dragged him to this evening of dancing at the Assembly Rooms looked positively gleeful at his discomfort. A quick glance at the two men he called friends told him there would be no rescue coming.

"Aunt Sorcha, I appreciate your help—"

"No, Joshua, I do not think you do." The silver-haired, fiery-tongued countess slapped his arm with her closed fan and shook her head.

Jamie choked on the mouthful of his own wine and then made his way off quickly with Alex in close pursuit. So much for stalwart companions. Within seconds he lost sight of them in the large, crowded room. Another slap of her closed fan drew his attention back to his godmother's narrowed gaze.

"What about Carlyle's get? She's quite comely," she asked. Using her fan once more, she pointed at the young woman a short distance away. "Good bloodlines and a decent dowry."

Lady Sorcha Irvine, Countess of Arbuthnott, was difficult once she put her mind and considerable will to a task. He'd been lucky to avoid her scrutiny even in the years since he'd ascended to his title, but she'd shown up on his doorstep just two days after he'd left his sickbed for the last time.

"I will keep her in mind." He tucked her hand on his arm, trying to lead her towards the tables where food was served. Once there, he steered her to a corner where they could speak.

"What brought you to Edinburgh this time, Aunt?" he asked. In spite of her younger days as the center of Edinburgh society, she avoided it and remained on her large estate outside the city. "And where are you staying?"

"I am staying with Lady Campbell. I did not wish to disturb your household at such a time."

"My household?" He may have raised his voice a bit. Several people close by turned at his question. "What do you mean by that?" He placed himself as a barrier to those who might hear and leaned closer. "What about my household?"

His godmother had always had sources all over the city, in places high and low and everything in between, and she'd never revealed any of them. It had confounded her husband, God rest his soul, who'd been caught in several embarrassing incidents because of her endless, secret sources.

"And with you still convalescing after. . . ." She simply stopped and stared at him. There in those dark blue eyes he recognized the guile of a wise woman. The intelligence of a master at manipulation. But the genuine concern he also found there broke him.

"I do not wish that to be public, Aunt Sorcha." Her eyes widened and then she blinked several times before nodding. "Although I do not wish to do so, I would call on you and explain the situation to you." He'd lowered his voice until it was almost a whisper. "But this must remain private."

"You are special to me, Joshua. So, come to see me tomorrow and we will talk."

He nodded, understanding that that casual beckoning held more power than being summoned by the queen herself.

"And, before you leave this evening, you will dance with the Baron of Carlyle's daughter Margaret. She is lovely and quite a bluestocking herself." She tapped that damn fan on his arm before stepping around him and calling out to a friend she saw. He could not help but laugh as she walked away. She heard him and came back, placing her hand on his arm and guiding him through the crowd milling at the edges of the larger dance floor.

"Come along, lad," she said. "I will introduce you to her myself, because I ken how willful and obstinate you can be."

"Aunt Sorcha—"

"Complain too much and I believe I see my friend Lady Brownley is here with her granddaughter Rose. I'm certain she would enjoy dancing with you."

He believed her threat and walked at her side without further argument. Better one dance than stuck the whole evening. As they approached his godmother's target, he noticed the young woman's expression before she could guard it. Miss Carlyle was no more interested in finding a possible husband here than he was in finding a wife.

Which somehow lightened his mood.

His godmother made the necessary introductions, highlighting in a very few words his bloodline, his holdings, and his title, even commenting rather vulgarly on his wealth. The only details she had not shared were his preferences on how to cook his beefsteak and which cravat knot he liked best. He realized he'd grossly underestimated Sorcha Irvine, Lady Arbuthnott's prodigious collection of knowledge of him.

Finally, a quadrille was called, and he led Miss Carlyle to the floor where other couples were forming their smaller groups. He hated dancing but would not make the young woman suffer for it. She did not force chatter while they formed their lines but held her words until the times in the dance when they paused in their movements.

"I apologize for my godmother's force of will, Miss Carlyle," he offered.

"She is quite. . . ."

"Forceful?"

"Just so, my lord. If I might be bold myself, I have heard that you traveled to Egypt."

"I have. Are you interested in Egypt, Miss Carlyle?" The dance would draw them into the rounds soon, but she turned and smiled at him.

"Oh, I am ever so interested, my lord," she said. "I ken it only through books, but to travel on the Nile River and see the great pyramids and ancient temples would be marvelous. Truly."

They parted for a few of the steps and when they returned to each other, her face was flushed bright from the dance, and her blue eyes sparkled.

"What was your favorite place there? Did you see much of Cairo?" Clearly, the young woman had a true interest in the far-off land. She took the pause of his reply as reproach. "I beg your pardon, my lord. I fear my mother ever despairs of my unseemly interest in books and history."

It was such an unusual thing to be asked about his travels to Egypt and by a woman that they continued speaking about it throughout the rest of the quadrille. He enjoyed it more than he thought he would but, after returning her to her mother, his head began pounding. An unfortunate but continuing effect of his concussive injury.

Seeking something to drink and something to prevent the twisting of his stomach which would begin if the pain grew worse, he glanced around the chamber to find the refreshment tables. The buffet tables were not too busy and he was surprised that Jamie did not stand before one of them, sampling one and all of the offerings. Josh took no notice of anyone else until a serving maid had placed a portion of sliced ham and some cheese on the plate he held out to her. He nodded thanks to her and only then met her gaze.

"Mrs. Lewis?"

ARABELLA HAD BEEN watching him since he entered. After taking on this job because she was certain he would never attend and never know, she nearly toppled in her surprise at his entrance.

He was in formal dress and she had to keep telling herself that this was the man who barely remembered to have his neckcloth in place while in his house. The one who constantly wrecked whatever style Duncan combed and shaped his hair into with his habit of raking his fingers through it. Now... now he looked every inch a nobleman.

A handsome, unattached viscount among a crowd of his peers and marriage-seeking mothers and misses. And Duncan's work showed off his broad shoulders and muscular form to its best—no padding like so many of the other men here needed. After seeing him in his usual day clothes and then for almost a week in a sickbed, this version of him was a very attractive change.

But, she'd known how attractive he was the first time she'd seen him—when she'd sought him out to see what the man she would target looked like. And, worse and more tempting, she'd felt almost every inch of him when they'd stumbled in his closet during their secret embrace and kiss. Taking a handkerchief from her sleeve and dabbing at her now-heated forehead, she knew she could blame the work and not her reaction to the man for the sudden beads of sweat gathering along the edge of her hair.

Then, she thought he'd taken notice of her when he drew closer to her position along the buffet tables with an older woman. The Countess of Arbuthnott was here? As Arabella watched, their conversation grew intense before they walked off together towards the crowd gathered to one side of the dancing floor.

What he did next surprised her—he danced with a young woman!

Though neither appeared happy to be doing it, she could see the moment his face brightened after the woman said something to him. She could not stand and gawp at them, but when she was able to track their progress, she found them smiling and chatting each time the dance steps brought them together.

Something hurt within her. A tightness gathered in her chest as she watched the couple. An envy, a wanting, a need deep inside her that she'd never felt before erupted into her awareness in that moment. Arabella had been focused on avenging her father since her earliest memories and had never considered any other path. Everything she'd done had been in furtherance of that purpose.

Seeing them, seeing him, forced her to realize all that she would give up in this endeavor.

Oh, she had neither the wealth nor the standing to be invited to a grand gathering such as this one or to socialize with people like these. But, she'd never sat with friends and chatted over tea. Or gone shopping with sisters. Or even considered searching for a husband.

She'd never permitted herself to want a family of her own.

Everything depended on the results of finding out the truth and discrediting the viscount. None of the conclusions if she was successful offered much hope for a customary happy life.

Now, as these lords, ladies, gentlemen and others born higher than her danced and plotted out their futures in this gathering, and as thousands of others living normal lives outside this did the same, it struck her what she would be missing. What she was giving up to satisfy the darker need on her father's behalf.

Rewriting the past would cost her any hopeful future.

The dance finished and the couples scattered off the floor and back to their small collections of families, friends and acquaintances. Her attention drawn back to her duties for this evening, Arabella adjusted some of the dishes and the cutlery as more hungry guests approached.

Serving tonight added to her coffers and, along with her wages, would provide her with funds for. . . after. So, when the viscount ordered her away, she was glad to find something to do. And if helping her former landlady's friend serving at this ball tonight was part of it, then all the better. Glancing up at those moving along the long tables of food, she saw him again.

Now, as he walked directly towards her, she knew he'd seen her. Would he be angry to find her here, working for another? At first, he held out an empty plate and she filled it with slices of ham and some of the cheeses in front of him. Then he raised his head and saw it was her.

"Mrs. Lewis?"

"Good evening, my lord," she replied to his greeting.

"Mrs. Lewis, I don't understand," he said. He placed his plate on the table. Seeing others walking towards them, she leaned over.

"May I explain later, my lord?" She hoped that he would be the understanding man in this moment.

He stared at her for a long moment as though searching for the truth in her eyes. A curt nod signaled his agreement and he walked away, his plate forgotten on the table.

The next hours passed slowly and Arabella caught sight of him several times. He stayed away even when no one waited for her to serve them. The event reached its end and the valets and maids in the dressing and cloak rooms were at their busiest in seeing everyone out. Since she was hired only to serve at the tables, her tasks finished sooner than some of the others and she gathered her things to leave.

The cooler night air refreshed her as she walked out into the alleyway behind the Assembly Rooms and made her way to the nearest street. Several of the other maids would be walking home with Arabella, since safety was more assured in numbers together and they'd arranged to meet at the end of the block. As she arrived there and saw the others, she gathered her cloak around her shoulders. Whoever controlled the weather in Edinburgh never understood that the air should warm in the spring, and so the chill and dampness threatened to make their walk very uncomfortable.

"Mrs. Lewis." The loud call startled her and the others. Turning around, she found a carriage sitting in the street and recognized the coachman.

"Adam," she said, nodding at him. The other women stared openly as she walked closer so the man would not have to shout. She suspected that his passenger was their employer, and it was confirmed just a moment later when William jumped down from the back and opened the door for her.

"Mrs. Lewis, his lordship will take you back to the house."

Now the women stood openmouthed in surprise at such a thing. If a nobleman, any man in truth, picked up a woman on the street it was for one purpose. She was about to decline when the viscount himself climbed out and nodded to the small group.

"My lord, I was, we are, on our way home." She did not want to be separated out and alone with him in the carriage. Well, what she wanted and what she must do, were different things but she understood that going with him would mark her in a way she could not allow.

"Come along, ladies," he said, stepping aside. "Climb in and we will see you home." The women—three maids and the friend of Euphemia, her landlady—gasped at such an invitation.

"Surely you cannot mean to—"

"Take your associates where they need to go? Aye."

He motioned for them to enter the coach and they did not hesitate a moment longer to climb into the well-appointed carriage. Standing alone on the sidewalk, Arabella gave up and did the same, taking a seat on one side. Before he entered, he looked at the women.

"And where are you going?" One by one they told him, as did she, and he called up the addresses to Adam. When she wondered if he would indeed take her to Euphemia's house, he added hers to the list. "Onward, Adam."

Soon, they were squeezed inside as the coach headed out of the New Town and back into the Old. The streets were not busy at this time of night and they were able to make their way without delay. No one spoke, the other women were clearly in awe of a handsome nobleman who invited them into his conveyance and drove them home, easing the discomforts that a walk in the cold night air would cause. If one or two or all the others batted their eyelashes at him, it was no surprise to her.

Soon, only she and Euphemia's friend Betty were left, and she expected to be left off last. Once again, she was forced to look at him in a different way when the carriage stopped in front of the boardinghouse.

"I would like to speak with you in the morning, if you're returning?" he asked as he climbed out to help her down.

"I will be there, my lord." She wanted to return with him now, but common sense stopped her. As she curtsied to him, he leaned in closer so only she would hear his words.

"Are you well? Is there aught you need now?"

"I am fine, my lord. I will explain everything in the morning."

"Very well."

He waited until she climbed the steps to the door before returning inside. Arabella watched through the small window next to the door as the coach pulled away. A sigh escaped her as she tugged off the cap that held her hair back and loosened the tight braid that controlled the length of her hair. As she turned to climb the steps to her room above she found Euphemia standing there, studying her.

"Are ye in trouble, lass?" the older woman asked.

Arabella kept the first several replies behind her teeth, unwilling to expose her secrets, even to a woman who'd helped her so much already. When she'd had no place to go, Euphemia Taylor had offered her a room in exchange for help in taking care of her lodgers.

The woman had been a godsend when Arabella had arrived in Edinburgh, friendless and without family. Mrs. Brander believed she'd had a position awaiting her, so she'd asked no questions. The weeks in between arrival and being hired were better for her because of the widow Taylor. But sharing the whole truth with her was not something Arabella could do.

"In trouble, Euphemia?"

"A rich lord, in his evening clothes and fancy coach, just brought ye back to my door in the dead of night. Ye stand at the door, staring with sad eyes, watching him leave." Euphemia came close, once more studying Arabella's face. "Ye have the look of a lass in love, dearie." She took Arabella by the shoulders and tugged her in. "And like a lass who doesna wish to be so." Euphemia's grasp eased. "So, I ask ye again—are ye in trouble?"

"I am not in that kind of trouble, Euphemia."

"A young woman alone in this city can find many kinds of trouble. I dinna mean to make things worse for ye. I have seen ye struggle with some great matter and I ken something weighs heavily on yer shoulders and yer heart." She lifted her hand and brushed some of the loosened tendrils of Arabella's hair out of her face. "I can find ye work, if ye'd rather not return to his household. With all the new families moving into the New Town there is always a need for housekeepers and such."

The conflict between her oath and the man she'd discovered grew deeper each day. But how could she live when her father had died, if not at the viscount's hand, certainly by his efforts?

"I gave my word, Euphemia. I need to finish what I promised I would."

"That and twa'pence will give ye an empty bed, an empty heart and twa'pence in yer hand." The kindness in the woman's pale blue eyes brought tears to her own. She'd been on her own for so long that the concern shown her by this woman reminded her of the absence of it in her life.

"I need to seek my rest," she said, brushing away the signs of her weakness. "I will be returning to his lordship's house in the morn."

Euphemia started to say something, thought better of it and nodded at Arabella. Then, the woman shook her head, as if arguing with herself and said what she wanted to say.

"Ye canna change the past, lass. Ye canna buy peace with yer own heart and soul." Euphemia gave her a sad smile and Arabella knew there had been something bad in her life. "Ye can only live yer life and lay claim to yer future."

Was Euphemia correct? Was this all a mistake that would, in reality, change nothing and cost her everything? She trudged up the steps, each one taking more effort than the last until she reached the landing at the top.

When the sun's light tried to pierce the thick fog that formed the next morning, Arabella was still tossing and turning in the small bed. The echoing sound of the bells ringing in the church steeple nearby was her only clue that it was day. She felt as badly as she surely looked for her eyes felt swollen and fought opening, and her head ached from the restlessness of the arguments that filled her thoughts when sleep should have.

The only good thing she'd done was to sort out what she must do in her battle of past oath and present. Now that there was a sort of familiarity between them and now that he planned to speak with her about his work and the missing papers, it was the perfect time to press him for information. To see what he would reveal about her father.

About their travels and the rumors she'd heard later after her father's death. About a treasure.

And, about the brooch in that sketch and what the part she possessed meant.

Chapter Twelve

As Arabella had expected, the household was running smoothly even without her presence. As it had before her arrival and would after she eventually left. Mrs. Mathieson greeted her and handed her a cup of tea before she could ask for one. She made her way into her room and put her bag down. On her return to the kitchen, she found a place set at the table for her with a plate of coddled eggs and toasted bread.

Her stomach rebelled a bit, but the first sips of tea settled it. Glancing around, she took note of who was here and who must be above and about their chores.

"Has his lordship eaten?"

"Nay, he has not asked for it yet," Mrs. Mathieson said.

"Not yet?" Arabella looked at the clock and checked again with her pocket watch. "'Tis late for him."

"Aye, but then he had quite the late night." Mrs. Mathieson winked at her and smiled. "His godmother—"

"Lady Arbuthnott?" She knew the answer but asked anyway.

"Aye, the countess showed up here yesterday and demanded he escort her to a ball at the Assembly Rooms last night. She even ordered him to get ready while she waited. Said she couldn't chance that he would escape!"

"Nay!"

"Aye! And I must say, between us, that his lordship dressed up well for it. Tall and in clothes that fit like, well, like his valet wanted them to fit!"

Mrs. Mathieson laughed and patted Arabella's hand. She bit her tongue when she almost revealed she'd seen him and aye, he had looked every bit as handsome as the cook described. Mrs. Mathieson was older and, unlike herself, was a real widow and had experienced married life. And from the few comments they had exchanged on that matter, the woman had enjoyed it.

Before she could offer a word about it, Mr. Pottles walked in. Standing at his arrival, Arabella nodded.

"Ah, you are indeed back as his lordship said you would be."

"I am, Mr. Pottles. Here and ready for duty." He would probably wonder for hours how the viscount knew she would return.

"His lordship would like to speak to you now and have his breakfast when he is done with you." Arabella frowned at his choice of words, but Mrs. Mathieson gasped.

"That sounds ominous, Mrs. Lewis," the cook said directly to her. "Well Mr. Pottles? Should Mrs. Lewis be concerned of her reception abovestairs?" Arabella smiled at the cook's boldness, something only dared of late.

"A butler does not ask his employer about his intentions, Mrs. Mathieson," he said. His countenance was that perfect, unexpressive butler's face that revealed nothing. Only his voice gave the slightest hint of his anticipation with his employer's coming actions. "A butler carries out his orders." He turned to her now. "Mrs. Lewis, his lordship is in his library."

The devil was on her shoulder for she picked up a piece of the toast and took a bite. A mouthful of tea washed it down before she wiped her hands on a linen square and walked out of the kitchen to the stairs without waiting for Pottles to follow or speak again.

Arabella stopped in front of the door and could not make her hand reach for the knob. Suddenly, all the possibilities about this discussion, the outcome of it and the links to her father flashed before her. After all this time, she wasn't certain how she felt. Confused over the man she'd come to know. Desperate for the truth of what had happened between her father and the viscount. Regret over what she had given up of a life she could have had and guilt at the same time over questioning her purpose. What a mess she was!

Beneath all of that anticipation ran like a river through her, its edge teasing her emotions, pushing her onward and leaving her unable to resist its pull. She gripped the knob as she knocked and then pushed the door more forcefully than planned. But the viscount was tugging at the same time, and she made an impressive entry by stumbling forward and landing directly into his arms.

"Here now, no need to fall at my feet. Let me help you." Her hands slid around his waist seeking purchase on his waistcoat since he wore no jacket but gripping the silk fabric did her no good. The viscount eased his arms from around her and guided her to stand. "There now. Come in and be seated."

Arabella smoothed her apron down over her skirts and sat where he'd indicated. He closed the door and then, surprising her again, he dragged his chair around the desk and placed it near hers. He lounged against the back of his chair and stretched his legs out, crossing them at the ankles. She could not help but smile as he raked his fingers through his hair, leaving it mussed from Duncan's handiwork.

"I'm afraid you have ruined Duncan's crowning achievement, my lord," she said. "He must have been insufferable after dressing you for the ball."

He laughed, it came so naturally to him, and repeated his small affectation.

"He did enjoy himself. More even than the day I left my bed and returned to my usual schedule." The viscount laughed again. "He had such high hopes for a repeat of his grooming this morn, but I disabused him of that quickly."

The room fell silent for a moment, and she decided to be the first one to speak on the matter between them.

"Euphemia Taylor took me in when I arrived here in Edinburgh looking for a position. When you told me to take some time away from here, the only place I could think of was her lodging house," she said.

"Clara." He shook his head. "I did not mean to chase you from the house." The viscount sat up straighter and reached out to touch her hand. "I meant for you to take time from your duties considering how many additional tasks you took on after my injury. More than were expected of you, but ones I appreciated immensely." Her skin tingled under his hand, and she fought both the urge to leave it be and the urge to pull away. Then he lifted his, ending their contact, and leaned back in his chair.

"I misunderstood," she said. She had been confused by his order and had not wished to begin a discussion when he'd given it. "So, I stayed with Euphemia." She shrugged. "I'm never good when left to my own devices, so when her friend needed help, I agreed."

"The lively Mrs. Betty Paterson."

She glanced at him, thinking at first he'd said "lovely" and realizing he'd actually used the word "lively" to describe Betty. Although even she could hear the humor that tinged his words, the flushing in his cheeks did surprise her. Was he embarrassed? Flattered by whatever Betty had said or done?

"Aye, my lord, Betty is that."

Now watching him, she could see that he was actually blushing. And, God help her, she thought he looked positively adorable as he did it. What had the woman done to earn such a reaction from the viscount?

"Betty works for one of the grocers who supplied food to the ball and her employer needed to also provide maids to serve it. I was available so I offered to help her." But he looked as though he was fighting against saying something, so she could not resist asking. "Did something happen between you after you dropped me at Euphemia's?"

"A gentleman never reveals a lady's secrets, Clara." He winked at her and she lost her thoughts. The way his eye twinkled and the dimple that appeared in his cheek as he winked a second time stole her very breath.

"Let me just say that Mrs. Paterson, Betty, as she insisted I call her, made it clear that she prefers younger men *when it comes to it*."

"Oh, good Lord, nay she did not!" The laugh escaped before she could stop it.

"Oh, aye, she did indeed." His whole face broke into a smile that made him even more devastatingly handsome. "She made certain to have Adam repeat her address several times so he would ken it, *if needed*."

"How did Adam respond?" From his words and tone she could see he thought it entertaining and took no offense from Betty's forwardness of manner.

"Well, with the way she was winking at him as she said it, I think she was casting a wide net. The only one she did not offer it to was William." She frowned, thinking on why William would be left out of her attempts. "But I fear he is too young for her tastes."

Arabella should not, she knew she should resist the urge to join in his merriment, but she could not. She laughed until her eyes teared and her stomach hurt. Knowing Betty and her bold words, she wished she had seen it.

"You should laugh more." Although he'd laughed with her when she started, at some point, he'd stopped and now was watching with an intensity that belied the humor they had spoken of. "It brings out the shimmer in your eyes and makes you look like a different person."

Dare she tell him it was true? That she was not the woman he thought but a conniving stranger here for her own purposes. That she was working on her own plan and lying to him with every word and action, even in simply doing her job. The joy in their shared laughter faded quickly as the truth flooded in.

"You would tell me if you needed anything, would you not?"

"I do not understand, my lord."

"Something Betty said last night only makes sense if you are in need of. . . funds. You would tell me if you were?"

His gaze softened then, a genuine concern that made her guilt tear at her from the inside. She wiped away the tears of laughter and cleared her throat several times while trying to come up with a way to explain without explaining.

"The salary you pay me is quite sufficient, my lord. I have enough to see to my needs and my expenses." She sat up straighter in her chair and clasped her hands on her lap to regain some control over herself. She would not tell him more than that—about how she saved every possible bit of the money she earned for the escape she would need to make.

"And if something were to happen to me, would you still have the means to support yourself? Could you find employment?"

Shocked at his question, she could not respond. To her needy ears, it sounded as if he cared. Though she'd planned for him to be recognized as the cause of her father's dishonor, his position as viscount and peer would protect him from their misdeeds in all the important ways as it had always protected those men high enough in society. He did and would still walk among the noblemen. He would continue in whatever endeavors he chose. He could move on and live a happy life because of his bloodline. If the matter was settled.

The truth struck her then. It would be settled in her opinion, but what if. . . .

"So, the attack on you was not coincidental?" she asked.

Now, he paused, not answering quickly, clearly contemplating his reply and choosing his words with care. How much did he know? Did he suspect her of being involved? The viscount stood and moved away from her, pacing the chamber slowly as she watched. Then he went behind his desk and lifted the leather satchel to the top of it. Reaching inside, he took out the sheet of paper she'd seen. The one she'd wanted to keep.

The drawing that had been in his bag.

"Someone is looking for this and will not stop until they find it."

"This sketch or the piece of jewelry?"

"The piece itself."

"Where did this come from?" Her voice shook when she asked that question. Was she holding something her father had created before his death?

"This was drawn by the illustrator who traveled with me. He was quite talented. He did most of the recording for the dig."

"Drawn when you found this?" She held her breath for the answer.

"This is a dream," he said, as he picked up and glanced at the drawing. He dropped it to the desk. "It does not exist. It is a fairy tale of old. The desperation of the obsessed." He rubbed his head, as if in pain, but it was not where he'd been hit. Instead, he pressed on his temples and closed his eyes for a moment. "People have died and will die if this chase continues."

"So, you did not find it? Does it truly not exist?" she asked. She fought not to reach for the place where the replica her father had given her previously hung. Mayhap that's why he had it made for her? If he had drawn this, he must have seen or known about the original one? Was the viscount lying to her even as she lied to him?

"Like every other fictional story, I'm certain there is some element of truth, but most of it is made up to encourage weak minds to seek it out. We saw this only in a carving at one of the ruined temples in Timgad."

"So, this brooch is why you were attacked?" She touched the drawing. She knew she had not been responsible for the attack, which meant someone else was. Someone else believed the brooch existed and they were searching for it and the treasure it promised its finder. "Or was there something else in your satchel they wanted? The notebooks and pages are torn and missing.

Could those have been their aim?"

Her father had never mentioned the design of the complete brooch or a link to a legendary treasure when he'd given her the replica of part of it as a pendant to wear. This might not have anything to do with him, other than the drawing itself.

"Though they ken I do not have it, they are searching for anything, papers or drawings, anything that could point them to it." He leaned over the desk and stared at the sketch.

"How could they ken about that?" she asked. If the viscount lied now and there was an actual artifact, then it could explain the sketch. Otherwise, how would others ken of it?

"This is not the first attack, Clara. Since I returned and parted ways with my partner Balugani, there have been attacks and burglaries of some kind every five or so years."

She stopped breathing at the mention of her father. It was the first time the viscount had shared anything about his past and she could almost not bear hearing it from his mouth. Gathering her control, Arabella forced the words to come out, needing and fearing what he would say in reply.

"Do you think this Balugani is behind it then?"

HOW WAS HE supposed to answer her question without breaking the rule he held himself to regarding Luigi Balugani? And more importantly, why would he even consider telling her the truth of it when his decision to lie about it had been made long ago? In his opinion, keeping up the lie remained the safest path to follow.

The man behind Josh's biggest accomplishment in his career as an archeologist and adventurer was the very man responsible for his humiliation. Bile burned its way up his throat at even the thought of him. No matter that he was having a conversation with someone about what was happening currently, a person who had no preconceived notions or knowledge of his past, he found himself resistant to speak the name of the villain aloud. But Balugani was. . . .

"He is dead, so no matter his previous sins, this attack and the theft of my documents does not lay at his door."

Clara let out a soft breath at his words. He examined her expression and realized that something was wrong. What a fool he was for allowing himself to think that her usual pragmatism could withstand such a harsh discussion.

"My apologies for bringing up such topics and distressing you. It must be a shock to learn that your employer has a dark, problematic past." Josh walked around his desk and sat in the chair next to her.

"I knew about your travels and the books you wrote about them. But attacks in the past and even more recently? I did not ken about those."

"I have done my best to keep those out of public view. At least until this one. They grow bolder now."

"What will you do?" she asked.

"Finlaggan and Hepburn are checking into several things for me. I have hired some—" how should he say it? "—some additional help to see to keeping the house, the area and the people who live and work here safer."

He wanted them safe. He needed her to be safe. If anyone knew what she'd seen and even that they'd spoken of the papers and sketch, and the Treasure, she would be in danger. Whoever was behind this would see her as a potential target, so he would keep her safe, even if it meant sending her away.

"Clara," he said, taking hands in his.

He'd not noticed that she was shivering, or trembling, until he touched her very cold hands. He was wrong to speak to her of all this. Wrong to need her to see him as more than the viscount who'd hired her to keep his house. Wrong to want more from her than her efforts in his service.

"I'm sorry to say that you could be in danger, too. If anyone kens that you not only saw that drawing but also read the documents with it, you will be part of this."

"That sketch? Why did they not take it with them if that's what interested them?" she asked. "Why leave it behind?"

He hesitated to answer her, for it would make the danger much more tangible and literally much closer at hand than she understood it was. But, since she'd very much been dragged into this situation, she deserved the truth.

"It was not in my possession until they left it behind. A warning to me—"

"My lord?" Pottles called through the door. "May I enter, my lord?" Several loud knocks followed and then the sound of another voice added to the growing fray outside.

"We will speak later—" Josh had barely released Clara's hand and stood when the door opened and Pottles stumbled into the room. His butler's attempts to stop the force of nature in the hallway from entering without being asked to as Pottles regained his footing and carried out his duty.

"My lord, the Countess of Arbuthnott." From the calmness in his voice now, Pottles was recovering quickly and holding the door as his godmother entered.

"What exactly is going on here, Joshua?"

Chapter Thirteen

A RABELLA MADE HER way to her rooms downstairs as quickly as she could. When Pottles entered the viscount's library trying to control Lady Arbuthnott's entry and not being able to stop her, Arabella jumped to her feet. While the viscount was speaking to his godmother, and trying to divert her questions, she slipped out without attracting their attention.

Now, she closed her door and locked it, leaning against it for the support it gave her now that her legs were trembling. Arabella tugged her watch out and could not believe that less than an hour had passed since she'd answered his call. It had felt much longer to her. And yet, if she'd heard correctly, he was late to visit his godmother for some pre-arranged meeting and that brought her to his doorstep.

That she'd worked for Lady Arbuthnott was not a lie, but she'd only helped out when Mrs. Brander needed her. There was no possibility that the countess would recognize or remember her, but she did not wish to risk it with such a formidable woman. So, she must avoid Lady Arbuthnott and avoid being exposed too soon. Leaving her room, she went to check on the maids to see if they had reached the bedrooms yet. The drawing room and dining room had been cleaned and new fires laid in each hearth. Edmee and Eilidh had moved through the upper floors efficiently and already the bedchambers had clean linens. They would visit the library once the viscount and his guest were done.

With the daily housecleaning nearly complete, she consulted Mrs. Mathieson about groceries and foodstuffs needed and about a new shop a few blocks away near the Grassmarket area. Feeling excited and restless, she decided a walk there would allow her to ease some of that tension. It would also allow her to examine their wares to see if the quality and selection they sold was appropriate for this household.

Keeping a brisk pace, she arrived at the shop and met the owner. Within a half-hour, she'd made arrangements for samples of some vegetables and spices to be sent to Mrs. Mathieson for her to try. As she made her way back to Dunalastair House, rumbles of thunder filled the air, threatening a storm. It took one glance overhead to see the clouds gathering right above her.

Laughing, she began walking faster, intent on getting to the house before the deluge hit. With her head down and her cloak pulled up, she never saw the man until she'd nearly run into him. Only his quick action, stepping aside and holding out his arm to steady her, kept her from falling. When she looked up to thank him, she wondered if this was one of the men hired by the viscount to protect the area.

The punch to her head from his fist knocked her to her knees. Arabella managed to get her hand up and blocked the second one. When he grabbed her by her hair and pulled her up, she feared the worst. He brought his face to hers, close enough to smell his fetid breath as he spoke.

"Do ye ken where it is?" He shook her head, sending shards of pain through it and down her neck. He kept her just off her knees so she could not steady herself or get hold of him. "Where is he hidin' it?"

"I do not ken what you want," she forced out. Even if she knew what he wanted, she had no idea of its existence or location.

"Tell me!" He growled the demand. When she said nothing,

he shook her head again until she moaned. "If ye ken wot's good for ye, ye better tell me now."

She drew in a breath, intending to scream, when his hold on her disappeared and she fell to the ground. Curled there, with her cloak twisted around her, the sound of others running towards her, calling out her name, gave her hope. But it was *his* arrival and the way he knelt next to her and lifted her into his arms that told her she was safe.

"Here now," he whispered against her ear. "I have you."

She let her head rest on his shoulder as he carried her, giving orders with each step to people she did not wish to see. Dizzy from the blow, Arabella could only feel the strength of him as he carried her and hear his breathing increase. Without realizing, she had clutched the lapel of his jacket and under it she could feel the rapid beating of his heart.

He stopped only once, at the front steps, when she heard Mr. Pottles direct him down to the servants' entrance. His indecision warmed her own heart and worried her at once. She was his employee and belonged in the servants' area. If he carried her into the main entrance of the house and placed her anywhere else, it was a statement no one would miss. A statement she was not certain she wanted him to make.

"My room, please, my lord," she whispered so only he heard.

One of the footmen moved ahead of them, opening doors and leading the way to her chambers. It took too much effort to open her eyes to watch their path, so she waited until they'd reached her door.

"Please put me down now, my lord," she said, releasing her hold on him as he allowed her legs to ease down to the floor. He did not remove his arms from around her for several long moments, not until Mrs. Mathieson arrived at her side.

"Here, my lord," the cook said. "Allow me to see to Mrs. Lewis."

Agatha Mathieson stepped to her, giving the viscount no choice but to back away. His hands lingered at her waist even after he'd begun moving, but the cook moved in, making it impossible for him. He stepped back and watched as Agatha guided her into her chambers, not moving from the open doorway.

"Lie down or sit?"

"Sitting, please," she said. Agatha pulled out the chair from next to her table and eased her into it. Arabella placed her trembling hands on the table, willing them to calm. They did not. Her hair fell over her shoulders, some still pinned up but the mass of it loose and tangled. Reaching up to touch the tender place—just above her hairline on the side of her head, she grimaced at the soreness there, even at a gentle touch. "Well, Mrs. Mathieson, how bad is it?"

"Aye, Mrs. Mathieson, how bad is it?" the viscount asked from the door.

"Give a woman a chance to check it, if you will, my lord."

Agatha retrieved the hand mirror from her chest of drawers and gave it to her. Holding her breath, Arabella peeked at herself. It hurt to move her hair out of the way, but she saw no bleeding and obvious lump.

"Let me help you," the cook said.

Arabella dared a glance at him there in the doorway. His stare was so intense it made her blush. As Agatha pulled the pins still holding the useless cap in one place, the woman freed the rest of her hair from the previously neat bun she'd twisted it into to hold it under that cap.

The sound he made as she shook the tangled curls free drew her gaze. It sent shivers through her, for he'd growled a sound that was so possessive she felt. . . claimed. He took a step towards her, crossing the threshold of her chamber before he seemed to realize it and moved back. This was not the man she knew. This man was dangerous to her, filled with strong emotions, wild unpredictable ones she could feel emanating from him even across the space between them.

The air grew tense, her body heated and something deep

within her tightened incrementally until she could not release the breath she held in. The ache in her head disappeared as the strength of this attraction grew.

"I do not think the surgeon will be needed, my lord." Mrs. Mathieson's voice broke into the strange bubble of intimacy. "There's no bleeding, but there will be some bruising. A little rest and a cold cloth will help now." Agatha turned and faced down the viscount. "Now, my lord."

"I will come back later," he said. "Clara, rest and we will sort through everything when I get back."

There was more to his words than a simple farewell. It was a promise. And in spite of her past and his, it was one she knew she was anxious to hear.

Josh took the stairs up to the first floor by twos. The sight of her battered face, her hair tangled and hanging around her shoulders, and the vulnerability in the way she laid her head on his shoulder as he carried her here all served to enrage him.

If only his godmother had not distracted him with her arrival which allowed Clara to slip away unnoticed. If only he'd given the new guards he'd hired instructions sooner, about her being a possible target and making certain to keep her in their sights, If only he'd. . . .

Dragging his hands through his hair, he leaned against the wall at the top of the staircase before going through the doorway to the drawing room and his library. His godmother was in his library waiting for his return. He'd run out without a word when he heard the yelling outside his window. It took less than a second to realize Clara was in danger. Though no one said her name, he'd known it was her.

He left the house at a full run as his godmother sputtered in disbelief and got to Clara just as the guard had reached and knocked down her attacker. The bastard disappeared into the dark shadows of the incoming storm.

Josh never wanted to feel the desperation he had when he

saw her there on the sidewalk, crumpled and dazed. He did not think. He did not consider the options. He did not weigh propriety against expediency. He simply acted—picking her up in his arms and carrying her back to safety.

Every shudder that coursed through her body tore into him and his lack of forethought pained him. For his lack of better planning, she could have died or been terribly injured. As he stood and walked through the door, he vowed that she would never be in danger because of him again.

He allowed himself a few slow breaths, trying to regain control before facing his godmother again. And he must have his wits about him if he was to avoid further commitments with her and see to Clara's safety. Opening the door, the sight of a calm Lady Arbuthnott drinking tea surprised him. Actually, the fact that she was yet in his library was unexpected. Being the woman she was, it would have been more like her to be in the center of things calling out orders and putting everyone in the places they needed or where she thought they needed to be. He closed the door and sat behind his desk, in the chair someone had moved to its usual position there.

Then he waited. The barrage of questions and opinions and directions and ultimatums should begin any moment and Josh thought himself prepared to handle, deflect or ignore whatever the lady aimed at him. The silence, other than the clink of her cup returning to its saucer, was unnerving.

"Is your housekeeper well?" she asked.

"No, Aunt Sorcha. Mrs. Lewis is not." No gasp of impertinence met his honest reply. "She was attacked and beaten just yards away from *my* house. Attacked because she is in *my* employ and for no other reason than that."

"Almost as a warning, it would seem," she mused. "Is this connected to your own recent encounter?" Before he could answer, she continued. "Which is connected to that old, nasty business?"

He was still sorting out how to say what he could say, when

she added, "That I thought was over and done and would remain in the past?"

"It is certainly connected to both, Aunt Sorcha." She could smell dishonesty at thirty paces, so he didn't bother to try. "It has all reared its ugly head once more."

"Bah! You have let this go on for too long, Dunalastair. You should be seeing to securing your title and inheritance rather than protecting a blackguard years after—"

She stopped when she met his gaze. She knew more than anyone else did about the cost of quieting the rumors of the past, but she did not know it all. There were lines he would not cross, vows he would not break, and she was growing extremely close to one of them now. From the widening of her gaze and the way her teacup stopped just short of touching her mouth, his godmother understood that.

"Pottles tells me your housekeeper—Mrs. Lewis—worked in my household? I do not remember the name." She sipped as she watched him.

"Mrs. Lewis is a war widow. She lived in the village at Arbuthnott and helped your Mrs. Brander as needed while Mr. Lewis served on the continent."

Josh reminded her of the basic details. He searched his memory for some other information about her background and realized he'd never read her letters or discussed other particulars with Clara. But he could explain how the left corner of her mouth lifted first when she smiled. And that she had one unruly lock of hair that could not be tamed. And that her droll sense of humor could withstand even Pottles' worst.

And. . . .

"Ah, she does sound familiar," his godmother said, interrupting the path of his thoughts. Her teacup now empty, she placed it on the tray. A dab of her linen napkin and she was done. "Has she need of a physician? I could send word to mine to come here?"

"It seems it is just some bruising, thank the Almighty."

"And now what will you do?"

"I will see to her."

They stared at each other in silence for a long moment. When she blinked and looked away, Josh knew she understood something of his plan and would not argue it. When she stood, he did as well.

"Have a care, Dunalastair. You have a title that will give you a certain measure of *protection* in this as it has in the other matter. This widow will have none. Remember that in your plan."

He walked to her and kissed her cheek. "I understand."

Josh rang the bell on his desk and Pottles promptly opened the door and moved aside for the countess. She took a step, stopped and motioned Pottles away. When the door closed, she turned back to face Josh.

"Being a person of some age and certain ailments and discomforts, I have made certain that my carriage is well-appointed and spacious. It will be waiting on the street behind the house at six of the clock in the morning for your use."

"Aunt Sorcha?" She surprised him yet again.

"They are watching you and your household and will follow your coach each time it leaves." She narrowed her gaze. "Send it to that Society of which you speak so often, to their building in the morning at your usual time but allow your footman to take your place," she whispered. Her flair for subterfuge was unfamiliar to him and he found himself marveling at the quickness of mind that concocted this plan as she spoke. "You may have use of mine, simply send it back to town when you finish with it."

"I am speechless," he said.

"You may have traveled the world and been feted and sponsored by important people, Joshua, but I have had some adventures of my own."

"Adventures, Aunt Sorcha?"

"Young people believe you invented excitement," she said as she nodded at the bell. He rang it. "Some of us have been seeking it since before you were born."

The door opened and she left without another word, leaving

him open-mouthed at her. . . confession? admission? . . . of some youthful indiscretions. After a few minutes of astonishment as she made her way to her carriage, his own planning began in earnest.

Here in the city it was too easy for strangers to keep watch over your comings and goings. But out in the country, where villages were close-knit and strangers recognized immediately, it would not be so.

With only one road approaching it, Dunalastair Manor was a safer place than here. Past Perth and Pitlochry, in the middle of the mountain wilderness and with a loch on one side, anyone traveling there from the small village would be seen and remarked upon and, with a bit of help, he would be warned of their presence.

He kept a small staff on duty, more to do with hiring the locals than any true need for it, so the manor would be stocked with the necessities, but not too many people. Those who worked here would not reveal his absence, and very few would know his whereabouts.

Or Mrs. Clara Lewis' either.

Chapter Fourteen

THEIR ESCAPE FROM Edinburgh, without being followed, seemed to have worked. Just before dawn's light reached the city, he and Clara boarded his godmother's well-appointed carriage that turned out to be well-stocked, too. And very comfortable. Clara slept through most of it, thanks to a dose of the same concoction he'd used during his recuperation. Ensconced in a pile of cushions, blankets and pillows, she roused only during a few of their stops for comfort or for sustenance.

Remembering how badly he'd felt just one day after his attack and injury, Josh wished he could have waited to travel. The need to get her out of the city forced his hand. At least, this coach was everything his godmother had promised. There was even a lockbox hidden under the floor panel that held a brace of pistols that made him less anxious about any interference along the way. With several changes of horses, they would reach Dunalastair lands by nightfall.

After they'd passed through Perth and took the road west instead of north for Arbuthnott, Josh rode up with the driver and kept a lingering eye on the road behind them. As each turn took them farther and farther away from towns and towards the mountains and lochs, he could breathe a bit easier. There was no sign of anyone following them. After stopping one final time,

Clara remained sitting up, looking pale but not overly so. She'd not eaten much at all throughout the day, other than a bowl of soup and several cups of tea.

"Better? Worse?" he asked.

She tried to smile. He could see that tempting left corner of her mouth twitch with the effort, but she shrugged instead. "I am not worse."

"Considering the number of miles we have traveled and how you began the day, I will accept that without argument." He moved to the edge of the seat and leaned across to take her hands in his. At least they were not as cold as Dunalastair Waters in winter. "And there will be time to rest and recover when we arrive and settle in."

At his words, a deep furrow crossed her brow. "I have duties to see to," she said. "I must learn this household as well unless you have a housekeeper employed here already."

"The coffers of the Viscount of Dunalastair have enough funds to employ a housekeeper in each of his households, Mrs. Lewis." He held onto her hands, warming them between his. Sitting on the edge also allowed him to lean his legs against hers, but she had not noticed that yet. "It matters not, for you are not coming to Dunalastair Manor as its housekeeper. You are a guest."

"I could not, my lord."

Her dignity drew her up straighter on her seat, but the discomfort and jostling, even of this well-sprung coach, caused her to lean back quickly. Josh stood up and placed one of the pillows behind her neck and head to support her.

"You were attacked because of me, Clara." He sat down but did not slide back in his seat. "I am responsible for the pain you are suffering, so I will provide you the place and the means to recover from it."

"My lord."

"Mrs. Lewis." He adored her stubbornness even when it was directed at him. However, she was wilting before his eyes, her face growing paler then and her hands clutched into fists fighting the pain. "Your pardon, Clara. I did not mean to add to your discomfort. We can discuss this when you've had a good night's rest."

"One night, my lord. One night, then I will seek my duties."

He allowed her to win this argument, but he had no intentions of her taking up her role as housekeeper at Dunalastair Manor. He might hope for something else, but he would see her treated as a guest during their stay.

"Very well," he said, tipping his head in deference to her declaration. "Rest now. We should be there within a few hours. Think about a hot bath and a soft, warm bed."

He'd meant the words innocently, about the hospitality he could offer her at the manor house, but his body understood its other, its true, meaning. But only a beast would think about his own needs when the woman he wanted was in such a sorry condition.

So, Josh closed his eyes and waited for her to sleep. It wasn't long, as he watched through slitted eyes, before her head began to lean to one side. He eased over next to her and adjusted her so she was supported by his body. He felt the moment she relaxed completely against him and smiled. And if his own muscles grew tight because he did not move until they arrived at the entryway, it was fine.

She did not wake as he scooped her into his arms and carried her out of the carriage.

She did not wake even as he greeted his very surprised staff and gave directions about her accommodations.

And she did not wake even as he laid her on the bed or while he waited in the hallway as Margaret, the daughter of the cook who worked as a housemaid here when needed, made her comfortable.

In spite of her plans to the contrary, Mrs. Lewis remained in bed for that night and most of the next day.

ARABELLA SPREAD HER hands out, skimming along the surface of the most comfortable bed she'd ever slept in. Somehow, she knew that the sheets were of the highest quality as well and she stretched her body, limb by limb, enjoying the feel of them on her skin. Shifting to test her body's discomforts, she realized she was fully awake when she rolled onto her side and her face touched the pillow. That yet hurt. The moan she released seemed to echo around her, indicating she was occupying a large room. So, having a care not to do it too quickly, she lifted her head to look at the chamber.

It *was* large.

With one this spacious, she could have shared it with three or four others and had enough space for each to have their own bed! Only as she sat up and the sheets slid down did she realize she wore only her shift. Tugging the covers back up, Arabella spied her threadbare robe lying across the bottom of the bed. As she grabbed it and pulled it on, she also noticed that her head did not pain her. Sliding her fingers through her tangled hair, the area was a bit sore and that was all. As her feet touched the floor, the door opened and a young woman of perhaps fifteen entered carrying a tray.

"Good day to ye, ma'am," she said, closing the door with her foot. "I brought ye something to keep ye until dinner as his lordship asked."

"Thank you. . . ."

"Margaret, ma'am." The girl moved efficiently, setting the tray on a table in the corner Arabella had not noticed before. Once the plates were arranged, the girl approached. "I ken ye were no' weel when ye arrived. Would ye like help?" Margaret held out what looked to be a sturdy arm, but Arabella waved her off.

"My thanks, but I feel much better this morning." She wasn't lying for she did feel much improved. She glanced at the girl's face as she laughed.

"Morning, ma'am? 'Tis ha' past six."

"It cannot be. I would never sleep through the day," she assured the servant. And she never had. Especially not when working as a housekeeper and not even in those exceptional weeks when she was on her own. Margaret did not contradict her, rather she stepped back and pulled the chair out, waiting for Arabella to sit.

"Och, I almost forgot to tell ye. The bath his lordship ordered for ye is being prepared now. Once ye finish wi' this, ye can ring for it there." She finished her shocking announcement with a nod to the bell pull next to the bed.

Arabella walked to the table and sat in the chair offered, stunned to be the one being served. The viscount had told her she would be his guest, but she thought he'd accepted her refusal. Once seated, she looked at the teapot and the tray. A smaller plate was filled with an assortment of cakes and sweets. Another with cold sliced meats and cheeses. Even another with thick slices of bread slathered with butter. Her mouth watered at the sight of the simple but plentiful feast before her.

It was clear he had not accepted her objections. She should protest and make it clear to him that. . . . her stomach growled so loudly it could not be ignored. She was going to protest this. Arabella took one bite of fresh bread slathered in butter and knew her protest would have to wait.

Arabella pushed her sleep-loosened hair off her shoulders and did not feel her necklace there. She dropped the bread and checked under the length of her hair and inside her robe. It was gone.

"Ma'am, is something amiss?" Margaret returned to her side.

"My necklace? Have you seen it?" Panic grew within her. She could not lose the only thing she had left of her father. She rose, running to the bed and searching under the pillows and bed-covers, seeking out a place where it could be.

"Och, aye, Ma'am." Arabella whirled around to face the maid. "When I readied ye for bed on yer arrival. 'Twas tangled in yer hair it was, so I careful-like removed it and put it there." She turned to see where the lass pointed. A small wooden box sat on the table next to the bed.

"In there?" She rushed to open it.

"Aye, ma'am. I put yer hair geegaws and the necklace in it for ye. Ye didna hiv one in yer things."

Arabella opened it and beneath several ribbons and hair pins lay her only prized possession. Letting out an anxious breath, she closed the box and placed it back on the table. She would have to put the necklace in a more secure place later, when she was alone.

"My thanks, Margaret." She sat down at the table set with food and tea and gave herself some time to calm down. "I was not able to pack for myself, so some of my belongings are still back in. . . Edinburgh."

She should not have overreacted to the necklace's removal, for now the maid knew something private about her. Which she could share with others, even the viscount. Arabella placed the cup down in front of her. Margaret had lost no time in tidying the bed and gathering towels and soaps and other supplies needed for a bath.

"I thank you for seeing to my care last night," she said over her shoulder. "'Tis something made and given to me by a beloved cousin, and I would not want to lose it. I appreciate that you've protected it for me."

After giving the girl permission, Margaret rang for the bath and Arabella finished eating.

Arabella had thought about refusing the food, or most of it, and the bath, but that would only make it awkward for the maid and other house servants who'd been given orders by his lordship. Understanding how that felt, she would not be the cause of it. She could take it up with the viscount when they spoke next.

Margaret was a soft-spoken lass with bright green eyes and a frequent kind smile. She also loved to chat as she worked. And work she did, proving herself a well-trained and excellent maid in all sorts of roles—from bedmaking to serving food to helping at the bath and then dressing.

As the girl carried out each task, Arabella could almost see a younger version of herself. Memories of working and learning tasks just to survive filled her thoughts. She'd actually enjoyed the hard work, for it took her mind off her own losses and earned coins to support herself. And, she learned enough in her duties to be ready when opportunities arose.

So that when Mrs. Brander needed help and asked her friend, the woman who'd taken Arabella in, if she could recommend someone, she had and Arabella was prepared.

And when she discovered the connection between Mrs. Brander's employer and the man she must find, she was ready to use that for her goal.

The best part was that if her scheme went in a different direction than the one she planned, she at the least had training and experience to find employment.

As she listened to Margaret chatter away as she worked, Arabella discovered the names of all who served in the household and bits about their background and personalities, too. By the time she was ready to leave her chamber, she'd learned many helpful details. How the Viscount of Dunalastair seldom visited his manor and lands. How this had been the maid's first sight of him. And even how surprised the staff were by his manner and calm demeanor, hinting that the last viscount had been more volatile in his nature and eccentricities.

This was all just while Margaret helped her dry and arrange her hair and dress! Most of it was without prompting which spoke of her inexperience rather than any lack of ability at her job. Before she left this place, Arabella would whisper a word of warning about the need for discretion to the lass.

After a lost day in that sumptuous coach, most hours spent in a sleepy haze, she'd thought it would take several days to regain herself. But apparently, eighteen hours in a row of deep sleep cleared the cobwebs from her thoughts and eased the pains from her body. As she looked at herself in the full-length mirror in the corner of the chamber, she was stunned to see the woman there.

The brown dress, modest in its cut, was almost the exact shade as her hair and eyes and it fit her well. She smiled as she remembered wearing it for her interview but with her hair arranged rather than covered with her white cap, it looked different. *She* looked different.

Should she insist on playing her part here? It was possible that the viscount had secured documents and such in this house, away from exposure and safe from discovery. Without knowing his plans and with an unknown amount of time here, she wondered if being his guest would be an advantage.

Worse, she wanted to be his guest here. To be at leisure and learn more about him. Aye, she still wanted the truth. Yet, she was beginning to want . . . too much that she could never have.

No matter, she thought as she pushed all that aside in her mind, her first step was to find out his plans.

"Margaret, do you ken where I can find the viscount?"

"Aye, ma'am, he is in the library." The girl said as she gathered up the wet towels. "The footman will show ye the way."

Of course, he would have a library here. He was a scholar, a historian, a writer, a viscount, and a man who loved learning and researching, and for that he needed his books. She startled and stopped where she stood as she noticed she'd not added *enemy* to that description.

Arabella opened the door and saw the footman at the top of the stairs. Taking in the length of this hallway, the two staircases leading up and down from this floor to the others, and the number of rooms she passed getting to the footman, it was obvious that house was much larger than his house in Edinburgh.

"I'm looking for his lordship's library," she said as she approached him. From the descriptions Margaret had given about the staff, this must be. . . . "Brodie?"

"Aye, ma'am, right this way," the tall, young man said as he turned to lead her.

"I will be fine on my own, if you could just point out the

way."

"His lordship said I was to wait and bring ye to him, Mrs. Lewis." The lad's posture and manners were impeccable, and his respectful tone undid her decision to make her own way.

Again, trapped by her need to be kind to the servants, she nodded and waited for his escort. Once she familiarized herself with the layout of the house, she could and would explore on her own, but for now she followed the man down an impressive marble staircase.

Lined with paintings and portraits, it went down two whole floors before ending in the entry foyer of the house. Costly carpets in designs she did not recognize softened the steps and the landing. She could usually tell truly excellent carpets by their weaving and patterns, especially the highly-prized Aubussons, but the ones here stymied her. They did not appear to be French nor even English in origin. She had not realized she'd stopped to examine them, until Brodie cleared his throat.

"Pardon me for dawdling, Brodie." He held out his hand to direct her to the right side of the foyer and then led her down one corridor.

"No matter, Mrs. Lewis. His lordship can tell you the details of them." She walked near his side so she could hear him.

"Not Mr. Pirrie or Mrs. Lyle?" The butler and housekeeper should be able to answer questions about the house, its furnishings and history.

"Ask his lordship, Mrs. Lewis."

"Ask his lordship what, Brodie?"

Chapter Fifteen

T HE FOOTMAN BOWED his head but not before Josh could see him blush. What had they been speaking about on their way to the library?

"My lord, here is Mrs. Lewis as you asked." Brodie stepped back, ready to return to his post.

"What should Mrs. Lewis ask me about, Brodie?" Why wouldn't the young man reply?

"The carpet, my lord," Clara said. "I was admiring the beautiful workmanship and colors but do not recognize the design or origin. These, at least, are not Aubussons?"

She stepped closer to him, in truth positioning herself between him and the footman in a curious move. He dismissed Brodie with a nod and watched as he walked up the stairs and back to his post a little faster than his usual pace.

"The household staff was quite stunned when I ordered these out of storage to replace the original ones my cousin, the previous viscount, preferred." He watched her as he revealed the truth to her. "William lived his entire life here. He never traveled farther than Perth. And he viewed those of us who did and items we sent back dimly."

"He did not like these?" She looked around at the patterns of the rugs and shook her head. "Did the man not have eyes, my lord?"

She must be feeling better for her words revealed a bit of spirit. Certainly, her color was better, no pale cheeks or tired eyes. Now, instead of only one errant curl, the lack of her cap and the way her hair was arranged with the curls loose in the back had him staring at her unhidden beauty.

"Eyes, aye, but some scruples against anything coming from the 'heathen countries' where I traveled."

She mumbled some words under her breath and though he thought he knew what she'd said, he could only laugh at her reaction.

"Forgive my rudeness, my lord." She met his gaze and stared at him. "I meant no insult."

His ability to breathe stopped as he lost himself in the depths of those dark brown eyes. And in that moment, he understood that he had hired her just for the chance to possibly see her like this—standing before him not as his housekeeper but as his guest. As a woman.

"I took none, Clara." He held out his arm. "Come, I will show you the library here. I use it as my office, too."

He felt her touch on his arm and fought the urge to take her into his embrace. But, he walked, concentrating his thoughts on putting one foot before the other to keep them moving along the corridor. For the first time since inheriting the title and properties entailed to it, Josh wanted to show off the wealth and comfort and luxury of this place.

He reached the door he'd left open and released her before it. The indrawn breath pleased him. They entered and he waited as she walked on into the middle of the main chamber.

Josh was only a child, a lad of ten years or so, when he visited here for the first time. He had to be chased out day after day, his father complaining that he needed to leave the books behind. He had never seen so many books as this. Not at the school then, and not until the university had he seen a collection like this one. For everything about his cousin he did not like, he could not but be pleased about his penchant for collecting all manner of books.

"'Tis a wonder you ever leave this chamber," she said as she faced him.

"Commitments in my life demand that I must."

"Seriously, my lord, why do you not spend more time here? You have your new project that you are writing. I would think this," she motioned to the surrounding shelves upon shelves, "would be more useful to you."

She looked at him then, truly looked him over and her brows tightened in question. He glanced down over his clothing to make sure nothing was wrong with them—and he realized her question.

"I cannot let down the expectations of my title here. My cousin would turn in his grave if I insulted him by not presenting as is expected of the Viscount of Dunalastair." He dressed every day he spent here in the finery a viscount should wear.

"But you do not do that at your house in Edinburgh."

"Ah, so you have noticed."

She began to say something, but he held up his hand to stop her and walked to the bell pull. When the butler answered the call himself, Josh ordered tea and coffee and then offered her a seat on one of the couches that were arranged around the large chamber.

"I cannot sit, my lord," Clara said. "I have overstepped myself and my place already." She gathered her hands before her and smiled. "As I told you in the carriage, I would begin my duties here, learning this household, after some rest. I have had that rest now and—"

"My lord," Pirrie called out as he entered, leading the footman in carrying their repast. He paused as Donald walked past to place the tray on the table between two of the couches. "Mrs. Lewis, I have not had the pleasure of welcoming you to Dunalastair Manor. I hope your stay is a good one."

Josh saw the surprise flood her at the warm words from his butler. So very different from the way Pottles had spoken to her.

"Mr. Pirrie, I—" She stopped and he could see that she was trying to decide whether to expose herself as a member of his staff or to remain simply a guest. "I thank you. My stay and care has been wonderful so far."

"Please send word to me or Mrs. Lyle, our housekeeper, if there is anything you need." The butler nodded at her and then walked to the door. After Donald finished placing the cups and pots and the accompaniments, the two bowed and turned to leave.

"Would you pour, Clara?" he asked, sitting on one of the couches.

Though she looked ready to begin disagreeing with him over her position here, she nodded and sat to prepare him a cup.

"Coffee or tea, my lord?" she asked as she lifted one of the cups.

"My name is Joshua."

"I ken that, my lord." She lowered the cup.

"Could you not call me by name. When you are my guest and not my housekeeper? When alone with me?"

"You are the Viscount of Dunalastair at all times, my lord, and I would not insult the dignity of your title, or you, by calling you otherwise. Whether alone or with others, you are the viscount." She paused and let out a shaky breath. He smiled at that. "Coffee or tea, my lord."

"Coffee, please." He relented, for now. "It seems to help my headache leftover from the injury." He was about to say milk and lots of sugar, but she added both, in the amounts he liked without him saying so. "Now, please help yourself and sit."

She'd stood up to bring him his cup and now remained standing as though making a decision. So, he pushed her a bit in the direction he wanted her to go.

"I found the carpets on the stairs and in the foyer at a market in Ottoman Turkey. The colors have faded a bit but are still strong." She poured some tea, with but a splash of milk and sprinkle of sugar, and then when he raised an eyebrow at her, she sat on the very edge of the couch opposite of him.

"These have faded? The colors are pristine, my lord." He would continue to work on that, for he wanted to hear his name on her lips.

"I brought or sent back a dozen. Bought in the markets of Marrakesh, Algiers, Egypt, Turkey, Persia and more. The ones in my chamber and several others in the upper hallways get little use so they are still closest to their original condition and colors. I can show them to you while you are here."

"About that, my lord," she began, placing her yet-untouched cup on the table. "I am recovered. We can return to Edinburgh whenever you are ready."

He drank the last of his coffee before speaking. He had a way to entice her to remain here, with him, but would it work?

"'Tis clear I have missed something in my review of the papers and records from my journey to Timgad all those years ago. At least the ones I keep in Edinburgh."

"My lord?" Clara sat up a bit straighter, if that was possible, and watched him closely.

"Most of my records and files from the journey and writing the manuscript are stored here. I've not done a thorough review since these attacks last happened."

"So, you will remain to do that here?"

"I will. Since it is remote and we probably were not followed, it gives me time to work on it openly."

"Then I will simply be a distraction and I should return—"

"You could be that and go back," he said, meeting her surprised gaze. "Or you could be of help to me?"

He could not count the number of emotions that flashed across her face in the moments after his offer—shock, fear, joy, and something that resembled hope all flitted over her features. Then she blinked several times and her expression emptied, giving him no clue. Some kind of conflict was happening within her over this—her prolonged silence and lack of response told him that much.

"I mean no disrespect, Clara. And if you preferred it, I will have you taken back to Edinburgh once the danger is over." He stood up and walked to her. Crouching down to meet her eyes, he smiled. "Truly, coming here, in the manner we did, was to protect you and allow you time to heal. If you would be more comfortable elsewhere, at my godmother's perhaps, I will make arrangements."

Her hand lifted and for a moment he thought she meant to touch his face. He remembered the feel of her caresses when he was injured, and he almost closed his eyes waiting for it. She dropped her hand to her lap and shook her head.

"Amid the warm welcome and care here, I forgot about the danger, my lord. I do not wish to stay with the countess though."

As she studied his face, she tilted her head and he saw that lifting corner of her mouth and wanted to kiss it. Kiss her. Take her in his arms. Stroke her skin and taste his way along the length and breadth of her. Peel off every layer of clothing she wore and take all the pins from her hair, until she stood, or laid, before him in all her glory. His body's reaction forced him to stand or his hardened flesh would be very apparent before her. As he did, she stood, too.

"I w-would like to help you, my lord." He'd never seen her hesitate in anything, so this was startling and exposed a vulnerability he'd not seen before.

"But?"

She walked away from him, circling the couch and approaching the nearest of the tall bookcases. Sliding her hand over one row of the books, he wished she was touching him with that gentle caress. He held his breath, imagining how her hand would feel on the erection that instead now pressed against his trousers.

"I ken how to read, my lord. But—" She met his gaze then, facing him, framed by the luxuries of this library and its carved mahogany shelves, crystal chandeliers and collection of priceless arts. "I do not ken how to do what you do, my lord. I do not ken history or archeology or other studies. I did not go to university or school as you have."

Josh walked to her. He wanted her to be part of this, part of discovering what he'd missed.

"I think your fresh view might see something my old eyes have missed in all these years of reviewing them."

"Old, my lord?" As that corner of her mouth lifted, he understood she would stay. "Ah. I can see the gray hairs growing in as we speak." She reached out and touched his temples. "And certainly, there." Her fingers grazed his hair, the lightest touch and yet his body turned to fire from it.

He could blame it on many things in his life—his single-focused need to remain in charge of his life, his refusal to immediately acquiesce to the demands to marry and never finding a woman who interested or intrigued him. But, the truth was that he'd never realized most of that until Mrs. Clara Lewis walked into his house and his life.

Oh, there had been a few short-lived relationships along the way, and many amorous or physical adventures in his travels, but he'd never considered any of the women or arrangements permanent.

Now? Now he'd barely had a minute when he had not thought about this woman since she'd entered his life weeks ago, no matter the folly of it. For considering her for any other place in his life other than his housekeeper or his mistress would be an affront to the title he held. And though the housekeeper was honorable enough, asking her to share his bed without a commitment was an insult to her.

His body renewed its demands as she moved closer to him, her fingers threading through his hair, mimicking his own habit but feeling much so much better. His nostrils flared, taking in her scent, and it fueled his need to touch her.

"Not so old," he said.

Josh wrapped his arms around her and drew her to him, smiling as she kept hold of him. He held her, just held her, feeling her own restraint and not wanting to push his desires on her.

Now that she would stay, there was time. When his body urged him on, he resisted, glad that he'd done so when a knock came on the library door. Clara released him and he turned towards the door, taking a long step away from her.

"Come," he said. Pirrie opened the door and stepped inside.

"My lord, Hutton is here, if you are available?" His steward had sent word he needed to speak to him before dinner.

"I will go, so you can speak with him in private," Clara whispered from behind him.

"I will meet him in his office, Pirrie." Pirrie bowed and left. When the door closed, he faced her. "This will take some time so stay here. Have tea. We can talk at dinner," he said. She'd still not given her assent to remain here.

"My lord?" *Joshua.* Just once he wanted to hear his name spoken aloud by her. "May I?" She nodded at the bookcase nearest her.

"Of course, you may. I am certain you have not read my accounts from Algeria or Egypt?" A strange light filled her eyes for a scant moment and was gone. "They were relegated to academia or to those archeologists interested in the scholarly details in them. They were not popular among the public." He tried to make light of it, but it still made his stomach burn in anger.

Josh walked to the bookcase closest to his desk and drew out two books—his personal copies of his works so far.

"These, as most of my library is, are too heavy to read comfortably anywhere but at a table or desk." He walked to the desk and moved aside most of the notes and documents strewn across it. Though several book cradles sat about the chamber, he grabbed his favorite, always close at hand and very portable, and positioned it where he'd cleared.

"This will help." Josh placed the first book, his detailed travelogue of his journey and discovery, well, rediscovery of the Roman city Timgad on the stand. "The king was kind enough to allow me the great honor of dedicating this and my second one to him." He turned to the dedication page. "His Majesty signed this copy."

"The king signed your book?"

She crossed the space between them and gazed from next to him at the signature, the only thing truly that had kept him from disgrace after. . . the debacle with Balugani. No matter the king's recent travails or condition now, he would always be thankful for the small honor and the very crucial help it gave him.

"The king himself."

"Here. Sit." He heard the underpinning of wonder and awe in her reaction and pulled the chair out from the desk for her. "I hope that once you move past the regal signature, the rest of it does not bore you to tears." She settled in the chair and looked up at him, for he had not moved away from her. "And Clara? I hope you will stay."

He touched his mouth to hers in a brief kiss and, even as his body and his burgeoning erection protested, he walked away. Without looking back. Trying not to hear her breathing. Hoping to forget her scent.

Chapter Sixteen

*G*EORGE THE *T*HIRD, *by the Grace of God, of the United Kingdom of Great Britain and Ireland King, Defender of the Faith.*

His title was listed out in full, under the stylish signature and in a different hand. Tempted to touch it, Arabella did not for fear it might rub off. Never in her life had she thought to see something that the King of Great Britain had personally signed. Leaning down closer for a better look, she read the inscription written at the top of the page, in the same script as the signature. A private note to the Viscount, well, Mister Robertson at that time, from the King himself.

Arabella leaned back in the chair and just stared at the incredible page. And marveled at this amazing moment when a commoner like her, with no standing in society and no claim to one, could look on and actually hold an item that had been held by a king.

She'd seen a copy of this book in a bookseller's stall in the market once, but the cost was too dear to even consider its purchase. Her father told her he'd sold his copy for money for food, so she'd never had an opportunity to read the actual words and events that had filled her father's life before.

Now, she could read the whole account and see how his lordship hoarded the discoveries and the opportunities of their journeys.

Damn him!

She'd almost convinced herself that she could not succeed in her quest—to find anything that would reclaim her father's honor. She was ready to return to Edinburgh and avoid the temptation that this man—Joshua Robertson—was to her, to her person, to her future. He made her want to give up. He made her want to. . . want him.

Damn him again, for she could not blame it all on him.

Every single time he was not what she'd expected, how her father had described him, she lost a bit more resolve as the temptation to take what she wanted grew stronger. He thought her a widow, so giving in to his obvious desire for her and hers for him should not matter to him. As a widow she had a measure of freedom, if she was discreet, to be involved with a man.

Knowing the outcome of how this would all end should be a comfort to her. The ending made it clear to her that there could be no long term, permanent connection between them. So, if it was all too clear to her, why did it bother her so much?

Restless, she stood up and walked around the perimeter of the chamber, only to discover that his library continued into two more chambers. The first, the area he used as his office, was not even the largest one. No, that description applied to the second room with its soaring high ceiling, with windows that let in so much sunlight that she squinted as she walked through. But her favorite one was the last one, the entrance of which was tucked off in one corner of the largest chamber. She'd thought it a service corridor or closet until she entered it.

Though there were windows on three of the walls, they were high up, allowing the light but not blinding the room's occupants. The fourth wall was a window, facing north and overlooking a private garden. Part of it was a door and part was a huge bay window, the base of which had been covered in a thick cushion for comfort. Pillows strewn across it would make it the perfect place to sit and read. And read and read for hours.

A thick woolen blanket lying across part of the base would guarantee warmth. The small garden outside the windows with its tall, thick hedges would assure privacy and protect anyone within from the winds.

Arabella decided that this would be the place she would stay forever if she could have. The smaller bookcases seemed less intimidating than those in the other two chambers and she walked along them until she found a small book—an atlas of plants found along the Water of Dunalastair—that she took with her to one of the two chaise longues that sat at angles to the window.

Though part of her wanted to return to the copy of Joshua's book, it felt too overwhelming, too shocking, to handle that copy and to finally read the accounts of his travel. Perhaps she was not as recovered as she'd first thought? So, perhaps sitting on this luxurious, comfortable chaise, supported by several pillows and covered with a thick, warm blanket was something she needed to do instead?

The last thing that occurred to her as an unexpected need to sleep pulled her down was that she'd thought of him as. . . .

Joshua.

THE FIRST THING she was aware of was a warm hand on her hip. Large and warm.

Then a kiss on her forehead. Lingering. Soft. Kiss. She lifted her chin, wanting to feel the kiss on her mouth.

Instead, the hand she'd thrown out to her side was lifted and that mouth touched the sensitive inside of her wrist. A kiss that became something else. A touch of his mouth then his tongue teased along the fold and ended with the pressure of a small nipping bite. Soothed by his tongue. She moaned as she opened her eyes and watched him taste her palm.

Waves of heat and shivers of ice raced through her blood and body as he continued his attention to her skin there. The tips of her breasts tightened with each stroke of his tongue and when he suckled on the tender place at her wrist, heat and an ache filled her core. She tightened her thighs against it, for it, savoring the way she felt awakened by the sensations he caused.

Arabella tugged her hand free and slid it into his hair then around his neck, pulling him down to kiss her where she wanted it most. Opening to him, she arched up as he plundered her mouth. His hand slid down and around her hips, lifting her until she was in his arms, held against his muscular chest.

And still he kissed her.

He lifted his mouth from hers but kissed his way along her jaw to her chin and then down her neck. As she leaned her head back, he kissed and suckled the tender skin above her breasts, making her lose her breath from the sheer pleasure of it. Then, he tugged one side of her bodice down and took the throbbing nipple into his mouth.

Her body ached. And wanted. As she shifted on his lap, he tormented her with his mouth. She could not believe that the feel of his teeth grazing over the tips of her breasts could make her feel such heat and such desire.

And make her want more.

"Joshua," she whispered, her fingers in his hair keeping him close to her, keeping his mouth on her doing those wonderful things. She opened her eyes then, hearing what she'd said and truly seeing what she was allowing him to do. It was the most exciting thing she had ever seen. His mouth on her breast.

"Clara." Her name was like a growl of possession. "Clara."

He was not with her—he was with the false woman she was in his life. Her hands dropped as the realization struck her.

She could not do this. Not with him. As she shifted away, sliding back up onto the chaise longue. He released her as soon as she moved at all. Though he watched her closely, he did not say a word. And she could not bring a single word to mind. The call from the other chamber gave her an excuse not to.

"Lord Dunalastair?" Mr. Pirrie's voice was getting louder each time he spoke the viscount's name.

Joshua, the man who had caressed her and kissed her and touched her in such an intimate way, now became the noble who carried the title. He nodded to her and walked out to stop his butler from getting any closer to save her from being seen in this state of. . . arousal and disarray.

Arabella slid her feet to the floor and the dress that had tangled around her legs during their encounter dropped back into place. If no one had interrupted them, she wondered how far she'd have let it go. How far he would have gone.

As she heard him speak to Mr. Pirrie, she accepted that she would not have stopped him. In spite of her deception, in spite of her original intentions, and maybe because of everything she'd learned about him, she wanted him, even if only until the truth was known.

Standing and gathering her wits, Arabella waited for him to return. Unsure of what to expect, her hands trembled as she heard his approach. No matter what she'd thought she would see, the open affection in his eyes nearly undid her.

"Dinner is ready." He held out his arm in a formal invitation.

"Already, my lord?" She had no idea that she'd slept that long but the small library was wonderfully cozy and comfortable, and she could imagine herself lost in there for hours. And that was before he woke her in such an arousing way.

"I came back from my meeting to find you gone. I thought you'd returned to your chambers, but the footman said you'd never left. When I finally found you in the small library sleeping, I spoke your name and you answered me."

"I did? I do not remember."

"Now I suspect you were sleeping more deeply than I thought. I kissed your forehead and you leaned up into me." He stared at her, studying her face and she found her gaze focused on his mouth. The mouth that had done wonderful, almost-unimaginable things to her. "I should have stopped," he said.

"I did not want you to stop."

"I will be direct with you, too, Clara." She swallowed several times before meeting his gaze. "I want you. I want to be more to you than your host. Or your employer." His hot gaze swept over her, making her shiver with excitement. "But I would be no better than Finlaggan if I expected you as my due and forced you to accept my attentions. I swear I will not take what you do not give freely, not here, not now and not later."

"My lord?"

"You are here to recover and, I hope, to help me look over the materials I have for a reason for these recent attacks." He took her hand and lifted it from his arm, entwining their fingers. "I do not wish you to be uncomfortable around me. Have I ruined things?"

"No, my lord," she said truthfully. Worry shone in his green eyes. "Joshua, all is well," He smiled when she spoke his name and it warmed her heart.

The viscount held out his arm once more and she placed her hand on his.

"Come along now. Mrs. Sommers has a bit of a temper if her dishes are allowed to grow cold."

He used his sense of humor to ease the tension between them and she was glad of it. They went to what he called the small dining room, which was a complete and utter lie. Larger than any she'd seen, it could have held a dinner for fifty and had room for dancing afterwards.

He walked her to a seat at one end of the long table and she slowed with each step. She felt like an imposter. Ludicrous and hypocritical because she was one twice over. She was neither a housekeeper nor the woman she pretended to be.

"I cannot do this," she whispered, tugging his arm. "I would rather eat in my room if you will not allow me to eat in the kitchen where I belong."

She glanced around to see not two, but four, footmen at their posts along with Mr. Pirrie, waiting to serve them, serve him. Arabella did not want to make this difficult, but he must understand this would not work.

"You are my guest, Clara. This room is where I want you to enjoy your meals while you are here in my house," he said. He pitched his voice so only she could hear his words. "The staff believes you to be my guest and will treat you as one. But better than they treat either Hepburn or Finlaggan, I assure you." He winked and her resistance began to melt.

How could she refuse such a plea? She could not and was about to say so when he added his final blow, the one meant to break down her opposition.

"If I have to wear these, the least you can do is be on hand to make it worthwhile."

She allowed her gaze to drift over him from head to toe. His valet here had done him up well. From the cut of his coat, to the fit of his waistcoat and his pristine, well-tied cravat, he looked every inch the viscount he was. In finer clothing than she'd seen him before, superior even to those he'd worn to the ball he'd attended with Lady Arbuthnott at the Assembly Rooms in town. Duncan would be jealous if he could see this valet's efforts and success at turning the adventurer into a viscount.

"Very well, my lord," she said. "I will try to appreciate your valet's—"

"Lachlan is my valet here when Duncan does not travel with me," he explained.

"I will admire Lachlan's efforts so that his work is not in vain and so that there is a witness to his success."

His laughter filled the expanse of the dining room. The deep timbre of it echoed also within her, making her warm and relaxed. And making her more certain that she would do as he asked.

Joshua continued walking with her to her seat and waited as one of the other footmen adjusted her chair beneath her. When he sat across from her, she was relieved that any conversation would not be called out along the length of this magnificent table. Still, it did not feel right to be here and to be served by his servants and she could not settle her thoughts as the meal began and progressed.

"I can hardly tell," he said, as Brodie lifted the now-empty plate from before him.

"Hardly tell, my lord?" Arabella dabbed at her lips with her napkin, trying to remember the proper way to eat at a society dinner. There were so many rules and if this household was the stickler Joshua described it as, she'd more than likely broken a number of them by now.

"I can hardly tell how uncomfortable you are."

"I apologize if I've embarrassed you, my lord." Clutching the napkin on her lap, she spoke in a whisper, knowing better than anyone that the servants heard every word.

"Pirrie? Could you ask Mrs. Sommers to come here?"

The butler was off in a near run almost before he'd finished his request. They sat in silence as the hurried footsteps in the corridor approached the dining room. No more than three minutes could have passed when the woman entered, following Mr. Pirrie. Impressive especially considering the size of the manor. Arabella could also see another woman standing just outside the door, waiting and watching.

"My lord," Mrs. Sommers said, curtsying to him. "Was there something wrong with the meal?"

"Nay, Mrs. Sommers. It was delicious," he said, gifting the cook with that smile of his. But she knew it was a genuine one, not something put on or fake. "Mrs. Lyle," he said in a slightly raised voice. "Please join us." The woman outside walked in and curtsied.

"I was just checking on the—"

"Mrs. Lyle. Mrs. Sommers, may I present Mrs. Clara Lewis, my guest for the next week or so." He glanced at Arabella then. "Mrs. Lewis, this is Dunalastair Manor's housekeeper," the newest arrival nodded at her, "and the cook."

She began to stand when the slightest shake of his head told her to remain seated.

"Mrs. Lyle, the hospitality and my chambers have been lovely. Mrs. Sommers, the meal and the treats on my earlier tray were delicious." She tried to say what she and Mrs. Mathieson would have liked to hear from a guest. The women murmured their thanks, but turned back to Joshua.

"Now that we have had the grand meal, I wish for something simpler for the rest of our stay. Simpler food and simpler settings if you do not mind?" Pirrie stepped forward then, as a butler would, believing he must speak for the others.

"My lord?" He, they all turned to face her. "I would gladly speak with Mrs. Lyle and Mrs. Sommers in the morning to inform them of your current preferences, in food and meals and such. If you wish?"

The women's widened eyes and curious expressions did not surprise her at all. The butler understood the context of her words. Even the coughs by some of the footmen revealed that they'd understood. And though they were all mistaken in how she came by such knowledge, they were correct in their assumption that she was not simply his lordship's 'guest'.

After all of them stared at her for just a second short of impolite, they looked at Joshua.

"That would be appreciated, Mrs. Lewis."

"Is there anything else, my lord?" Pirrie asked.

"Nothing other than my, our thanks for a lovely dinner."

Only after they walked away could she dare to meet his gaze. She suspected what she would find but was surprised to see something more than simple desire or wanting. Something deeper and more terrifying to her peace of mind and her plans. If she was not careful, this could go from being a simple pretense to accomplish her aims to something that would turn her life and plans upside down.

An awareness of him, his nearness, his breathing, his smile, him, filled her through the rest of the dinner. And after a French dessert pastry she was not familiar with and some tea, Joshua offered to escort her to her chamber. A walk in the garden, both the small one off the library and the larger one he said was impressive, would have been a welcome thing but a crash of thunder and the sound of rain precluded that.

Her heart raced as they approached her bedchamber. It was beating so hard she thought he could hear the rapid tattoo of it. As they passed him, Joshua dismissed the footman at the stairs with a nod. The viscount stopped before her door and lowered his arm, releasing hers and reached out to open her door. Margaret opened it the rest of the way, waiting for her to enter.

"Sleep well, Mrs. Lewis, for I will be a devil of a taskmaster in our work tomorrow."

And he was gone. That wicked promise that could mean several different things and each possibility made her breath hitch in anticipation as she tried to appear calm in front of the young maid.

Arabella had just gotten into bed some time later, when the knock came. Margaret immediately went to it and Arabella had to remind herself that she was the guest here. When the lass curtsied, she knew Joshua was at the door. Was he boldly going to enter and leave no doubt in anyone's mind what her role here was. . . or would be?

When he had not entered after several moments of hushed conversation with Margaret, Arabella pushed herself up against the elaborately carved headboard of the bed, drawing the covers along with her, and waited for the reason for his visit. Margaret shut the door quietly and carried something to her.

"His lordship brought this for you, Ma'am." Arabella accepted the. . . book. "He said ye might find this one easier to read."

She turned the book over to find it was a copy of his, but unlike the one downstairs in the library, this one was not signed by royalty. This one she could handle without fear of damaging it or the precious inscription of the other.

"Thank you, Margaret," she said. "Leave the lantern for now."

"A book?"

Arabella heard the girl muttering under her breath in disbelief as she left. By now, her declaration in the dining room was commonly known throughout the hierarchy of the backstairs and she had taken on another role, another false one at this moment. But the look in his eyes as he promised to be a hard taskmaster made her body heat, the tips of her breasts tingle as though being touched by his teeth and tongue and that place deep within her throb in need of. . . something.

Her body would not relent in its arousal, so Arabella opened the book he'd given her and began to learn more about the man just down the hall. By the time dawn broke, a weak rainy dawn, she'd read almost half the book.

Chapter Seventeen

JOSHUA HAD LIED to both himself and to Clara. He had no intention of requiring much from her at all that next day. A hint of pain colored the areas under her usually vibrant eyes with a shading of gray and reminding him of the recent attack and its results. She arrived at the breakfast room and its size must have pleased her for there was no argument about eating there.

Too many years of scraping by on the small amount of an allowance he received or the money he earned as a diplomat in Italy had given him the habit of non-extravagance that he could not break. This manor house, his cousin's sanctuary of excess, made his skin crawl, with its gilding and carvings, sumptuous furnishings and priceless paintings. Even when he'd inherited the title, he'd refused to use the larger townhouse in the new section of Edinburgh that his cousin had leased and never used. The house near the university was his own possession, not linked, entailed or beholden to the estate.

His.

Owned not leased as many of the newer properties were. Paid for by his work, his efforts and his humiliation.

"I ken 'tis not for a gentleman to remark on a lady's appearance in anything but glowing terms," he said, motioning to the footman to fill her teacup. "But, you do not look as recovered as you claimed you were." Her left eyebrow raised in the same manner that the corner of her lip did when she smiled, yet Joshua did not fool himself that she was pleased about his taking note as he had.

"Coffee, please, Martin," she said, moving her cup nearer to the edge where the footman could get it more easily. She knew his footman's name already?

"That bad?" he asked.

She waited for her cup to be filled and placed in front of her, dribbled some cream in and a few pieces of sugar and stirred it until it blended smoothly. The sigh she let out after the first sip was nothing short of erotic. The sound that should escape a woman's mouth while she was being pleasured.

The sound he craved hearing.

"'Tis my own fault, my lord."

"How so?"

"I could not resist the book and could not stop once begun."

She did not seem happy about it. Indeed, Clara seemed bothered by her weakness. His pride surged. He cared not the reason why she could not resist reading his book, he smiled that she admitted it.

"Was it what you expected? Had you heard any of the tale before?" He was about to ask another question when he realized he was not giving her time to answer. "Forgive me, you are the first non-academic and the first non-historian who I've given a copy to."

"And the first woman?"

"Nay, not the first," he said. "Thomas, Mrs. Lewis prefers coddled eggs and some toasted bread." Since he'd already informed Mrs. Simmons of Clara's tastes in breaking her fast, everything was on the sideboard, ready to be served. The footman made up a plate and placed it before her. Her surprised and pleased expression assured him that he needed to thank Mrs. Mathieson for that information about Clara's eating preferences when they returned to Edinburgh.

"Ah, the Countess of Arbuthnott was the first woman," she said. Nodding at Thomas as he stepped away, she took a bite of the toast and chewed. "Did she read it?"

He watched as she devoured the eggs and scraped up the liquid bit of yolk with the edge of her bread. He caught Thomas' eye and nodded for him to get more. Though she looked ready to refuse, she accepted it with a smile at the servant.

"I do not think my godmother has read anything but the fashion magazines since leaving her finishing school as a young woman." She laughed at his words, then shook her head.

"I do not think you should ever underestimate the Countess." Though she knew they'd traveled in his godmother's coach, Clara did not know the whole of his godmother's involvement or the extraordinary confession she'd made to him about her younger days.

"I agree with your sentiments and I would never." He finished his coffee and motioned for Thomas to the empty plates away and go. After they were alone, he asked the question that had burned inside him since she'd made the comment about his book. "So, you have avoided my question long enough. What did you think of my book?"

A very strange expression filled her eyes at his question. Bloody hell, he hated it! And he'd pressed her for an answer.

"'Tis true, I am shamelessly seeking compliments."

She laughed, banishing the look of desperation as she gave him a reprimanding glance. "I have never read a book by someone I ken."

"For some reason, knowing you are reading it makes me nervous. If we are done here, perhaps we should go to the library and discuss it?"

"It happened that way, my... Joshua?" she asked. "Your interactions with the Bey? Traveling by camel through the desert? Discovering a clue on a map that led to Timgad? Your words created such a vivid image, I thought at times that I was there with you."

"I tried to make it an entertaining tale rather than a stodgy, dry tome of facts and figures." That had been the true struggle—writing something worthy of academic review, something acceptable to the serious-minded yet available to the general public if they so chose.

"How did you find the map that led there?"

Her voice grew tense as though this question meant something more to her than the others. Joshua realized they'd not moved from the table. He stood and retrieved the pot of coffee from the sideboard where it sat. Clara intercepted him and held out her hand to take the pot.

"I should do that, my lord," she said. "Here. Allow me."

Joshua sat down and moved his cup to the edge and watched her for some sign of what had upset her in some way. He let her do this small task because it seemed to comfort her. Once she returned to her chair, he spoke about the map.

"As I mentioned in the book, my assistant actually found the map, tucked in some old book he found in the Bey's collection. He smuggled it out and I was able to study it and have it translated for our use."

"This assistant?" she asked. "He did the illustrations in the book?" There was the brittle tone again.

"Aye, he was quite talented." Joshua forced his own voice to show only indifference as they spoke about the man who had cost him everything. Whose behavior on their travels had insulted the Bey and endangered everyone in their group.

"You said he'd died?"

"He died some years ago, if I remember correctly. We fell out of touch not long after our return from Egypt and the Middle East."

She began to ask another question but stopped herself.

"I do not mind your questions, Clara. What do you want to ken?"

"How did you meet this illustrator? This. . . ?"

"Luigi Balugani." He practically had to force the name

through his teeth, and she noticed. She lost some of the coloring in her cheeks making the shadows beneath her eyes ever more apparent. "Actually, my cousin introduced us. He sponsored Balugani in some art project and discovered that the man had a gift for languages, surely a benefit to have if one is traveling on the Continent and in Africa."

"Did he help you write the book?"

"Other than the illustrations and some of the translations, nay. The man had no patience for. . . ." He stopped himself once more, for he could not explain too much without endangering all he'd protected for so many years. "It would have been like putting Mrs. Sommers and Mrs. Mathieson in the same kitchen to cook a meal together."

He smiled, hoping it would bring this part of their discussion to an end. Her expression was closed, but he was sure he'd overwhelmed her and pushed her physically before she was recovered enough.

"Might I suggest that you may wish to seek your bed, Clara? You are paler now than when you arrived here to breakfast." That she did not argue spoke of his correct assessment of her condition. "May I escort you back to your chamber?"

"Nay, my lord, I can manage it on my own." She pushed up from the table and he stood as she did. The door opened as his attentive servants reacted to a guest's departure from a room.

"I will be in the library all day if you feel better, Clara. Join me there if. . . when you feel up to it."

"I am not used to having time to sleep the day away. It does not feel right to me."

He walked over to her and leaned down closer.

"You are not used to being waited on or taken care of. You are used to serving. But allow this for now. I will ken you are better when the impertinent Mrs. Lewis returns."

Tears glimmered in those lovely brown eyes and he did not wish her to be embarrassed, especially before the staff. So, he stepped back and nodded to her. Again, that she gave in and left was more of a sign of her weakened condition than her agreement with his assessment. But it was not fun to pick a fight when she did not give him one.

IT ONLY TOOK a few hours of rest before she felt remarkably better. Arabella did not go to the library first. Instead, she went belowstairs to speak to Mrs. Simmons and Mrs. Lyle. As she expected, they covered their initial horror at her arrival with politeness. If she'd not expected their reaction, she might not have seen it. . . but she had and did. Mrs. Lyle welcomed her in the parlor of her rooms and Arabella instantly longed for the simpler chamber she had in Edinburgh.

And she mourned it, for she knew she would never return to it.

"I ask your pardon for invading your privacy, Mrs. Lyle, but I thought it might be easier and less uncomfortable to speak with you both here." The two women exchanged a knowing glance between them—but what did they know? "I have heard that his lordship spends little time here?"

They both looked at each other once more but did not answer her. So she plowed ahead, breaking their reticence with her own truth. Well, the one she could share.

"I have only been with, worked for, Lord Dunalastair for several months and in that time he never once mentioned Dunalastair Manor."

"So, it's true then?" Mrs. Lyle finally asked. "You are the housekeeper in his city residence?"

"Aye." The women nodded. So they had heard about her. "Does the staff ken?" she asked.

"Mr. Pirrie does, but he won't make any trouble for you," Mrs. Lyle said.

"Is that how you found out? Mr. Pirrie?" Who probably heard about her from his counterpart in Edinburgh.

"Nay, Coira's nephew works in the Edinburgh house and was praising your manners on his last visit."

"Ah, I'd forgotten about Adam," she said. "He's a good lad. A good worker."

"He mentioned your name so many times, how could we forget it?" Mrs. Sommers asked.

"Has he brought you here to replace me then? Am I to be sacked? Or are you spying on all of us?" The questions burst out of Mrs. Lyle in a rush, then she clapped her hands over her mouth as she realized it.

"Mrs. Lyle, nay to all of those," Arabella said. She reached out and patted the older woman's hand. "I am here after... an unfortunate incident at his lordship's house in Edinburgh. As his guest. To recuperate from... an injury."

"But wasn't he just injured there, too?" Mrs. Sommers asked. Clearly, some news did make it to the wilds of Scotland.

"Aye, he was, but I cannot discuss that." She turned to Mrs. Lyle. "I can assure you I am no threat to your position here."

"So, you are returning with his lordship when he leaves?" The woman was so focused on the possibility of losing her job, she would hear nothing else.

"The fact that both of you work here all year, every year, with or without his lordship's presence or visits speaks of his commitment to keeping you, all of you, on as staff."

They looked stunned as they accepted the truth that she had already learned about him—Joshua Robertson, Viscount of Dunalastair, was loyal to those who served him. As much as she wanted him to be otherwise, she could not deny that fact about him. Loyal, too, to those he called friends.

Loyal even to those he considered enemies, if his reluctance to blame her father when given the opportunity to do so told her anything.

"And you will return with him to Edinburgh?" Their knowing eyes confirmed they understood, as she did, that she would end this visit as more than his guest.

"Nay."

The word hung on the air as she realized the truth for the first time. When she left here, it would be alone. What path this would take, she could not say, but the ending of it would be without him. She knew that now.

"Does he ken?" Mrs. Sommers' eyes filled with concern.

"Of course not, Mrs. Sommers. He is a man. A viscount after all. But we women understand the way it is in this world. And there is no other way this could end but with me gone." Mrs. Lyle reached out and patted Arabella's hand after her declaration.

The strangest thing was that this unusual conversation had clarified things for her. Even if Joshua Robertson had done what her father had accused him of, there was no proof of any of it. Indeed, if she put together what she had learned from him and what she'd already known before she stepped foot in his world, Joshua had suffered in some way over the journeys he took and the books he'd written about them.

Though his friends had no idea, she'd listened in to their conversations whenever she could—during their visits, during their frequent stops to check on his condition after he was knocked unconscious and beaten and more. Arabella knew that there was some shame he'd endured, and now having seen the inscription by the king, she understood that the monarch had somehow intervened on his behalf.

And now, even if she found something new, something un-expected, to use against him, she doubted she would have the strength to use it. The only proof she'd discovered was that which she saw with her own eyes. With his actions, he'd proven himself to be the opposite of every bad thing her father had told her over the years.

'Twas worse than that. He was patient, intelligent, had a sense of humor while not suffering an overblown opinion of himself in spite of his education, wide-ranging travels and the ancient title he carried. He was careful and prudent in his business dealings and other decisions. He respected his godmother and treated those in his employ well.

Glancing at these two women who had not appreciated that

part of him until now, she felt guilt of her own. Overwhelmed by these shifts within her and not ready to face any more, she nodded at the cook and housekeeper and stood.

"His lordship prefers plain but hearty meals, nothing too rich, good wine, better ale, and fresh bread. He takes his coffee and tea with an ungodly amount of sugar and milk." She smiled at that. "He likes his meals earlier, more like a working person and less like a lord."

"Mrs. Lewis," the cook began. Arabella waved her off, knowing if she stopped now, she'd start crying.

"Nevertheless, no matter what you place before him, he will be appreciative of your efforts and will thank you." She walked to the door and turned the knob. "I will let you get back to your duties. I am certain you both are very busy."

"Mrs. Lewis, if you have need of anything, just ask," Mrs. Sommers said.

"Anything, Mrs. Lewis. Anything at all," Mrs. Lyle added.

Arabella nodded and left, intent on finding a place to be alone for a bit, to gather her thoughts and to accept that she was done trying to find him guilty of her father's accusations. Instead of going up the stairs to the main floor, she found her way to a door leading outside. The day looked fair enough, with big, puffy clouds racing across an impossibly blue sky and no hint of rain.

Trying to figure out her location, she walked along the path and it brought her to a larger one, one that split into two that led either to the right and the stables, or to the left and the extensive gardens. As she reached the place where it diverged, Arabella saw that the right one branched off once more and that led along a stream to the loch. So that was the one she took.

Arabella walked for some time, not truly paying heed to how far she traveled since she'd come in one of only two possible directions and she could turn and go back at any moment. Reaching a clearing, she stood in the sunny place along the banks of not the loch, but Dunalastair Water as it was called there.

As she stared out at the never-still surface, Arabella watched the undulating currents in the middle spread across and swirl to the edge of it. The sound of the water splashing and the sight of the sun-dappled ripples held her attention as one after another of her problems pushed forward in her mind to be solved. The process had been spurred on in that moment with the two women and now continued until she'd made several more decisions and discoveries.

The most startling one was that she realized that she may have been the cause of the attacks beginning again. Someone else or others still hunted for the legendary treasure and believed, though she was not clear on the reason for it, that Joshua knew something more than he admitted. Just his connection to the original expedition and being the only survivor of the team would be enough to draw the attention of anyone searching for any artifacts or plunder. Anyone that desperate or deluded or diligent could have discovered her own identity and been misled into believing that she was now working with her father's former partner.

Arabella kicked at the stones along the edge of the water. Picking up several, she tossed them one by one into the loch. As she watched each one first skim along for a few inches then sink into it, she reviewed her decisions.

She would help him while they remained here, looking for anything that might give him an idea of who was chasing the treasure.

When they finished, or when he decided to return to Edinburgh, she would leave. If she couldn't do that from here, she could go back, gather her belongings and disappear from there. Mrs. Clara Lewis would be gone and never found again.

With a little help, she could find another job to support herself elsewhere, perhaps Glasgow or even Inverness if she wanted more distance between them.

If luck was on her side, he would never know her real name.

If he found out, he would not want anything to do with her anyway for the deception she'd brought into his life.

And the rest of it?

As she threw her last stone over the surface, she accepted that she wanted this time to be with him. To be a person as close to her true personality as she could. To give in to the feelings that grew stronger with each and every encounter. To be with him and enjoy what that meant.

Even knowing it would be a time that could never last, she wanted it with him. She wanted him. She wanted to create memories that would last her a long time. She nodded at the flowing water as if it could understand her struggle and her intent.

Arabella might have five days or six at the most before she would walk away from all of her lies and live a life as the one person she knew the least.

Years as a dependent daughter, losing first her mother and then her father after he taught her the bitterness of failure.

Years in desperation, trying to make her own way, while planning her father's revenge.

Months discovering that her target might not be the right one.

Weeks learning she'd trusted the wrong man in her life and was living someone else's scheme.

Days accepting that she wanted to let it all go—the vengeance, the plotting, the scheming, the living to destroy *him*—and find a life of her own.

Only hours since realizing that she had fallen in love with the one man she could never have.

But, she could have him for these next days before anything else happened.

And she would.

Chapter Eighteen

J OSHUA COULD NOT believe the change in Clara.

Was it because she was feeling more recovered? He knew not. But, as they talked about their search of his documents and records, sitting comfortably next to one another on the couch in his library, he cared not.

In the three days since he'd watched her standing at the edge of Dunalastair Water, staring for more than an hour before she turned and saw him, everything had changed.

The impertinent Mrs. Lewis had returned and Joshua found himself laughing for the first time in a long time. Over nothing. Over everything she said or did. And more than that, she'd worked some miracle and the meals had improved, the tension in the household had eased and he was enjoying his stay.

"Well?" Her voice broke into his musing and made him realize he hadn't heard her question. "You are miles away, Joshua. Is something wrong?"

"Nay. I was just thinking how much help you have been to me with these." He held out the notebook she'd found, along with the long-forgotten letters filled with scrawled threats he'd received. "I had thought these lost."

"When did you receive them?"

He tried to remember but with her so close and seemingly

comfortable at his side, Joshua was having trouble remembering what day it was. But, he focused on the question asked and looked at the letters again.

"I received the first of these when Balugani was still alive and, honestly, I discounted their importance because I was certain he had sent them." Her smile faltered for a moment, and he waited for a pithy comment about the stupidity of doing such a thing. "But this last one, I think that was actually after he died."

"So someone else was involved?" Clara slid up to the edge of the couch and read the letter again, comparing it to the others. "This handwriting, such as it is, looks similar to the earlier ones."

She turned to face him, holding it out to him. He took hold of her hand and kissed her wrist and palm before plucking the paper from her fingers. That tempting corner of her mouth lifted and she smiled at him, allowing him to kiss her hand while he pretended to study the letter.

"This is why we do not get very far in this work, my lord."

She only used his title when he kissed her or when he was trying to convince her to kiss him. Her avoidance of his touch or kisses had disappeared even while they walked back to the manor from the loch, and it had not shown its face since. He respected her reticence by never approaching her when servants could see or hear them. And, if she seemed the least bit uncomfortable, he kept his distance.

But when she welcomed him, he could not help but to taste her mouth and tease the places he could. What this would mean when they left here he knew not, but Clara Lewis was important to him. And he would sort it all out in a way that would keep her at his side. He could imagine his godmother's reaction when he told her—one of many who would be surprised, and furious or opposed, to what he wanted to do.

A viscount did not marry his housekeeper. Plain and simple and easy to understand, though now difficult to accept. She had neither the breeding nor the connections for such a marriage. She brought nothing to this match. A common woman should not be allowed to marry a man with an ancient and proud title as the one he carried.

All of those and more would be thrown his way when his plan was known.

But Hepburn would be happy for him and Finlaggan would live in fear of her, which Joshua would enjoy. He should feel terrible about that and yet he did not.

Clara leaned back against him, and he savored the feel of her against his body. Kissing the back of her neck caused her to tremble and his cock to rise, so he did it again. Tracing the shape of her ear and then nipping the bottom of it sent more tremors through her. And when she leaned into him and angled her head so he could reach more of her neck, Joshua took the opportunity.

"Come to me tonight, Clara." He whispered the words against her ear, and she shivered. Joshua traced the graceful curve of her neck from her ear down to her collar on the modest gown she wore. Unexpectedly, she turned her face to him and met his mouth in a torrid kiss. Their tongues played, exploring and tasting, until they were breathless. When she lifted away, he whispered his invitation, his plea, again.

"Please come to me."

She let out a shuddering breath and stared at him, studying his face for a long, few moments before gifting him with a nod.

She must know how he felt about her. Not just the desire that had built slowly and was now his constant companion, but also the genuine affection he felt for her. He liked her. He liked everything he discovered about her. He wanted to spend his life with him.

One last kiss and then he gently moved her to sit beside him. Reaching over to his other side, he lifted several notebooks and held them out to her.

"Your next task, should you decide to accept it, Mrs. Lewis." She took hold of them and slid off the couch.

"If you do not mind, I will use the desk. 'Tis easier to open the notebooks there."

He watched her walk away, admiring her curves and the graceful way she moved with each step. He would never forget seeing that feather in her hat sway in time to her hips with every pace she took. Now, he admired the curls that Margaret had apparently convinced her to leave loose as they bobbed against her neck and shoulders.

His hands itched to pull every last pin from the mass of curls she somehow tamed in an intricate twisting of locks that were then woven around the top and sides of her head. That might be the first thing he did when she came to him. Unpin her hair until it surrounded her. Then he would peel off each layer of her clothing until she wore nothing but her stockings and the length of her hair around her. Joshua must have made a lustful noise, for she stopped and glanced over her shoulder at him.

He cleared his voice, shifted to allow his erection more room in his trousers and tried to read the paper at his side. All the words faded away as he watched her settle in the chair—*his* chair—and begin to examine the first notebook. Now that she'd said aye, all he could think of was her. His flesh throbbed again, aching with desire for her that heated his blood.

Naked in his arms. In his bed. Touching her. Tasting every curve of her body and inch of her skin. Finding the places that aroused her the most. Satisfying the need he could see in her gaze when she did not think he was watching her. His flesh grew impossibly hard and more insistent, so he ran his hand over it while thinking of thrusting it into her warmth and filling her. Pressing his palm harder, pleasure filled him. Her gasp drew his eyes to her.

Clara was watching him as he touched his erection. Her mouth opened and he could hear the sound of shallow panting breaths as he moved his hand along his length. He was being a beast, an unrepentant beast, allowing her to witness this. Her body was still, only her hands moved, forming fists with every caress of his cock but she did not look away. Her acceptance of his invitation had freed him in some primitive way when his only thought was to make her his and keep her with him.

He would do that in just a few hours.

ARABELLA COULD NOT take a breath in. It was not that she'd tied her stays too tightly, though it felt as though she had.

Nay, the sight of him, Joshua, touching his obviously erect. . . hardness took her breath away. She clenched her hands trying not to reach for him or say something shocking. She'd felt his flesh against her several times since she'd begun accepting his caresses and kisses and fondling these last few days. There was no doubt what it was nor of what it meant.

Staring back at him as his hand rested on the bulge, she almost offered herself to him here and now. The aching deep within her seemed timed to his movements and her core throbbed in need. . . of something he could do for her.

Though not a widow nor ever married, she was not an innocent. And in spite of a less than encouraging experience just a few years ago, she understood, as did her body, that this night with Joshua would be nothing like the last time. And her body wanted it as much as her heart wanted him.

Even if it was for only a night or two.

As it must be.

Some movement outside the library broke the spell of intimacy between them and Joshua stood up and made his way with some awkwardness to the shelf nearest him. The soft knock on the door found them yards away from each other.

"My lord," Mr. Pirrie said. "Mr. Hutton asked if you might be available to speak with him."

"In his office or elsewhere, Pirrie?"

"The stables actually, my lord. If it is convenient for you?"

She saw him look out the window at the cloudy, windy conditions before he turned his glance downwards. He smiled at her then, a wicked one that her body understood. Her thighs clenched at the heated throbbing between them.

"A walk to the stables might be just the thing I need right

now, Pirrie."

Arabella thought he would follow the butler out, but instead he walked directly to her, standing so as to block Mr. Pirrie's view of her. Her breasts swelled as he leaned closer and spoke softly to only her.

"We will get no sleep this night, love. So, if rest is what you need, you'd best seek it while I'm busy with estate business."

The heat caused by his words filled her body and she felt the flush of it in her cheeks. Her body shuddered at the boldness and readied for. . . him. Her mouth went dry, and she slid her tongue over her lips trying to moisten them. This time it was his body that reacted. A subtle thrust of his hips which pleased her immensely.

He stood up straight and shifted on his feet. Her eyes noticed that he was yet rather large despite his efforts to ignore it. And he turned his body and angled out the door behind Pirrie, trying to hide the obvious from his butler.

Once the door closed, she waited for a moment or two before breaking out in laughter. This was exactly what she wanted and wanted to remember of him.

After a fruitless hour of staring at the pages of the notebook and thinking only about his whispered warning, she considered going up to her chamber. The restlessness grew within her and she knew she would never be able to sleep now. She decided she needed a walk outside in the cool Highland afternoon.

Arabella laughed as she made her way outside the main garden and let the winds buffet her along the path. It took some time to ease the tension within her but the cold breezes coming off the loch and river managed it.

And it took only a moment of hearing the chiming of the clock in the hallway when she entered the house to finish up working on the notebooks to fill her once again.

She was, they were, one hour closer to dinner. Which brought them closer to the night.

Which brought her so much closer to his bed.

IT WAS A wonder that the table did not burst into flames from the heat in her eyes as she looked across it at him. All the good work that the winds had done to cool him down, indeed the addition of a quick rain shower had worked wonders, only to take one look at Clara and he was on fire again. If he had learned anything about her, at least her own body was betraying her as much as his.

If the servants were paying attention, they knew something was different. How could they not when every time he or Clara began a topic of conversation, the words just stopped because they lost track of what the topic was. Then they would laugh until they met each other's gaze and the heat built once more.

His servants were as well-trained as any, but even they fought the smiles as the sexual tension intensified with each passing minute. Although Mrs. Sommers prepared less formal meals after Clara had spoken to her, they were always delicious. Tonight's was just one course of four dishes, all of them his favorites, but they could have been hay from the stables for all he tasted them. Each one had been removed quicker than the one before and by the time the table was cleared, he did not remember any of them.

Finally, when offered coffee and tea, Joshua asked for a tray in his chamber and walked around the table to hold out his hand to Clara. He held his breath until she placed hers in his and let him guide her from the room.

Try as he might, their steps began at a normal pace but then sped up so that they were almost running up the final few to the landing. Thomas, on duty there, turned and walked away, returning to the main floor rather than remaining there near the bedchambers.

At her door, he pulled her into his arms and kissed her, possessing her mouth in an imitation of what would happen between their bodies soon. Then he stepped back and nodded to her.

"I will be waiting."

Joshua watched as she entered her bedchamber and closed the door. If he'd read the signs of her body, her arousal, her attraction to him, it would not be very long until she came to him. He entered his chamber and made the final arrangements in what he hoped would be a comfortable and different scene for their night.

He could not wait to see her face when she saw it.

Chapter Nineteen

T HANKFULLY HER CHAMBER was empty when she entered it. A pitcher of steaming water and a bowl sat near the banked fire and her lantern and candles were lit, showing that Margaret had prepared the chamber. Arabella could not have faced the young maid knowing where she was going and what they would do this night.

Everything would change irreparably as a result of the walk down that hallway to his chamber. Nothing would ever be the same. Yet, this was actually only the first irreversible step that she would take in the next few days. As the anticipation built within her, somehow she understood that this may be the only one she had any control over.

Perhaps that was part of her decision to go to him? To claim a measure of power over her life and her person before everything spun out of control. No matter the whys and why nots, she wanted this night. . . and she wanted him.

And he was waiting for her just a few chambers down the hall.

Arabella considered what to do next and how to prepare and what to wear, and realized that none of that mattered either! Since she had only her three plain gowns along with a black utilitarian one that belonged to her housekeeper's uniform and only plain undergarments, there was nothing more appealing that she could wear.

So, dressed as she had been, she opened the door and walked down to his bedchamber. Being his guest and not his housekeeper had meant that she'd not seen all the rooms in the house and his was the most mysterious. Though he'd promised to show her the imported carpets throughout the house, including one in his chamber, he'd not yet. . . .

Damn, but she was nervous if she was thinking about his carpet!

She released her hands, already clasped in a death grip, and shook them until she had feeling back in her fingers. Trying to calm her raising heart, she let out a breath and took several slow breaths in, releasing them as she approached his door. Before she could knock, the door opened.

"You came." There was a touch of vulnerability in his voice as though he thought she would not.

"I have." Just seeing his expression and hearing his hint of uncertainty eased the tension within her about whether this was a good thing to do. It was.

"I have a surprise for you," he said as he reached out and took hold of one of her hands. He was not in his dinner clothes any longer. A silk version of that robe he'd worn, she thought he'd called it a kaftan, this one was in shades of dark green and it made his eyes seem to glow. "Close your eyes and let me guide you." He kissed her hand and then guided her within.

She took several steps inside and began to notice some unfamiliar yet pleasing scents. Even behind eyes tightly shut, she could tell the chamber was not well lit, less so than the corridor behind her. The door closed behind her and she waited for his next instruction. She felt his body behind hers and his hands slid over her arms to rest on her shoulders, which made it easy for him to adjust her position. Excitement of a different kind built within her, adding to the heightened anticipation that had filled her for hours.

"You seemed very interested in the details of the places I've visited, so I thought I would show you the things I liked best about them." So close that she could feel his breath on her neck, he rubbed slowly down her arms as he held her against him.

"Like your kaftan?" she whispered, wanting to open her eyes but waiting on his word.

"Aye. I have many of them." His hand moved from her arm and she felt the smoothness of silk against her cheek. "Some for simple comfort and some for the pleasure of their feel on your skin."

This was not the pragmatic scholar. This was not even the kind employer. This man was a surprise to her. Shivering, she leaned back on him and let him touch the silk robe along her neck.

"Open your eyes, love."

They stood at the opening to the smaller of two rooms in his chamber and the scene before her was like one out of stories of old. Once he'd closed the door, she felt the warmth and there, in addition to a fire burning in the larger hearth of the main chamber, were two other small metal containers in which wood and something else burned.

"What is burning in those?"

"Some incense I brought back from Marrakesh. The bazaars there have the most wondrous scents and tastes. I prefer this one."

"It is intoxicating," she admitted to him as she inhaled the heady aroma.

"Some of what men smoke there is just that. Not like the tobacco from the West Indies. More spice-based. More pungent."

"And you have tried it?"

"When you travel with natives in faraway places, you tend to try their customs and practices."

"And?"

"I have been told that I apparently have the tendency to sing loudly when I have." She laughed at that. That was something she would like to see.

"But not when you drink excessively?"

"That only happened at university and I have no desire to remember those experiences."

She had never seen him inebriated or even slightly drunk, though his friends had been. Smiling at the thought of him singing while drunk, she also realized that no matter that her father was from another country, he had never seemed to enjoy customs or foods or drinks outside of his own, if those stories of his were true.

Almost as if her gaze had ignored the most important part of this scene he'd laid out, Arabella gasped at the corner of the rest of this chamber.

Traditional furnishings were absent completely and replaced by a very low chaise longue sitting on the plush and colorful carpet surrounded by pillows and cushions in all manner of shapes and colors. The only thing in common was that they seemed made of the same silk as his robe. A table, small but only inches off the floor, was covered by pots and glasses and plates, and even from here she could see and smell some of them.

"I have some of the delights of the Turkish markets shipped here to Scotland. Through one of my business endeavors with people my cousin detested, but some of the fruits and syrups and sweets are like tasting heaven and worth the cost." He released her and turned her to face him. "I cannot wait for you to try them. To see your reaction. To taste them on your tongue." His gaze dropped along her body until it rested just above her thighs. "And to lick them from other places."

"Joshua." His name came out as a breathy whisper.

"Will you undress for me, Clara?" He moved back from the large alcove and leaned on the side of an enormous bed. Carved in some dark wood, with four posters holding up a canopy. Dark green silken sheets covered the largest mattress she'd ever seen. "I would, but I fear the damage I would do them in my haste."

The slight tremor in his hands gave her the courage to do as he'd asked. She'd never been undressed before a man for this purpose before. Her hands shook, too, as she reached up to unpin her hair.

"Nay, leave that to me."

The gown she wore was a simple one but the buttons down her back would present a challenge for her. Before she could ask, he was there, kissing her while his hands slid around her bodice seeking the back of her gown. Despite the obvious fumbling, he managed to open the row of buttons on the back of her dress. Arabella hadn't realized she'd grabbed hold of him until he stepped away and she pulled the silk tie of his robe free. The edges of his kaftan separated, giving her a clear view of his body, from his shoulders, down his chest and stomach to his hips visible just above the loose pants worn low. The dark curls of his chest continued along his belly and disappeared beneath the edge of that decadent garment.

"Undress," he said, his voice now low and gruff.

Arabella tugged the top of her gown forward and let it slide down her arms and then down her hips and legs before stepping from it. Once she untied her petticoat, that slid away next. As she reached for the ties on her stays, he moved a scant inch as though he would do the rest before shaking his head. With his gaze staring into hers, she loosened the garment and pushed it down.

Her shift was thin and must reveal everything to him, but it was the only thing between them. He nodded, a slight lifting of his chin really, and then his mouth dropped open as she removed that last barrier.

SHE WAS BLOODY beautiful. Standing in the light thrown by the flickering flames, his eyes were drawn to her curves—from breasts that he knew would fit perfectly in his hands, to a narrow waist and then flaring out to hips he loved to watch move. The deep pink of her nipples and the brown tuft between her legs stood out from her fair skin and his mouth watered at the possibility of tasting her.

But, he would not be the ravening beast that his body wanted. He wanted to savor this time with her, make it pleasurable for both of them. So, Joshua turned back to the bed and picked up the soft, pink kaftan that matched the color of her nipples. Walking to her, he could not wait to see her reaction to the feeling of pure silk sliding over her breasts and belly.

"Lift your arms," he said. Gathering up its length, he tossed the opening over her head and guided her hands into the sleeves on each side. Then he guided the luxurious fabric over her body, using his hands to smooth it as it dropped into place. Though it eventually covered her body from shoulders to feet, the flowing material followed every curve. "What do you think?"

"It is. . . sinful."

He was so hard he would not last if he touched her. And yet, he must. Stepping closer, he just let his hands glide over her, enjoying her body and thrilled by her reaction. Her eyes closed and she panted with his every stroke. But he did not want to just rush this. He pulled his need for her under control, intent on wooing the curious, intelligent woman first.

And he would have, with the samples he'd gathered of the teas and fruited syrup and honey-coated sweets, and with the drawings of smaller villages as well as the Bey's palaces that he hoped she'd enjoy. Except that when she reached out and stroked him in the same way—sliding the back of her hand over his chest and flicking her thumb across his own previously-unsensitive nipples on her path to his trousers—he knew he and his control were lost.

She imitated the way he had slipped his finger beneath the edge of her bodice in the small library and moved her fingers into the knot holding his pants up. Loosened, they dropped to the floor. When her hands teased her way into the coarse curls that were very close to his erection, that randy flesh shifted on its own, seeking her touch. He clenched his jaws, trying to remain still under her attentions, intent on his plan. It would have worked, until that moment when her fingers curled around his length and his semblance of control dissolved.

He wrapped his arms around her, pulling her closer and kissing her as he walked them back to the bed. Sitting first, he took hold of her by the waist, leaned them back and pulled her up to straddle him. Joshua was willing to give up or postpone his grand plan for her seduction, he'd be damned if he would not do the one thing he'd done in his imagination dozens of times.

Reaching up, he began pulling out the hairpins that held her woven plaits in place. Between the pressure of her heated flesh sliding on his cock and the feel of her loosening hair around his hands, his blood heated and his heart pounded. He needed to bury himself deep inside her.

And claim her body even while she claimed his heart.

When he pulled that last pin, it was like watching a waterfall pouring over its edge. The neatness of the way she wore it gave little warning of its true nature. Thick, curling locks of the darkest brown hue tumbled over her shoulder and down her back. The length of it rested on his thighs and flowed around her, and he tangled his hands in the curls and tugged her to him with it.

"Kiss me," he whispered against her mouth.

Joshua opened to her and reached down to see to her pleasure, gathering the robe up and allowing him to touch and caress the most private part of her. Her folds were wet and she moaned against his mouth as he caressed her, sliding one then two fingers deep into her inner passage. She was tight but her channel eased as he massaged there. From the tightness he'd encountered, he suspected that she had not had relations in some time.

"Tell me if I am hurting you," he whispered as he guided her hips up and positioned his erection under her.

He had thought to go slowly, but as she slid down his length and he sank into her, he lost that battle. Rolling them over, he pushed up on his elbows and watched her face as he drew almost all the way out before thrusting back in.

"I have waited so long for this," he said, his flesh hardening even more with every stroke.

"As have I." Arabella canted her hips, allowing him in deeper. Nothing about this was anything like the last time. Or any time before.

That she could remain standing as he'd watched her undress was a miracle. Her body heated and some awareness blossomed within her, tightening and twisting with every glance from him that touched her like a look and caress. Desire filled her and she wanted him.

Now, she could feel as his flesh swelled with each thrust of his hips. It created such a delicious friction and she wanted to enjoy every moment of it. But as he set a pace, faster then slower, deeper with each stroke, whispering words that inflamed her more, she lost herself to the sheer bliss of it. To feel so cherished, so intimate, was something she would remember forever.

Then, he urged her to fly and she did, the tension spiraled free and wave after wave of pleasure raced through her blood and a cry of release echoed around them. He thrust once more and then his own moan sent another surge of heat as her intimate muscles clenched around his flesh.

She lost sense of time and was uncertain how long they lay there in silence, the beating of their hearts finally calming. He seemed fascinated by her hair and the feel of his fingers combing through her curls was soothing even while thrilling to her. He eased out of her body but held her close as he turned them on their sides, then tugged her robe back down over her. Facing each other, meeting his gaze, in the afterglow of passion was more comfortable than she expected.

Over the next little while, he never stopped touching her, sliding his hands over the glossy fabric. Sated and relaxed after all the tension that had built between them these last days dissipated, she did not believe she could have moved a muscle now.

But she had questions about all the special things he'd arranged, and she wanted to know about the various beverages and foods and where he'd gone and what he'd done. His hands moved in a slow, methodical path from her head, down her shoulders and back and up again.

Arabella did not remember anything after the third or fourth time he massaged her in that way. Opening her eyes, she found herself alone in his massive bed in an empty chamber.

Chapter Twenty

"AH, SO YOU are finally awake?" His voice came from nearby, so she pushed up on her elbows and looked for him. And found him. "I did not eat much at supper, so I asked for something more substantial to supplement the desserts and concoctions," he explained.

With his bed-tousled hair and one of those sweets in his hand, he wore the guilty expression of a lad who'd just been caught being naughty. It made her want to devour him and the treats he'd promised. He stood and approached his bed, and only then did she realize that he'd covered her with those silky sheets when he'd left her side. Rubbing her hands over them and allowing them to glide over her skin, she wanted these, too.

"You have been hiding these, all this, from me?" She sat up and slid off the bed's high surface, landing on her feet just as he reached her.

A wicked idea struck her as the robe flowed over her skin, doing wonderful things to her breasts and other places. She reached out and brought his hand to her mouth, searching his fingers until she found what she'd been looking for—evidence of his crime. She opened her lips and teased the tip of his thumb with her teeth before drawing it into her mouth and licking the remnants of its sweetness with her tongue. Her body reacted when he watched her wetting and licking and sucking until the last bit of sugary flavor was gone.

"Marchpane?" But there was something different in its making than what she'd taste here in the confectionary on the High Street.

"A Persian way of making it."

She touched her tongue to his thumb, seeking another taste of it. "Did you eat it all yourself?"

"There is—" He stopped and cleared his throat. "There is more for you to taste."

She was close enough to him that she felt the moment his flesh rose between them. Arabella glanced down to see the evidence of his arousal tenting out the pants he wore. Though she had been asked to perform that wicked task once before and had, at the time, sworn never to repeat it, the sight of his erection and the thought of licking him made her mouth water. He had intimated using some of the treats on her in such a manner.

He lifted her in his arms and carried her into the smaller chamber and placed her on the chaise. Designed more like a bed, its rounded side sloped up gently and she was able to turn on her side with her arm resting on it. Her body fit its curve and it reminded her of stories of ancient Romans eating like this.

Joshua pushed a short, padded stool over and sat between her and the table. He held out a pink confection in the shape of a flower to her. When she reached for it, he pulled it back and shook his head. Dropping her arm, he nodded and moved closer, holding the petals of the rose to her lips.

"Use your teeth. Take one petal at a time."

Her breasts swelled against her kaftan and the nipples tightened into buds as he held it to her mouth. Biting off one piece as he'd said resulted in a burst of nutty sweetness in her mouth and she moaned. His eyes never left her mouth as he turned the sweet after each bite to offer her the next petal.

"Marzipan from Persia. They use several different flavored sugars to deepen the flavors of the sugar and almonds."

When he'd fed her the last of it, he held out his fingers to her and she licked off every bit of sugary bits. Then he leaned over and kissed her, his tongue sweeping over hers and tasting what she'd just chewed.

"Less rosewater." A kiss. "More citrus." His tongue plunged deeply and swirled around hers. "Delicious."

When she thought he would touch her, ease the throbbing that made her lower body feel heavy and aching, he sat back and lifted up a small metal cup. She arched against the torment of the silk on her breasts.

"This is made with a syrup found all around the Mediterranean Sea. Tell me what you taste." He held the cup to her mouth. "Open and lean your head back."

So intoxicated by the smell and the heat and the pleasure racing through her, she did as he said, leaning back against the chaise and opening her mouth. Joshua tipped the cup and poured some of the thick mixture onto her tongue. Thick, rich and fruity, it coated her tongue, and she licked it onto her lips.

"What do you taste?"

This was so thick that it did not dissolve away quickly. Flavors exploded on her tongue in layer after layer. It was so decadent and luxurious and added to her anticipation coursing through her body as she waited for his mouth on hers. Every part of her waited for him.

"Do you need more?"

"It tastes like your incense." She savored the spices and ingredients trying to sort through them. "Sweet, but it's not sugar." He smiled, not giving her a hint. "Dates?" His brow rose waiting on her answer. "Rosewater?"

"Let me try."

His tongue teased along her lips, licking the syrup there and then plunged inside, repeating with his tongue what he had done inside her body with his cock.

"Fruit molasses," he whispered. She offered her tongue to him, and he kissed her open-mouthed until she could not breathe.

"Aye, rosewater. Aye, dates." He tipped the cup and let another bit dribble into her mouth and down her chin. "You missed the best one, love."

With nothing more or less than his mouth, licking the sticky liquid from her tongue and lips and down her chin and across her neck where it had spread, he created an inundation of sensation that rushed over her. Her thighs clenched against the waves of pleasure throbbing in the folds there and deeper still. As she cried out, he did not stop, his wicked mouth nipping and tasting his way down, peeling the neckline of her robe until he feasted on her aching and needy breasts. Arching her body to keep his mouth on her, his hand slid down the silk robe, rubbing it against her curls and surprising her. He pressed the heel of his hand on her mons and let his finger slip in between her legs, caressing her through the silk until she screamed out her pleasure. When she could finally breathe once more, he whispered one word to her.

"Chocolate."

She could watch as he moved away but do little else. Every bone in her body had given up from the exquisite crisis of desire he brought her to once again. He knelt, his erection clear to her, and reached for a bottle of golden liquid which he added to the syrup, stirring it with his finger to mix it. Her body quaked just at the sight.

"This is the way I prefer it," he said.

He sat back on his heels and held out the cup to her this time. Arabella pushed herself to sit up, but it took great effort—and he looked inordinately pleased by that. Taking the cup, she sipped the concoction.

Whisky. He'd mixed in a fine whisky and the flavors mixed well, each liquid enhancing the other. The whisky deepened and filled out the smokiness of the syrup. The undertones of fruitiness in the *uisge beatha*, as it was sometimes called, blended with the flavors of the dates and molasses and burst on her tongue. She took a mouthful of the delicious drink this time, letting it trickle down her throat as she swallowed slowly. Without pause, she drank the rest of it. Opening eyes she had not realized she'd closed, she met his hungry gaze as the heat of potent mix spread through her body. She knew from his expression what he wanted to do next.

But she wanted her turn.

Emboldened by his frank desire and his openness in his affection and probably the whisky, too, she placed her hand on his chest and pushed him back. Following him until he slid off his stool and into the cushions, she looked over the plates and bowls on the table.

"What is this one?" she asked, choosing something that looked like a filled chocolate. When he did not answer her, she knew it would fit her purpose. "Take those off."

Her voice was clear, but her body ached at the thoughts running through her mind. Could he tell she was already aroused? When he had not moved, she bit into the edge of the candy and felt the liquid within dribble down her chin. Perfect. Now, she knelt up and over him, watching as his manhood pulsed under her gaze.

Even the palms of her hands ached to hold his flesh and caress it, so she did. Encircling his width and sliding her fist up his length and down it. He stretched out on the cushions and put his hand behind his head, just watching her, daring her with his gaze, to do it.

Lifting the sweet and holding it several inches above the thick, ruddy tip, she squeezed the chocolate layer until it wept its filling down onto his rod. As the liquid trickled down over its satiny smooth length, Arabella tightened her fingers around the base of his erection and stared at the arousing sight. Her mouth watered and she swallowed several times as she lowered herself towards him.

"Just remember you brought this on yourself, my lord," she said.

EVEN NOW, ALMOST two days later, he remembered and wanted

to stir her boldness again. Clara dozed on the chaise after their last bout of pleasure, covered only by her hair and a silken sheet she seemed to favor. Any attempt on her part to dress since she walked into his chambers had failed, for now that he had seen her naked, wrapped in silk or in her hair and in nothing at all, he removed anything else.

As her attempts to match him act for act succeeded, he lounged naked on the cushions next to her. *Fair is fair*, she'd said more than a few times in their time out of time here.

Their bedsport had been a surprise to him—she denied neither him nor herself whatever appealed in the moment. The use of the sticky sweet concoctions had been followed by the flavored whisky and several other treats. He only knew that he would never look at Mrs. Sommer's gravy in quite the same way again. Or Mrs. Sommers for that matter, fearing she would read their guilt on their faces.

A bath had appeared in the dressing room twice since they entered here, and trays of food were delivered at some regularity, all without the need to pull the bell. Pirrie delivered whatever he requested, and he asked for anything Clara wanted. Books, papers, flowers, no matter what it was.

Joshua had never done anything like this before. Certainly this was a longer visit than he'd ever made to this place. Most contacts were done through his factor or man of business. When he'd inherited the title on his cousin's death, he resisted everything attached to it and to his cousin.

For William Robertson, the tenth Viscount of Dunalastair, had been the one to force Luigi Balugani on Joshua. His cousin had made his funding and support based on Josh's acceptance and continued involvement with the ill-reputed Italian. And though the previous viscount was separated enough from the affair not to suffer from the debacles that followed, his cousin's prestige and position had done little to protect or rescue Josh.

Only finally inheriting the title and the king's patronage had given him the ability to escape. And even that had not prevented the rumors and the cuts direct from polite society. The knowledge that there were innocents involved that needed far more protection than he did held him firmly to his resolve about how to handle it all. He could not protect them from Balugani's ignominy, but he could keep them from suffering because of Joshua's true failures.

Clara let out a breathy sigh and turned onto her side. The sheet slipped allowing him to gaze upon her lovely breasts. Though he could rouse the randy fellow, he was deeply satisfied and could also simply appreciate the way that she lay draped over the chaise. He had tired her out, for even the not-soft knock at his chamber door did not wake her. Grabbing his more-traditional banyan from the chair as he walked to the door, Joshua pulled it on and tied the belt before opening the door.

"Good afternoon, my lord." Pirrie made certain Joshua was aware of how scandalously late in the day it was for him to be walking around in a dressing gown. "Mr. Cameron has sent a message from Edinburgh."

Joshua glanced down at the tray Pirrie held. The demands of true life and commitments would not be held at bay any longer. He took the letter and opened it, reading it quickly. Cameron was succinct and without his usual flourishes and excessive details. Most likely because of the news it imparted.

The villain who'd attacked him had been apprehended and the authorities were waiting for his return to process matters.

Relief warred with regret that their idyll was indeed at an end. Oh, their time together was not over—far from it—but it would be some time before they could be together in this way. Arrangements must be made. Announcements published.

"Thank you, Pirrie. Please prepare for our departure at first light in the morning."

"Very good, my lord." The butler left and Joshua knew the household would move swiftly and efficiently to pack their belongings, prepare the coach and make plans for the journey back to Edinburgh. Before the servant reached the stairs, Joshua called him back.

"Send up baths for myself and Mrs. Lewis after dinner in our chambers."

Pirrie controlled the twitching right brow that was making a valiant attempt to raise itself in reaction to the formal request. They'd made do with one bathtub several times now, but Joshua thought they should begin to reclaim their separateness until things were more formalized between them.

Bloody hell, he was not ready to do that yet.

"Never mind, Pirrie."

"So, no baths after dinner then, my lord?" The butler lost control over his brow then and it lifted in a mocking salute.

"One bath. After dinner. Here."

"Will you be dining downstairs, my lord?"

"Aye, we will."

"Nay, we will not," Clara said from the other chamber.

"Nay, we will dine here," he said to the butler who clearly had heard Clara's words.

"Very good, my lord." Pirrie turned after bowing and walked away. Stopping at the top of the staircase, the man looked back at Joshua as though giving him another chance to change his mind. Joshua closed the door, afraid his butler would laugh at Mrs. Lewis' influence. For in spite of the man's absolute adherence to his role as the perfect butler, riveling only Pottles in that, he was a bit softer around the edges and had a good sense of humor. Leaning against the closed door, he read the letter once more to see if he missed anything before going to Clara.

The lack of specific details made sense when Joshua thought about his attempt to leave the city undetected and to remain that way until his, their, return. His solicitor wisely did not reveal more than the most essential information.

Still. . . .

"Will you return to the man, the viscount, I knew when working for him in Edinburgh now?" Clara asked. Sliding gracefully off the chaise and wrapping the sheet around her, she walked towards him.

"Is he different than the one here?" he asked.

Clara glanced around the chamber that, after two days of carnal abandonment, looked more like a sultan's rooms with its luxurious and sensual décor than a Scottish nobleman's bed-chamber.

"If you had spoken of furnishing like these or the special dishes and drinks you had prepared, or your preference for Persian or Egyptian silk kaftans over a good Scottish woolen banyan, I would have thought you daft." She stood before him and lifted up on her toes to kiss him. Something about the kiss was so poignant it hurt him.

"Nothing could have prepared me for the adventurer who loved the places he visited though he never mentioned them. Nothing forewarned me that the historian hid a sensual side that could rival a rake of prodigious efforts." He smiled at that, for that had surprised even him. She reached up and kissed him again but this time he held her close. "I only saw the hardworking, intelligent, loyal nobleman who did not take himself too seriously and who tried to be good and fair to those he knew."

Clara took the letter from his hand and stepped back to read it. He thought that he could read her expressions now, after months together in Edinburgh, but especially after these last two intimate days. Yet, whatever the expression was that flitted across her features as she held the letter back to him, he did not recognize.

"We have the rest of the day and one more night before we must leave our little secret world behind and return to the real one, Clara. I want, I need to sort out the business of the attacks and find whoever is behind this."

"I understand. I do," she said. But that expression—part loss, part resignation, and part regret—remained in her eyes.

"Once I do and everything is settled, we will—" She pressed her fingers over his mouth to stop his words.

"Nay, Joshua. Make no promises until everything is handled."

Somehow this was important to her, for he could hear a sense of desperation in her voice. So, he relented and smiled at her.

"We have tonight," she repeated, dropping the sheet and walking into his embrace as he opened his banyan and wrapped it around her.

"We have tonight," he said.

But he knew there would be more. A lifetime of days and nights if he had anything to do with it. That night was filled with tenderness as he showed her with his touch and with his whispered words the depth of his feelings for her.

And when he carried her back to her chamber, so she would wake there and not be as embarrassed as she would be to be found in his, he said the words he most wanted to say. Words that no woman had ever tempted him to speak. Whispered as she slept, just before he left her.

"I love you, Clara Lewis. I love you."

Chapter Twenty-One

ARABELLA STRETCHED AGAIN, lifting her arms over her head as far as she could as though trying to touch the ceiling in the beautiful chamber she'd occupied for this visit. Well, for most of her visit if one looked past the debauchery of the last two and more days. The memories of those exquisite days and passion filled nights made her body shudder. She existed in a half-aroused state the whole time and he could bring her to completion with barely a touch.

Memorable, certainly which fit her purposes exactly.

Wearing only her shift and stays, she waited for Margaret's return, hoping that between the lass and Joshua's valet they could find her missing hair combs. She would return as his housekeeper, gather her belongings and leave under cover of night. That way, if he did discover anything about her from the man they held, she would be long gone from his life.

Mrs. Clara Lewis, widowed housekeeper, would walk out of his house and Miss Arabella MacGibbon, unmarried daughter of the late Sarah MacGibbon and Luigi Balugani, would regain her life. She would leave her father's false hopes behind and go her own way.

She brushed the surprising tears away. She needed to finish this and do it well. For herself and for him. And for the first time

ever, the man involved was not her father. Holding the last
vestige of him in her trembling hand, she heard the knob turn and
she spoke over her shoulder to her maid.

"I hope you had some luck finding them, Margaret. Could
you please help me tuck this under my neckline?" She held the
two unhooked ends of the necklace over her shoulders for the lass
to connect and place where it would be secured and unseen.

"I am not Margaret, but I would happily play lady's maid for
you, my love."

Her breath stopped. Her hands froze in place and she prayed
he would not look. *Pray God, do not look.* But her luck had run out
and her escape would not be a clean one. Nay, all hell was about
to break loose around her. His indrawn breath was her only
warning.

He'd taken hold of the ends of the chain on which she wore
the pendant, and he lifted the whole thing free of her, getting a
close look at it. Arabella stood and faced him, seeing the disbelief
on his face. Replica or not, it damned her forever in his eyes. He
stiffened, and took a breath and the lover was gone, replaced by
the nobleman who realized he played the fool.

"Where did you get this?" he asked, his voice low but more
unnerving than if he'd shouted the question. When she met his
gaze, she could see his stunned expression as he was trying to sort
it out in his mind. "I asked you where you got this?"

"From my father." Arabella was surprised that her own voice
did not tremble as she answered him.

"This is the missing half of the pendant," he said. Shaking his
head, he seemed to be silently arguing with himself.

"This is a replica, my lord." His nostrils flared at her address.

"Your father?"

There was no other way out of this now. The wild and crazy
thought that occurred to her was that this way might make the
break between them cleaner, harsher aye, but complete. She
began to say her father's name, but he spoke first.

"Luigi Balugani."

He imbued the name with such hatred and rage that she flinched at the sound. He tucked the necklace in his coat pocket and then his hands clenched into fists.

"Margaret!" he yelled. The lass came at a run, looked from Arabella to him and back again and curtsied so low she nearly tumbled over.

"My lord?" The young woman was terrified and stared at this man that neither of them knew.

"Get Mrs. Lewis dressed and down to the coach."

"Aye, my lord!"

He turned to leave but he stopped and faced her, his hand on the door. "Your name?"

Margaret gasped and stared at her, stark confusion and fear lay on her usually kind features. He'd done it on purpose, a way to humiliate Arabella when he'd shielded her before.

"Arabella MacGibbon."

He was gone but the sound of him tearing his way downstairs, yelling out orders and reprimands as he went, echoed back up to her.

"I dinna understand, ma'am? What did he mean?"

Arabella would be gone and never be seen here again, so she tried to ease the girl's fear.

"It matters not, Margaret. I have taken advantage of his lordship's good nature and he has discovered my transgression." She patted the girl's hand and smiled around the tears. "Here now, let's finish with my hair so I can dress and leave, and this disruption will be over."

It took a bit longer to manage with the way the poor lass's hands shook and ended with each section of her hair being a different thickness. The arrangement looked haphazard at best, but, when her cap was placed over it, it hid the worst and would do until she could fix it. She gathered her small bag of personal items, ones he'd given her during her stay here since they'd left so quickly and left most of her things behind.

A thick, dark pall hung over the house as she made her way

down to the entry. Arabella could not help but look once more at the delicately-patterned carpet there, remembering the similar one in his chambers. Brodie held out her cloak and placed it around her shoulders. She put her bag in his hand and tied the laces and pulled her hood up onto her head.

"'Tis a miserable morning, Mrs. Lewis. You will need that cloak, I fear," Pirrie said as Brodie took her bag out to the coach.

Arabella glanced out the door and saw a thick, Highland mist that the pre-dawn sun could not pierce. The viscount was nowhere to be seen. "Thank you for your concern, Mr. Pirrie. And please thank the staff for their excellent service during my visit. I will not forget it."

The butler nodded to her and opened the door as Brodie opened the coach and helped her to climb inside. In a way, the viscount's demand to leave so quickly had given her fewer witnesses to stare and point. She settled back against the seat and waited for his lordship to enter. The steps were closed up and the door secured closed, leaving her the only passenger inside.

She knew there would be a reckoning between them, so as she passed the first hours alone, half asleep, half in dread, she found the tension growing worse by the mile. At first, she thought he might have remained behind, not wanting to travel with her after he knew her true identity. But at one of the places along the loch, she heard him call out orders to the coachman and then to the footman. But she never saw him out the windows.

When the coach slowed to a stop sometime later, she righted her cloak and adjusted her cap inside wanting to be ready for whatever was happening. The door opened and the footman lowered the steps. Through the dreary rain, she saw that they were in the yard of an inn.

"Mrs. Lewis, watch your step here. The mud is quite thick."

He helped her not only climb down but to rush through the yard and into the inn. When they stepped inside, the warmth struck her. But Brodie led her through a small, crowded area to a hallway and a chamber there. Opening the door, she found a private room, already set with a meal on the rough table there.

"Through that door is. . .a. . ."

"Thank you, Brodie." She understood. Arabella saw to her comfort for she barely had time before they'd left. Coming back into the small room, she found the viscount standing by the other door watching her.

HE'D RIDDEN IN the rain, trying to ease the rage that flowed through him at the betrayal dealt him by another Balugani. Joshua did not wish to even speak to her until he believed himself in control. And with the haste in which his ability to think logically had disappeared this morn, he was not certain he could yet.

Arabella MacGibbon had been living in his house, serving him as housekeeper and even sharing his bed and he'd had no idea. Searching her features now with a knowing eye, he could see no trace of her father except the color of her hair and eyes. He'd met her mother long ago but could not remember enough details to decide if their resemblance was stronger. She'd been just a girl when he'd tried to clean up the mess left by her father and he'd paid little notice of her, if he'd seen her or any of the others at all.

The door to the commode closet opened and she walked in, catching sight and pausing, half in half out of this small chamber. Then he watched her take a breath, enter and sit at the table. Without a word from him, she poured ale into two of the cups and placed one on the side of the table closest to him and one before her. Sitting down then, she repeated it with the pot of steaming stew that awaited them, sliding one over towards him and placing a spoon next to it.

The aroma of the tasty stew that this inn was known for should have reminded him of his hunger, but the sight of her quashed that. Soon, only the sound of her spoon scratching along the metal bowl broke the silence, though she was merely moving the stew around the bowl and not actually eating it.

He dragged the chair out and sat down at the table. She flinched at every move he made as though she expected violence from him. A dark part of him, one buried so deep he had forgotten it was there, could have been stirred to it at one time, but too much had happened, first to him and then between them for him to raise a hand to her.

"Stop it," he said, when he reached for his cup and she moved back. "You are in no danger of my fist, Cla—" He stopped, realizing he was about to use her false name. "Miss MacGibbon." She recoiled as though he had indeed struck her. "So, you sought a position in my household knowing much more about me than I ever suspected. Why?"

"To avenge my father." Her words shocked him.

"Avenge what?"

"He died, alone and in poverty because of you. I wanted to find proof of your perfidy and expose it." Whatever he'd thought she might confess, this was not it. And Balugani had not died in that manner.

"I had nothing to do with his death." This past just never died, the lies never ceased, no matter his efforts to bury them.

"He told me—"

"He was a consummate liar, among other faults, Miss Mac-Gibbon. He fooled me for too long and he has apparently fooled you as well." He poured more ale and drank it in one long swallow. "How does it feel to be played for a fool?"

He slammed the cup down and her reaction was both more and less satisfying than he'd hoped. But he cared little as he realized something about her arrival in his life now that he knew who she was.

"You were the catalyst. You showed up and the attacks, the robbery, began. Are you in league with the ones behind those? Or are they in your employ?"

"Nay!" she cried out. For the first time since finding the price-less artifact being worn around her neck like some common decoration, she was alarmed. "I had nothing to do with those. I would not harm you, Josh. . . my lord."

"And when you found whatever proof you were searching for? What then?" he asked.

"You stole everything from him, even the money he should have earned from the illustrations for the book. I wanted to prove it."

"And then?" he asked again.

"I would be able to live my own life knowing I had cleared my father's name."

She was not a stupid person. Indeed, she was one of the quickest wits and most intelligent people he'd known. So how could she have believed. . . .her father. She believed him because he was her father. Because she needed to believe him.

He reached for the pitcher again and stopped. Something had changed between them. Their flirting had become something more serious and she'd resisted him until. . . .

"Mr. Lewis never existed?" She shook her head. "My god-mother would have told me if you'd lied about working at Arbuthnott."

"I did work there, as I said, and learned the duties of a house-keeper."

"That's an elaborate ruse and not a dependable one if you are seeking vengeance."

"I was only trying to survive after my parents died. My moth-er went first, and my father died of a broken heart some months later. Her friend took me in. Vengeance does not put food on the table nor pay your rent," she said, a bitter edginess in her tone that made him look closely at her. She lifted her cup and drank deeply then, the first time she had taken in anything since their arrival here.

"But when I found out that the countess was related to you, it was easy to ask questions, pretending to be in awe and curious. I even saw you once in the distance, when you came to visit." She laughed, but the sound was rough and disturbing. "I thought that things were happening that were meant to happen to give me my chance. So, when Mrs. Brander mentioned you were looking for a new housekeeper, I came to the city and waited for the chance."

And unbeknownst to him, everything she needed had actually worked out and he'd hired her, bringing his enemy's creature into his house. . . and into his bed.

"What changed?" he asked.

"I learned that my father must be wrong. You were not as he described you, not the villain. Not the ruthless nobleman who took advantage of his employees." She shrugged. "I changed."

"So, without proof of your father's accusations you decided to ruin me in another way? Allowing your seduction in an effort to lay claim to some of my ill-gotten wealth?"

Joshua knew the accusation was false, but his pride got in the way. The one thing that had been honest between them had been the attraction that flared like lightning in a summer storm. Instead of anger, she replied in a flat voice.

"I was leaving. I had no intention of staying with you, of making any claim on you at all."

"And I was about to propose marriage to you."

"I ken," she said. "You are too honorable for your own good." She smiled, a joyless one, and shook her head. "As I told Mrs. Lyle and Mrs. Sommers, this could not end with us together. Not for a viscount and the daughter of the man he'd blamed for all his problems. Especially if the truth was known, as it is now. My only choice was to leave."

Brodie opened the door, interrupting anything else she had to say. and told him the horses had been changed and the coachman and he had eaten and were ready to get back on the road.

"Miss MacGibbon, it is time to leave."

She sat up and followed Brodie out without argument or delay, leaving him in a stunned silence at the table. Her words, her explanation disturbed him, for he knew the other side of every story her father had told her. And he knew how persuasive Balugani could be and how he'd lied and manipulated his way out of so many predicaments that it still shocked Josh.

If she had grown up listening to those lies, it was no wonder to him at all that she'd believed it. Though anger made him want to refuse to accept her account, he realized that his former friend had created the perfect weapon for his vengeance. If she'd been less intelligent but just as determined, he might have ended up with a bullet in his head. Instead, he'd ended up with a talented, efficient, knowledgeable, bold and brave housekeeper. And the perfect woman for him.

Whichever of the ancient gods they'd insulted those years ago while digging at Timgad must be laughing from on high at this turn of events. His own part in this farce did not leave him blameless, but he contented himself with knowing that he had done his best to protect Balugani's true victims. Even if none of them were aware of his actions. Even if the woman waiting in the coach had no idea yet of her father's true crimes. At least he could rest easily in the knowledge that he'd tried to fix what Balugani had done. And what his own cousin William had covered up, nay, enabled.

Joshua summoned the innkeeper and arranged for the rest of their meal to be sent to the coach, along with several heated bricks. She would get hungry eventually and they had many hours yet to travel this day. If not the stew, then perhaps something in the basket Mrs. Sommers had packed would entice her to eat.

And give her the strength to face the past she had no awareness of but that played against her even now.

Chapter Twenty-Two

ARABELLA FOUND THE thick leather portfolio on the seat opposite of her once they'd left the inn. It had not been there when she'd left the coach so Joshua must have put it there.

With the storm clouds that filled the skies and followed them along the journey south, she needed to light one of the lanterns to be able to examine it. Something urged her to put it aside. A feeling of impending danger spiraled within her, growing stronger every moment that she held the portfolio in her hands.

She could see in his gaze that he did not believe she plotted with others to hurt him. And that was the only legal accusation that she could face in this whole endeavor. She might be able to convince him to let her go. Joshua had the replica of part of the brooch and that might lead him to the other half. He could find whatever treasure her father had claimed was his and have his reputation be restored by its existence. If it existed.

But her fingers glided over the surface, toying with the leather tie that held the portfolio closed, keeping its secrets from her gaze. Finally, she pulled on the tie and opened it. Pulling the contents out, she laid them on the seat next to her and began.

Though the handwriting was mostly Joshua's, the pile included reports drawn up by others, including private investigators and solicitors, and worse, law enforcement authorities in several countries. It was clearly Joshua's work, all of it laid out in a logical way to detail charges against her father and then the proof of his misdeeds.

Her stomach turned as the depth of his crimes struck her. Nothing could have prepared her for the truth or for the way the man she called father had left a trail of innocent victims—women, children, and others—as he sought riches and power and advantages in each and every situation in which he found himself.

Joshua had not threatened her father. Nay, it had been Luigi Balugani who had threatened and blackmailed *him*. Worse, as he tried to account for and manage her father's transgressions, the rumors her father always started made Joshua look like the guilty party.

Assaults. Robberies. Rapes. Bigamy. Destruction of property and people lay strewn in his wake.

The evidence of his three marriages—concurrent marriages that each resulted in children whose bastardy would be held against them sent her stomach into revolt. She barely knocked on the roof of the coach and got them to stop before she began heaving. Only his strong arms held her out of the muck along the edge of the wet and muddy road until the spasms ended.

She would never be able to look him in the face again. How stupid she'd been to accept her father's tales for so long! And it had taken her too long to realize Joshua's true nature.

If only she'd talked to him, told him the truth. If only. . . . The tears flowed freely then as memories of the years of hating and planning to act against him bubbled up within her. The loneliness and the hollow feeling of being alone. The sorrow of losing her mother and relying on her father in the months after. She'd always believed his tale of losing her mother broke his heart, but the records she'd seen showed the falseness of even that claim.

In the midst of her sobbing, Joshua was there, holding her in his arms, whispering words that made no sense in her ear. How long she cried, she did not know, but she was still in his arms when they arrived back in Edinburgh at his house.

And somehow, she must find the strength to pull herself together and leave him before any more harm was done to him by her family.

When he tried to carry her inside, she refused. There would already be too much shocking news within the household and more scandal surrounding him was the last thing he needed. Still, he bolstered her with his arm around her.

"Come, I ken where Mrs. Mathieson keeps her broth for times just like these," he said.

His kindness made her want to cry again and she fought that urge as they climbed out of the coach in front of the house. By the way he tensed up, she knew something was wrong.

"Brodie, see if the doors are locked. Gavin," he said to his godmother's coachman, "take Miss MacGibbon—"

The snick of a pistol being cocked behind them stopped him.

"Gavin, climb down nice and slow-like. My employer would like a word with yers. Inside now." She knew Joshua would try to protect her, so next words were chilling. "My pistol is pointed at Balugani's daughter, my lord. I would hate if it went off and hit her."

Rough hands shoved them towards the downstairs servants' entrance and the only thing that kept her from screaming was his hold on her. Their few escorts led them into the kitchen where the actual numbers of these invaders doubled. And, sitting in Mr. Pottles' chair was the man who must be their leader. He had the appearance of a shopkeeper or businessman rather than a ruffian. Sharp blue eyes met hers and he tipped his head in greeting to her and then Joshua.

"Ah, my lord, welcome home. Sit him there, lads, and bring the lady closer to me." Joshua looked as though he would argue but the cold, metal barrel of the pistol against her face stopped him. "Tie them up and put them with the others. A few banged heads is all that happened to them, my lord. Nothin' more than that—if they behave. If *you* behave?" Joshua's curt nod answered him.

Only when Brodie and Gavin had been bound and the door of the storage closet opened did she see the others there. The terror on the maids' faces tore at her. Another horrible crime laid at her feet and brought about by her belief in her father's lies.

"Ye dinna look anything like yer father," the man said, staring at her. "I will tell ye that when we saw Balugani's get walking up to the house as bold as a whore plying her wares on Bells Wynd, we could not believe it. Could we, Robbie?"

It was her fault. They'd been watching and she led them right here. She dared to look at the viscount and mouthed an apology.

"And the way that yer papa denied kenning anything about the treasure! He swore up and down and in between, to anyone who would listen, that he didna hiv the map." He slammed his hands on the table and laughed, but it was mocking. "Robbie, remember how he swore on his deathbed that he'd lost the map?"

Deathbed? She looked at the man at the word. He'd been with her father when he died? But she'd come home from running an errand for him and found him. . . already dead. "Who are you?" she asked. Perhaps if she knew his name, it might trigger a memory of meeting him before?

"Dougal Dubh at yer service," he said. Was his name based on the dark color of his hair or the black heart that must beat in his chest to be such a villain? "I am yer papa's long-lost partner, come to claim what he stole from me."

"Let her go—" Joshua began to rise when several pistols aimed at him.

"Sit yerself down now, yer lordship. We are just here for a friendly talk and then we will be on our way. No one gets hurt," he paused and looked at her then. "If I get what's mine." Her throat seized up with terror as he stood up and walked to her side.

"I must say ye hiv grown into that name. No simple Betty or Maggie for ye. Nay, yer papa said only a fine name for his get. And I'll be damned if he wasna right." He leaned in close to her face and whispered. "So if ye tell me where ye hiv it, 'twill save us all a bit o' trouble, Arabella, my love." He spoke her name the way her father used to—with the accent of his native language, but from this man it was clearly meant as a vulgar threat.

Joshua was halfway across the table before three of the men wrestled him back into the chair.

"I can see his lordship might be tempted to do something very rash, lads. Why not tie him so he doesna act the fool?"

She wanted to scream out, but it might distract one of the men holding the pistols, so she watched in horror as Joshua was thrown to the floor and tied as he struggled against them. They lifted him back onto the chair and held him there.

"Hear now, lads! He's a lordship and ye must hiv a care wi' him." The man turned quickly back to her, and she could feel his breath on her face. "Now, as I was saying, Arabella, my love. I want the trinket yer papa gave ye when ye were just older than a bairn." He looked across at Joshua, pretending to speak to only him.

"Imagine my surprise, yer lordship, when I recently discovered that my partner Luigi had lied to me." Turning to her, he whispered again. "Imagine he lied, lass. Can ye?" She shivered as fear threatened to overwhelm her at the threat in his every word. Joshua began to struggle against the ropes holding his arms behind his back and the men around him.

"As it turns out, the trinket is the map, and he gave it to ye! If I need to find it on yer person, someone might get hurt." He smiled as he nodded at the others standing around them, waiting on his word. "My lads are not kenned for their gentle manners, Arabella, love. Who kens what could happen once they lay their hands on ye? In search of my property, of course, but things happen, ye see?"

"I have it." Joshua's voice was calm and very, very cold.

"I think ye are lying, too, my lord. To protect yer ladylove here," the man said.

"It is in my pocket."

"'Tis just a necklace," she said. "He made it to look like a carving he saw."

"Lads?"

They tore at his coat roughly and to her horror, they used more force than needed to find it where he'd put it this morning. As the one called Robbie drew it out and handed it to the leader, he took it in his hands as if it was the most valuable thing in the world instead of a worthless piece of painted clay or whatever her father had used to create it.

"What did he promise ye for this, Arabella? Or did he slip ye a few bawbees for it when yer were polishing his knob?" He reached over and traced his gloved fingers over the edge of her bodice.

"You bastard!" Joshua yelled as he tried to get to her. "Stop this."

The next thing she knew, he was on the floor, being held there by two ruffians while another cocked his weapon in warning.

"You have what you came for," she said. "Please go."

"But lass, we dinna yet. We came for the whole of it." The man stood up and grabbed her by the arm and dragged her up. "Let's go upstairs and get comfortable until his lordship kens what I mean."

"That's all we have," she cried out. "My father lied about it. There is no buried treasure to find. It's all a lie."

The man just waited and watched Joshua.

"Weel, if that is all there is, there would be no need for us to hiv a look in his lordship's chambers then."

"Stop this now," Joshua called out.

The man stopped near the door and held her tightly. His grip was like iron, holding her close at his side.

"I think yer lordship is about to tell us the truth." He watched as Joshua was dragged to his feet for a moment. "I think the best place for this discussion is where I can be comfortable, mayhap with the lovely Arabella at my side."

"Ye mean under yer cock!" one of the men yelled. The others

laughed as he pulled her closer and leered at her.

"All in good time, lads. All in good time." He began up the stairs dragging her with him as he called back. "Robbie, Bertie, bring him along. The rest of ye make yerselves useful. There must be something valuable hidden away in the cupboards and drawers."

Arabella thought about struggling against his grip, but the result would be that they both tumbled down the stairs. So, she walked with him, struggling to keep up with his longer strides as he took two steps to her one. Soon they were on the first floor, and he walked directly to Joshua's bedchamber.

Strangely, when they reached it and went inside, he was very calm and stood waiting as the other entered with Joshua.

"Leave her be and I will give you what you seek. I give you my word."

"SIT," THE LEADER said to her, shoving her in the direction of the large chair near the hearth. She stumbled over to it and fell into it. The man looked at Joshua and motioned to him.

"I need my hands free," he said.

"Just tell me where it is, and I can get it meself."

"It cannot be done that way," he said. "I will not risk her safety. My hands. . . ."

The man was not stupid, and Joshua was betting on that to get them out of this alive and well. He dared only a quick glance at her to make sure she would not interfere. She had no idea, and neither had he until he'd seen her necklace this morning, that it was the missing piece that fit with the priceless brooch in his safebox to make the map.

He'd sworn it was gone for so long, he could not believe that she'd had it all along. Her father would never have revealed its authenticity to her, and he had kept it from the men who'd killed him to protect her. That was probably the only good thing Balugani had done in his life.

When they freed his hands, he did not delay, going to the

panel in the wall and triggering the pressure points to open the secret enclosure. As he reached in, the man called Dougal Dubh pulled him aside and grabbed the items hidden there. It took him moments to find the brooch. He stared at it just as Josh had many, many times before, probably convincing him that it was real and in his grasp after all.

"Those will do you no good. The treasure does not exist."

"So says ye."

"Luigi made up the story. He said it would increase our prestige and notoriety. The Treasure of Trajan? A tale for children and fools," Joshua said quietly to the leader of this band of villains.

The man took a step towards Joshua and growled at the insult. At least with his hands freed, Joshua could defend himself. But, before anything else could happen, the sharp sound of police whistles started and they approached quickly.

"You might want to take what you have and leave now."

The leader was not stupid enough to get caught here, trapped inside while more and more police could gather outside and, with a signal to his men, he did exactly as Josh suggested.

He ran to Arabella and pulled her into his embrace.

"I did not believe the rest of the brooch even existed until I saw your part of it this morning."

"But I thought mine was a replica of something my father saw." Clar. . . Arabella said. "And he never mentioned a treasure."

"I have had and denied ever having that piece to keep it out of the hands of those seeking the legend. Although your father was convinced of it, I never believed a treasure existed. I still do not." He searched her face. "Are you well?"

"I think I am." She looked overwhelmed and exhausted. . . and beautiful to him. But when the excitement of this calmed and she remembered his accusations, could she forgive them?

"I would not have allowed him to hurt you. I knew the police were coming."

"How?"

"I'd sent a message ahead to Finlaggan." He could feel her body shake against his. "But you are unharmed?"

"Aye," she whispered as she fainted.

He caught her and placed her on his bed. Finlaggan came rushing in, followed by police and watchmen and the guards he'd hired. All his staff was accounted for and, other than being tied up, they were not hurt. Mrs. Mathieson came to sit with Arabella while he sorted out things with the police. No mention of the true target of the robbery would ever make it into the official report due to Finlaggan's father and his influence. It would take days to get his household calmed, but everyone was alive.

It was nigh on morning when he got back to his bedchamber and found it empty. Arabella was gone.

Gone, before he could explain and ask her forgiveness.

Chapter Twenty-Three

S HE HADN'T EXACTLY hidden from him, but she hadn't told him either. While Joshua was busy dealing with the legal authorities and seeing to the other servants, she slipped out. Arabella made no secret of it, going down to her chambers and packing the rest of her clothes and other belongings in a bag. But no one noticed a servant in black moving through the household, especially with so many additional people milling about both inside the house and on the grounds.

When he'd not even tried to contact her at either Euphemia's or Betty's, as they'd both told her, she thought he must have seen the wisdom in letting her go her own way as she'd always planned. Now that the recurring threat of her father's legacy was no longer an issue, he could finally return to his life and finish his current book. Though nothing she did would remove the taint from his reputation, she would know the truth of his honorable acts to mitigate her father's crimes.

So, she was free, too. Free of vows and promises that chained her to a past that was a lie. Now, all she needed to do was choose her path. Her funds would last her for several months at the least while she decided.

"Mrs. Lewis?" Her host laughed. "I mean Arabella," Peigi said. "I am going down to the shop to open for the day."

"I will come down shortly," she said.

The young woman had lost no time, taking the money from the settlement that Lord Finlaggan had given her and buying a half-share in the successful dressmaking and sewing business. When Arabella thought about moving forward, she visited Peigi and was welcomed to stay as long as she needed to. And, as she always found helpful, working and staying busy felt better than sitting around worrying.

Though Peigi said it was not necessary, Arabella made the beds, cleaned the kitchen and put away the laundry before going down to the shop below the apartment near the center of Leith. She was glad for the young woman who'd gotten a second chance and was doing well. As she entered the back room from the stairs, she called out to Peigi to let her know she was there. She was about to see which work needed attention first when Peigi called her to the front room.

"How can I help you, Miss Anderson?" she asked, smoothing down her apron as she walked through the doorway.

Looking as out of place as someone could, there he stood in the middle of counters covered with bolts of fabrics and boxes of ribbons and other notions. He looked different from the viscount she'd worked for and the one she'd loved. This one was not the dandy but was dressed well. Stylish, except for his tousled hair that would just not be tamed. When he faced her, the first thing she noticed was the silken neckcloth that looked familiar. Even knowing she must not change the decision she'd made, it was difficult to face him, to speak with him, in a calm manner. But she would.

"How can I be of assistance, my lord?"

"It is good to see you, Miss MacGibbon."

"And to see you, my lord."

"May I have a moment to speak to you?" Then he ran his hands through his hair. "Bloody hell, I cannot do this!" He turned to her and scooped her up in his arms. "Where can we speak?"

With a nod from Peigi, he carried her upstairs and stood her before him.

"How did you ken I was here?" she asked. She hadn't exactly forbidden Euphemia and Betty from telling him where she was, but she'd made it clear she needed some time before seeing him.

"Finlaggan," he said.

She could not understand how the earl could have known. . . . She smiled as she realized the obvious connection. "Peigi."

"Aye. She sent word to him just to let him ken you were safe."

"And he told you."

"Do you mind?"

"Not really. 'Twasn't a secret."

"Arabella, you left before I could tell you, about the brooch and about your father and you need to ken the rest of it. I'm not certain you remember some of the things you said after reading the portfolio." So overwrought by the truth of her father's crimes, she had fallen to pieces. "I was furious when I gave that to you without explanation. I thought you were involved." His hands tousled his hair.

"And do you still believe it?" He had raised some awful accusations. And after what they'd done together, for days, he must think she had seduced her way to get closer to the supposed riches.

"It took less time than you might believe for me to realize it was my anger and pride speaking and I hope I can convince you to forgive me for doubting you." From the skepticism in his gaze, Arabella knew he was in doubt of her answer. "Please forgive me. I do not believe that you were part of any of it. We were both caught up in a terrible coincidence and I did not realize the true danger to you."

He walked over to her and held out his hand waiting for her to take or refuse it, him. At least he did not believe her complicit in that part of the plotting against him. She took his hand and he kissed lightly on her knuckles. At least they would end as friends or not as enemies which was more than she could have expected when things went so disastrously wrong. She offered him the chair while she sat on the small couch and wait as he sat. Not certain of what he would say, she waited on the promised explanation.

"For years, since we returned from Algeria and the first book was published, it's all anyone cared about. Even when the rumors flew that I had not traveled there or that I fabricated the whole thing for fame and fortune. But they still wanted to find the treasure. The riches. Some simply seemed to want the thrill of seeking and finding it. Many tried to buy my cooperation, certain I knew the true location or how to find a map or path leading to it. Others tried blackmail, threats, and more." He turned away for a moment, shaking his head. "I wish I'd never heard of that goddamned desert or about the city. It would have saved me such trouble. It would have saved so many others." He faced her and she saw desolation in his eyes. "You need to understand my part in it."

It was then when he stood and began the pacing that she knew would happen as he explained. This was a recognizable habit of the viscount she knew from Edinburgh.

"I could blame it on my age, I was young when I took up my post in Italy—a minor position for the government in Rome. I could blame it on many factors, but I became aware of certain behaviors of your father's after several months traveling and working with him." He shook his head. "I was beholden to my cousin for my income and so, when he advised me to find ways to smooth it over, I did."

"You were not the one committing the acts."

"Nay, I was not." The pacing began anew. "Then he grew bolder, more violent, greedier. We had to leave Italy sooner than I'd planned because of him. Then, in Algeria, he insulted one of the Bey's officeholders by seducing the man's daughter."

It was so difficult to hear, even though she'd read the documents that outlined everything. Arabella tried to remind herself that she was not responsible for her father's sins any more than Joshua was. Still, she could not help but flinch while listening to the details.

"I am sorry for distressing you with these lurid details. But, instead of standing up to my cousin and your father, I did not. I wanted the fame and the fortune. I wanted the glory that came with the adventures and discoveries. So, I began paying off those involved and turned a blind eye to what I could not manage with money."

"Again, these were not your sins, my lord." She would not blame anyone else after finding out the truth.

"When we came back here, it was getting worse. That was when I found out about the other wives—I still think your mother was the only legal marriage and only because he was forced to it."

A sound escaped her at hearing that truth. She'd had so many misconceptions about her father but this one hurt more than any of the rest. "He said theirs was a love match."

"I am sorry you had to learn about it this way, Arabella. He'd gotten her pregnant before we ever left for Italy. My cousin was his sponsor even then and when I discovered and informed him of Luigi's disgraceful behavior towards her, he forced the matter."

After reading about his other wives in the reports in the portfolio, she had feared she would have to add bastardy to her growing list of sins. His gaze was filled with sadness as he watched her then.

"When I discovered the breadth of his crimes, I used funds from the sales of the first book to make restitution and to support those manipulated by him. Then he began the rumors that I had lied about the travels into Africa and along the Nile. Sales dwindled and it became harder to see to everything." She saw the guilt he should not bear there in his eyes, and she wanted to comfort him, to absolve him of her father's sins. She did not because he needed to get this out.

"My cousin died around then, and I was able to get funds

from the estate to make settlements on those who needed it. I paid him one—"

"You paid my father?"

"For the last several years of his life I did. But it was conditional on him agreeing to certain parameters."

"Let me make a guess. . . ." She did not have to, for she remembered his drinking and gambling increasing suddenly. A bequest, he'd said, until it ran out. "He must do as you say?"

"He signed the documents only to get the blunt he needed. No other reason, for he had no remorse. No sense of guilt. But the confessions he signed forced him to remain here in Scotland, for he would be arrested in five countries if he was found on the continent."

He stopped then and walked to her. Taking her hands in his, he tugged her closer. "I want you to ken that everyone has been taken care of." He kissed her hands. "Except you."

"Me?"

"I lost you." He smiled then. "Your mother told my man of business that she was moving with you to live with a relative. Apparently, she died but we never got word, leaving you in the care of a man who cared about naught but his own arse."

Arabella leaned into him, savoring the closeness while knowing it would end soon. She was a shallow woman with desires and love for a man who could not be hers.

"When you walked into my life, I had no reason to be suspicious of you. Actually, for some reason I could never explain, I went against my very experienced butler's advice to hire a woman I did not ken."

He kissed her, a gentle touch of their mouths, yet one that reignited the burning need for him that had been tamped down to a slow burn within her.

"I fought him every day to keep you near to me. In spite of his warnings, in spite of my godmother's warnings and my friends, some part of me kenned that you were the perfect woman for me."

"You did not ken the real me, my lord. I was pretending, living as a woman I was not."

"You pretended your passion?"

She felt the heat of blush fill her cheeks as images of them together filled her mind. "Nay, never." His expression was insufferably male when he met her gaze and grinned.

"You were not truly running my household?" Before she could argue, he added, "which is now in complete disarray and the staff is threatening mutiny."

"Even Mr. Pottles?" she teased.

"Pottles' experience at the hand of the villains changed him. He was asking about your return." He grew serious then. "Of course, your role as my viscountess will keep you too busy to serve as housekeeper. Your oversight will be invaluable in hiring a new one."

"My lord—"

"Joshua."

"Joshua—"

"Arabella." He loved teasing her like this. At Dunalastair Manor, it would lead to pleasurable interludes. "I think I did see the real you. When you had nothing to prove and just were Clara Lewis, I saw what makes you, well, you. That's who I want to marry." When she tried to object, he placed his fingers over her mouth. "Unless you tell me you pretended to love me, you must marry me."

"There will objections to a marriage between us. Serious and appropriate objections, Joshua."

"I do not care." He leaned in and whispered against her neck. "If there are issues that we cannot deal with here, I ken the perfect place where we could ride out the storm. Sultry breezes, hot sun, sweet and fruity drinks that serve other purposes, and very few clothes are needed there."

Arabella wanted to refuse. There were so many good reasons that this would be a bad idea. But looking in his eyes and seeing his love shining back was a hard thing to argue with.

"Do you love me? Just say it and put me out of my misery." He slid his fingers into her white cap and pushed it off her head. He wanted to loosen her hair, she could tell, but he waited for her word.

"I heard you," she admitted. "I heard you say it that morning."

"I am all about turn-about being fair play, my love. There are consequences to not holding up your part." Her body remembered and shuddered against his. "Tell me."

"I love you, my lord." He growled against her mouth. "I love you, Joshua Robertson."

"I love you, Arabella."

"And say you will marry me."

She sighed. How could she refuse him? She did love him and he loved her, no matter that he knew more about her past than she did. When she looked at him, she saw the hopefulness in his green eyes and understood she had no choice.

"I will marry you, my lord."

"My God, Arabella! Do you ken what this means?" She shook her head, unsure to what he referred. "Pottles will have to call you '*my lady*'!"

He laughed loudly and she smiled at the very thought of it. Then he gathered her closer and whispered to her. "*My* lady."

"My lord."

"I do like the sound of that, my lady."

"As do I, my lord. As do I."

Epilogue

Batna Province
Algeria
Spring, 1816

S TANDING JUST WITHIN the tent and out of the worst of the
constant heat, Arabella watched as Joshua walked towards
her. His head and face were obscured by the long scarf he'd
wrapped in the style of the men here. It protected his pale
Scottish complexion from the burning rays of the sun. And it gave
her a chance to have her turn, but she never stopped at just
removing the scarf.

That night they'd begun with them taking turns in removing
the layers of lightweight fabrics they now wore to deal with the
desert heat and ended up with them entwined naked together,
cooled only by the breezes that blew through the open panels of
the silken tent.

"We will have to change our usual garb next week, my love,"
he whispered to her after a bout of rather lovely passion. "And
you will have to control this insatiable need you have for my
body."

"Is someone visiting? Finlaggan, finally?" she asked. The earl
had resisted all efforts to get him to leave Scotland and visit
Timgad. *Hot as the devil's arsehole*, he'd said as he turned down
invitation after invitation. He'd turned into quite a priggish earl
since they'd first met and Arabella had sworn to sort out why. "I

do not ken why I must get into those woolen dresses. Pray tell me you do not expect stockings, too?"

"Aye, he's coming and you'll get dressed like a proper viscountess while he's with us."

"Even stockings? But Joshua—" He swatted her bottom and she arched against him.

"He may be one of my best friends, but I draw the line at him seeing you undressed."

"Undressed? But I wear at least six layers whenever I leave the tent."

"And no undergarments. No stays. Layers so diaphanous that they flow over your breasts and show every curve. That slip into the crevice between your legs when you walk."

"You demanded I wear those."

"I promised you that you could wear them."

She rubbed up against him, draping a silken sheet between them and enjoying the feel of it on her skin.

"True. And garments such as these have such advantages in the dry desert heat."

Their marriage had not been quite the scandal she'd thought it would, but it was unusual and did stir up talk. Arabella was certain he encouraged some of it to give him the excuse he wanted to leave Scotland and travel around the Mediterranean. The wars on the continent had ended late in 1815 and travel had become easier. So, they'd left a year later on an extended honeymoon.

It was like nothing she had ever imagined even though his descriptions were detailed.

They traveled to the places he'd visited and written about in his books: remarkable places, different cultures, sensual foods, unusual tastes. She'd told him that she would follow his lead and try anything, and he'd made it his task to fulfill her desire for new experiences.

And he'd been gloriously successful in his endeavors.

Arabella had finally understood why he'd never mentioned

the precious goods and foods and more that he'd kept hidden away at Dunalastair Manor. And why he'd avoided visiting there.

Guilt.

As much as he loved the experiences he'd had on his travels, the guilt he'd felt for not seeing the truth about her father tainted his enjoyment of the parts of those cultures he'd sent or shipped back to Scotland. So, rather than enjoy them as much as possible, he'd hidden them and the part of him that enjoyed the tastes and sensations and hedonistic pleasures he'd found.

After the robbery, he'd had his man re-examine each of the people who Joshua had "saved" after her father's actions. Once finished, they'd married and Arabella had convinced him that his duties to others had been honorably discharged. Freed of that responsibility, Joshua had allowed the joys discovered on his trips back into his life.

In their lives.

And, if they had converted the bedroom adjoining theirs into a room identical to the alcove in Dunalastair, well, so be it. And if deliveries from all sorts of foreign places arrived for them, 'twas not a bad thing. And if they disappeared for days into their own personal oasis, no one, least of all the staff—including their new housekeeper—complained.

Calmed by the breezes and her husband's slow and gentle caresses with the silken sheets she loved so much, she was drifting off to sleep when he spoke.

"I do have a place to show you before they arrive."

"A new place?"

"Aye," he said. "A small lake in the hills to the south. I can finally teach you to swim." She had wanted to learn but the ocean was too big and some of the bathing pools they'd visited were too small. "It's just right."

"Sounds lovely."

"The best part?"

"What is the best part?" she asked, intrigued at the thought of swimming with him outside. Their adventures in bathing and the huge bathing tub he'd had designed for their private room was scandalous. But they'd never been in water together outside.

"It is located in a very private area—one road in and out, so no surprise visitors."

She shivered then, imagining all sorts of things they could do together in such a place.

"I've been told that after the sun sets, under the stars with the cool breezes to dry our skin—" She shivered again, thrusting her hips towards him this time as he aroused her with his deep voice. "—is the best time to go there."

"It sounds like a lovely idea, my lord." She rolled onto her back and his attentions turned from soothing to stimulating. "If you wish to go there, I am, as always, your obedient wife."

"Obedient wife, you say, my lady?"

"Of course, my lord."

"Open your legs." He rolled closer and leaned over her, sliding his hand across the slight bump there to reach her curls.

She smiled at him, enjoying this playful prelude, and let her legs drop open. She guided his hand where they both wanted it to be and closed her eyes. His clever fingers moved into the intimate folds as he whispered.

"I think you are only obedient when it's something you want to do, my lady." He touched a place that made her body tremble.

"I have always said it is a gift to be married to a smart man, my lord." Her hips rose to meet the stroking and she could feel everything in her tighten.

"A smart man with an obedient wife," he whispered. "Nothing could stop them." He stilled his hand and she groaned in frustration. She was so very close to going over the sensual edge he was taking her to, and she wanted to reach it now.

"A smart man would ken better than to tease his obedient wife."

"Oh, did you mean this?" He stroked again, moving deeper into her folds. "Or this?" he asked as he thrust one, then two, and finally three fingers inside her channel. "Or mayhap this?"

His wicked thumb pressed on the aching, throbbing bud and release tore through her, tightening her entire body before tremors made her shake with pleasure. When she could finally breathe, she turned on her side and smiled.

"Was there anything else this smart man would like his obedient wife to do?" She knew what they both wanted. His smile warmed her heart as much as his touch had heated her body.

"Love me, my lady," he said as he opened his mouth for her kiss. She paused when she made him breathless and hard, and smiled as her hand slipped down from his chest to his belly and lower.

"I do, Joshua."

"It's all I ask, Arabella. An obedient wife to love."

Arabella knew she would not always obey his every order, but for now, she would.

About the Author

Award-winning, *USA Today* best-selling author **Terri Brisbin** is a mom, a wife, grandmom! and a dental hygienist and has sold more than 3 million copies of her historical and paranormal romance novels and novellas in more than 25 countries and 20 languages around the world. Her current and upcoming historical and paranormal/fantasy romances will be published by Dragonblade, Harlequin Historicals and independently, too.

Visit www.terribrisbin.com for more info about Terri, her works and upcoming events.

Connect with her on FB at facebook.com/terribrisbinauthor or on Instagram at instagram.com/terribrisbin.

Milton Keynes UK
Ingram Content Group UK Ltd.
UKHW021420290424
441932UK00025B/233